"I love Paige more and more with each book. Just when I didn't think it was possible to love her more!"
— BEKAH HAMRICK MARTIN, author of *The Bare Naked Truth: Dating, Waiting, and God's Purity Plan*

"*Paige Rewritten* is a shining example of Erynn Mangum's signature character development of witty and relatable characters. With a strong and genuine voice, she uses humor and smile-evoking romantic tension to reveal a surprising depth of biblical insight. Her superb plotting and believable twists keep readers engaged until the final, nail-biting page."
— XOCHI E. DIXON, freelance writer; speaker; Bible teacher

D1602730

ERYNN MANGUM

Paige Rewritten

A PAIGE ALDER NOVEL / Book 2

TH1NK, an
Imprint of
NavPress

NAVPRESS
Discipleship Inside Out®

NavPress is the publishing ministry of The Navigators, an international Christian organization and leader in personal spiritual development. NavPress is committed to helping people grow spiritually and enjoy lives of meaning and hope through personal and group resources that are biblically rooted, culturally relevant, and highly practical.

**For a free catalog go to www.NavPress.com
or call 1.800.366.7788 in the United States or 1.800.839.4769 in Canada.**

© 2013 by Erynn Mangum O'Brien

All rights reserved. No part of this publication may be reproduced in any form without written permission from NavPress, P.O. Box 35001, Colorado Springs, CO 80935. www.navpress.com

NAVPRESS, the NAVPRESS logo, TH1NK, and the TH1NK logo are registered trademarks of NavPress. Absence of ® in connection with marks of NavPress or other parties does not indicate an absence of registration of those marks.

ISBN-13: 978-1-61291-321-6

Cover design by Studio Gearbox
Cover image by CSA Images

Scripture quotations in this publication are taken from the New American Standard Bible® (NASB), Copyright © 1960, 1962, 1963, 1968, 1971, 1972, 1973, 1975, 1977, 1995 by The Lockman Foundation. Used by permission.

Mangum, Erynn, 1985-
  Paige rewritten : a Paige Alder novel / Erynn Mangum.
    pages cm
  Sequel to: Paige torn.
  Summary: Paige is still overcommitted but making more time for God when Preslee, the sister she has not spoken with in almost a year, returns wearing an engagement ring, the youth pastor asks her to take a job at the church, and an old boyfriend resurfaces.
  ISBN 978-1-61291-321-6
  [1. Christian life—Fiction. 2. Responsibility—Fiction. 3. Dating (Social customs)—Fiction. 4. Sisters—Fiction.] I. Title.
  PZ7.M31266532Paf 2013
  [Fic]—dc23

                            2013011791

Printed in the United States of America

1 2 3 4 5 6 7 8 / 18 17 16 15 14 13

OTHER NOVELS BY ERYNN MANGUM

To *you*, my dear friend — may you learn with me as I discover how big our God is, how much He loves us, and how perfectly He provides for us — even when we don't see it at the time. I love you and I'm praying for you!

Acknowledgments

To my Lord and Savior—may this book bring You honor and glory and be used to draw people closer to You.

To my loves—Jon and Nathan—I adore being your wife and mama. You two make every day exciting and meaningful. ;) I love you more than I could ever say.

To my family—Mom, Dad, Bryant, Caleb, Cayce—I love you all. Thank you for bugging me about my deadlines, bringing me coffee, and watching my crazy kid. Sundays with you all are the highlight of my week.

To my in-law family—Greg, Connie, Allen, Vicky, and Tommy—I am blessed to be a part of this crazy bunch!

To my friends—Shannon Layer, Kaitlin Bar, Jen Fulkerson, Leigh Ann Trebesh, Eryn Beechem, Melanie Larson, Thalia Chan, and Jamie Poore—I treasure you so much. Thank you for the love you have shown me and my family. I love you all!

To my amazing publisher and my incredible agent—the NavPress Super Squad and Tamela Hancock Murray—you guys are the best!

Chapter

1

My mom likes to say that good things come in threes. "Remember that time we went to see *The Phantom of the Opera*, Paige?" she always says to me. "Not only did our seats get upgraded for free, but we won those tickets to go see *Wicked* and we met Mariah Carey!"

By *met*, Mom meant "saw from a distance," and to this day, I still swear it was not Mariah Carey.

And if it was her, then I really feel the need to tell her that cornrows are not a flattering hairstyle for her.

I'm curious what Mom would say about my current situation. I really don't think I am looking at three good things.

Maybe three confusing things.

But not good things.

"Well?" My boss, Mark Lawman, is sitting in front of my desk, looking at me expectantly.

I don't know what to say. I stare at the paper he gave me that lays out a new job description of my duties, the biggest difference being the huge raise he is offering.

On the one hand, I am excited about the prospect of

more money. Saving is kind of a high priority for me at the moment after a few lean months, thanks to saying yes to too many things.

On the other hand, it will solidify my role in this adoption agency as a secretary for life when all I really want is to be an honest-to-goodness counselor.

I don't necessarily like the mental image I have of myself at ninety-four, sitting at this same desk, answering this same phone in a warbling version of my voice. "Lawman Adoption Agency, this is Paige."

Mark must see something in my expression because he clears his throat and stands. "Just think about it, Paige." Then he hurries down the hall to his office, leaving me with the paper and my cluttered desk.

I reread the new job description. Basically, all he did is include transcription work, but that is something I already do thanks to a much extended maternity leave our regular transcriptionist has been taking since about two years ago.

I figure we can pretty much consider her retired.

I set the paper down with a sigh and go back to my lunch of bagged salad and the text message I was reading when Mark interrupted my lunch break.

IT'S JUST DINNER BETWEEN OLD FRIENDS, PAIGE.

Luke Prestwick, my best friend Layla's older brother, has a very skewed view of the past apparently. "Old friends" implies that there is an ongoing friendship.

Something he ended nearly five years ago.

Right then my phone buzzes again, and I look at the message, worrying that it is Luke again.

HI PAIGE! JUST THINKING ABOUT YOU. HOPE YOU ARE HAVING A GOOD DAY!

It is from Tyler Jennings.

"Well, that's a pretty smile."

I look up to see Peggy, one of the two counselors who work at the agency. She is standing in front of my desk, holding a microwavable cup of chicken and rice soup and a spoon.

I shrug and try to wipe my face clean of emotion. "Soup day?" I ask her, trying to change the subject.

"I'm not that easily distracted, Paige, and yes. It's cold out."

Cold is a relative term in Dallas. Particularly in March. Really, what she means is that it's raining outside.

I peer out the front window and sigh. Nothing like a drizzly day to make you wish you were home watching HGTV shows in fuzzy sweatpants instead of sitting in an office chair in a skirt.

My phone buzzes yet again. Peggy smirks at me. "Look who is Miss Popular."

It's Luke again.

REALLY, PAIGE, I JUST WANT TO CATCH UP AND FIGURED THIS WEEK WOULD BE A GREAT TIME SINCE IT'S YOUR BIRTH-DAY ON FRIDAY. ☺

I can't decide if I'm flattered or confused by Luke Prestwick remembering my birthday. Four years ago I would have been overjoyed.

"So?" Peggy taps my desk with the end of her spoon.

"What are we so-ing about?" Candace walks in from the hallway leading back to her office. She is absently crunching a celery stick, which means there is yet another wedding or baby shower or some milestone coming up in her ridiculously huge extended family. Candace crash diets before every event.

"Nothing." I shake my head. These two are way too curious about my personal life, and having been "shrinked" by them before, I am in no hurry to have it happen again.

Last time they were critiquing my innate need to say yes to every single thing anyone asked of me. It got to the point where I didn't even have time to do my devotions I was so busy.

So, yes, they were right about that, but there isn't anything to tell right now. Tyler and I have been on one date. Apparently, this is the prime season for software developers, so he is slammed at work.

I shrug off Peggy and Candace and they finally exchange a look. "Okay, fine," Peggy says. "We'll do this your way." Then they look at each other again and go back down the hall to their offices.

Finally.

I glance at the clock. I have five more minutes in my lunch break, so I text Tyler first.

THANKS! HAVING A PRETTY GOOD DAY. I HOPE YOU ARE HAVING A GOOD DAY TOO!

It sounds horrible. I stare at it for three of my five remaining minutes before finally just sending it because I can't come up with a different way to word it without sounding even more like a chirpy little girl.

Then I click over to reply to Luke and just stare at the touch-screen keyboard for the next ninety seconds.

I WILL THINK ABOUT IT.

I push send. No smiley face, no exclamation point. Maybe he'll get the message and recant his constant pleading over the last two weeks.

That is another thing. He can't bother to visit for two

years, but now that he came back for his parents' anniversary party two weeks ago, he can suddenly stay in town? He tried to talk to me the whole night of his parents' party, but things just got crazy.

And I've been doing a great job of avoiding him since then.

I've been doing a great job of avoiding a lot of people.

Including my sister.

I finish the last bite of salad, throw the bag away, and sigh, thinking of Preslee. She and Luke must have tag teamed this because I've gotten almost as many texts from her as I have from him. And they could have been sent by either one of them, the messages sound so alike.

I really need to talk to you.

I know I hurt you in the past, but I have changed!

I think about that last text I got from her three nights ago. *I have changed.* What does that even mean to Preslee? Or Luke?

No, the past is where it should stay. In the past. I've moved on from both of them, and I am content now. I am doing great in my walk with God, I am good with the awkward are-we-dating-or-just-really-good-friends teeter-totter I'm riding with Tyler, I am happy hanging out with Layla and occasionally helping her with wedding stuff, and I am okay with my current job situation. So what if I don't use my college degree and am not doing anything to counsel people like I've always dreamed about?

Okay, I am sort of okay with my job situation.

Regardless, I don't need any more speed bumps in the road. I am finally at a good place. I just want to stay here.

The rest of the workday passes by slowly since I spend the

majority of it on hold with the people who service our copier. The stupid machine goes out at least once a month, and rather than pay for a new one, Mark just prefers to have me call in the repairman, Flynn, who is never available until at least four business days after the copier breaks.

"I just need someone to come by Friday," I say, eyeing the teetering stack of papers waiting to be copied. Today is Wednesday. "Friday at the *latest*," I annunciate.

"We'll do our best, ma'am!"

That means they will be here by next Tuesday.

I hang up, feeling useless and thinking about how a lot of people would kill for a gigantic raise for a job that essentially consists of answering the phone, waiting on hold, answering e-mails, doing paychecks, and getting prospective adoptive parents and birth parents bottles of water or coffee.

It is a no-brainer job.

At the moment, I can't decide if that is a good thing or a bad thing.

"Well, I'm out of here," Peggy announces at five o'clock, coming down the hallway and pulling on her raincoat and a wide-brimmed hat.

I look out the window and it is barely drizzling.

I think Peggy misses her hometown of rainy Seattle a little too much sometimes.

I dig my purse out from the desk drawer, turn off my computer, and stand too. Normally I teach Bible study on Wednesday nights to a bunch of high school girls, but this week is spring break in Dallas, so Rick, our youth pastor, took most of them on some sort of retreat and canceled Bible study.

"You really should come with us, Paige," he told me at Layla's parents' anniversary party.

"I can't take a week off work."

"It's only four days."

Rick does not understand what a normal nine-to-five job looks like.

I follow Peggy out, looking forward to a nice, quiet night at home. Just me, Westley, Buttercup, and a takeout container filled with General Tso's chicken from one of the local drive-thru Chinese places. It is three dollars for a huge box. Which sort of scares me because it is so cheap and the kid working the drive-thru always looks like he is plotting someone's murder, but that's why I drive through instead of going inside.

I don't ask questions; I just hand over the cash and keep my door locked.

Candace was the first one to suggest the restaurant. "Oh it's amazing!" She raved for days after she'd been there the first time following one of her niece's weddings. Really, that is the only time I take Candace's restaurant suggestions since every other time she is on a diet and looking for low-fat, low-calorie, and low-taste food.

I wave at Peggy and slide into my car, drive to the Chinese food place, buy my container of chicken with a side of broccoli and rice from the creepy boy, and drive home.

Layla texts me almost as soon as I pull into my allotted parking space at my apartment complex. PANDA EXPRESS TONIGHT?

I look at my three-dollar container of mystery meat covered in General Tso's sauce and am suddenly a little repulsed. Especially when I think of the delicious, no-MSG orange chicken.

I call her, gathering my purse and the takeout container.

"Is that a yes?" she answers.

"I just bought a huge box of General Tso's chicken."

She makes a gagging noise. "From that nasty Chinese place? Gross, Paige. Look, I'm leaving right now. I'll get you decent Chinese food and be there in . . . I don't know. Fifteen minutes?"

It will at least give me a chance to change into comfy clothes and get the movie going. Layla and I watch *The Princess Bride* at least once a month. Usually it ends up being just background noise while we talk, and then we both get quiet during our favorite scenes. I walk a few steps over to the Dumpster and toss in my takeout box before going up the stairs to my apartment.

I open the door exactly fifteen minutes later and Layla smiles at me, her hair glistening with rain droplets. She holds up a sack and the smell of Chinese food takes over my house.

"Thanks, Layla." I close the door behind her. I don't bother offering to pay her back. I will just buy next time.

She sets the bag on the kitchen table and starts unloading it, talking a hundred miles a minute. Typical Layla.

"So Peter told me yesterday that he wants me to move into his apartment after we get married and I'm like, absolutely not, you know? I mean his apartment is okay or whatever but it's a *guy's* apartment. It's cold and dark and smells kind of weird if I'm being totally honest. Plus have you seen his kitchen?"

She looks up at me and apparently that question needs an answer.

"I've only been to Peter's apartment once, and I definitely don't remember the kitchen." I turn on the TV and start the movie.

"Well, I told him we should move into mine instead."

Layla's apartment, in my opinion, isn't much to talk of either. The apartment itself is fine, but there's a long, dark, creepy path you have to take all the way around the building from the parking lot. I call it Murder Alley.

Layla calls it a relaxing walk after work.

She hands me the Styrofoam container and sits down on my couch, propping her feet up on the coffee table and weaving her fingers together. "Jesus, thank You for the real food we are about to consume and may any fat contained therein make its way to our boobs and not our hips. Amen."

I snort and shake my head, joining her on the couch.

I nod over at her box of orange chicken. "No more vegetarianism?"

"It calls to me," she says, tone sad, spearing a bite.

"Vegetarianism?"

"Chicken."

I nod. Layla's strike lasted about three weeks. That is longer than the no-more-bottled-water strike, the I-will-only-wear-100-percent-cotton strike, and the waking-up-early-to-do-Pilates kick. That one lasted two days, and then she decided Pilates was created by someone who hated human beings and their hamstrings.

We eat our chicken in relative silence, watching the beginning of the movie we know so well.

"So," I say, after I've finished most of my meal.

"So," Layla echoes, looking over at me.

"I haven't had a chance to tell you," I say slowly, thinking about it. That statement is sort of a lie. I've *had* the chance to tell her what I am going to say, but I've just chickened out.

Seems fitting to tell her over a dinner of poultry.

"What?" Layla looks back at the TV.

"Luke's been texting me."

Her head snaps over at me. "Are you okay?" she asks, eyes worried. "Oh, Paige, I swear I had *nothing* to do with this!"

I nod. "I know."

"How did he even get your number?" she rants.

I shrug. There are any number of people at the party who could have given Luke my number, but my bet is on Layla's parents. They made no secret about how disappointed they were when Luke broke up with me. "We'll always consider you our other daughter!" Mrs. Prestwick cried, mashing my head into her shoulder the day after the dumping.

"It doesn't really matter," I say now. "That's not all, though."

"That's not *all*? What, did he ask you to marry him or something?"

I don't mention how he's been asking me out. Layla and I have spent the past four years not talking about Luke and that is good for us. Layla loves her brother and so she should. I don't want to make things awkward in the Prestwick house.

"Preslee is in town," I say quietly.

Layla just stares at me, openmouthed. "Preslee. As in, Preslee Preslee? Your sister?"

Layla was there for all of the Preslee saga as well. Layla has been through too many sagas with me.

I nod.

"Wow." Layla leans back into the couch.

"That's not all," I say again.

"Okay, Paige, seriously." Layla shakes her head. "I'm not sure how much more I can take. You're singing a duet on Sunday with Zac Efron? You discovered you're allergic to chocolate? You found that dog with the two-thousand-dollar reward I've seen posters for all over the place?"

I laugh and Layla grins at me.

"Mark offered me a raise. For the same job I already have."

"Offered. As in you didn't take it?" She gives me a confused look. "Paige, this might just be me, but usually when someone offers you more money to do the same thing you're already doing, you generally say yes." She shrugs. "That's just been my experience though."

I sigh and rub my forehead. "I don't know what to do."

"Well, let's start with Mark since that seems the easiest."

This is why we are good friends.

"Okay." Layla straightens up, crossing her legs under her body and turning toward me. "You don't want more money. Why?"

I laugh. "Layla."

"What? It's a valid question."

"I don't want to die being a secretary." I bite my lip.

"Why not? It seems like a fairly mild way to go honestly. What's the worst that could happen? A gigantic paper cut? A stapler to the forehead out of frustration? Maybe dying of boredom?"

"Layla, I didn't mean literally dying *because* of being a secretary. I just meant . . ." I watch Westley as the Man in Black tries to find out if Buttercup still loves him or not. "I don't want to be a secretary forever."

"Well sure. But there's a lot of things I don't want to do forever. For example, I hope that at some point someone invents sunscreen that doesn't smell like a tropical rain forest, because one day I have high hopes of wearing sunscreen and

perfume without knocking people over from the sheer weight
of scent around me."

"You have the strangest goals."

"At least I'm honest."

"Well, here's me being honest then. At some point in my
life, I'd like to use my degree."

She shrugs. "Degree usage is overrated. Next."

"Next what?"

"Next topic. Let's talk about Luke."

"Let's not." Like I said, not talking about Luke has
worked out really well for us for the past four years.

"I think you just need to tell him, 'Dude, you missed the
train. I have a great life, a great new guy, and all is right in
the world that you have no part of.'"

I look at Layla, eyebrows raised. "Harsh."

"I like you without Luke."

"So it seems."

"And I like you with Tyler. Are you with Tyler?"

"Well—"

"And as far as Preslee goes, I'm not going to get involved
with that one." She pretends to wash her hands and holds
them up. "You need to figure that out on your own."

"Thanks for all the help," I say dryly.

"I don't have a sister unless you count yourself." She
reaches for the remote. "I can't help you there. Now shut up,
this is my favorite part."

She cranks the volume just in time for Westley to kill the
R.O.U.S. and sighs sweetly when he looks up at Buttercup,
all bloodied and hair mussed.

"Seriously. That scene right there shaped everything I
wanted in a future husband," she says.

*   *   *   *   *

I climb under the covers later after Layla leaves and pull my
Bible over to my lap. I just finished reading through James.
It's time to find something new, so I turn to Galatians since
Rick's wife, Natalie, and I were just talking about some verses
she was trying to memorize from there.

Verse ten of the first chapter screams at me: *"For am I
now seeking the favor of men, or of God? Or am I striving to
please men? If I were still trying to please men, I would not be a
bond-servant of Christ."*

I close my Bible, frowning. What does that even mean?
And surely there is some caveat in the later part of the book,
because isn't part of life pleasing people?

Chapter 2

Friday morning I open my eyes, blink at the white ceiling, and realize yet again how awful birthdays are when you live by yourself.

When I lived at home, Mom would always wake me up with a birthday cinnamon roll with a candle in it, sing happy birthday, and give me a present to open that was something I got to use on my birthday before I opened my real presents that night.

Usually it was just something little, like a cool pen or a cheap necklace or something, but it was still special.

I miss my mom on my birthday.

I get up, take a shower, and pull on a cream-colored gauzy tunic-style top with black leggings and boots. It is maybe a little winterish for March, but we are on day four of constant drizzling rain and it feels weather appropriate. Plus, it is one of my favorite outfits, and you should always be allowed to wear your favorite outfit on your birthday.

I eat a quiet breakfast of Raisin Bran just like I always do, but it just feels more depressing today since Raisin Bran, for all its high-fiber benefits, is nothing at all like a cinnamon roll covered in melting icing with a candle in it. My phone buzzes and I click open the text message.

A little dancing yellow smiley face wriggles around on the screen singing happy birthday and then a sign pops up. HAPPY BIRTHDAY! — TYLER

I smile. Layla has also texted.

HAPPY BIRTHDAY, O ELDERLY ONE.

I am three months older than her. Which means I have three months of being told how old I am before she moves on to other insulting nicknames.

I get to work and Peggy smiles at me as I put my lunch in the refrigerator. "Happy birthday, Paige. Anything fun planned for tonight?"

Luke asked me again to go out tonight and I never texted him back, so I am hoping he got the point. Tyler hinted about dinner earlier this week but sent me a text right after his happy face one telling me he had a huge meeting this evening at five o'clock.

I AM SO SORRY PAIGE. CAN I MAKE IT UP TO YOU TOMOR-ROW NIGHT? YOU SERIOUSLY HAVE NO IDEA HOW SORRY I AM.

I shrug to Peggy. "Not that I'm aware of." As of right now, I am planning on treating myself to the Cheesecake Factory, getting it to go, and going home and watching a movie.

Takeout.

Takeout is a sad word on your birthday.

I work all morning, watch the copier man, Flynn, wrestle the copier all afternoon, finally copy all the teetering stack of files, and turn off my computer at five o'clock. Candace showed up with birthday chocolates in the morning that I've already eaten half of, Peggy hands me a box of gourmet cupcakes, and Mark gives me a gift card to Panera.

"They have a new strawberry salad," he says as he puts his hands in his pockets. Mark is one of the most awkward gift givers I know.

"Thanks," I say. Because really, what else can you say when someone gives you a gift card to a restaurant known for its bread and pastries and suggests a salad? I can't decide if that's a subtle hint that I need to watch my weight, or if he is just trying to figure out something to say.

He finally goes back to his office, and I put the gift card in my purse as I sling it over my shoulder and gather up the chocolates and the cupcakes. I wave at Candace as I head out the door and open my car door, meeting a blast of warm air.

For being such a drizzly day, it is still warm out. I put the chocolates and cupcakes on the seat next to me and start the engine and the air conditioner, debating between using my new gift card tonight or sticking with the Cheesecake Factory plan.

My phone starts ringing right as I am mentally putting *mac 'n' cheese* in the pro list for Panera for the fourth time.

I don't recognize the number, so I answer it. Maybe I have "won" a Visa card worth one thousand dollars again like the last time I answered an unknown number.

"Hello?"

"I was hoping you'd answer."

Luke.

I bite back the urge to push the end call button and bite my tongue instead.

"Happy birthday, kiddo," he says, voice warm and friendly.

You would think the man would take a hint. I've barely returned any of his texts, I pretty much ignored him the whole night of his parents' anniversary party, and I danced with Tyler the whole night.

You'd think he'd see that there is the potential of a relationship with Tyler here and that I am finally happy again and he should just go back to California or wherever he is now living.

At least I think there is that potential with Tyler. Apparently we'll see after the crazy time at his work is over.

"Hello, Luke," I say, because he is obviously waiting for a reply from me.

"Any big birthday plans?"

I think about how to answer this without blatantly lying. "I'm not sure yet," I say, hoping maybe he'll misread that to mean I am expecting a surprise party.

"Great. You should come out to dinner with me."

"I think not."

"You're just sitting there in your car. That's a terrible birthday."

I immediately jerk my head around until I see him parked two spaces over, smiling at me through the raindrop-streaked window all stalker-like, phone to his head. He waves the hand not holding the phone and flashes a smile.

"Hi, Paige."

"What are you doing here?" I demand.

He shrugs. "I'm considering adoption."

"Go away, Luke. I have plans."

"For what? Dinner alone? No birthday cake? No candles? No singing?" He *tsks* into the phone, shaking his head. "That's the worst birthday I can think of."

No worse than sitting here in my car talking to my ex-boyfriend two parking spaces over from me. I try staring him down but it doesn't work. He just smiles bigger.

"I like your hair," he says.

"What?"

"Your hair. It's long. I like it like that."

"You know what, Luke? You had your chance. Go back to California." I hang up the phone, don't look at him again, turn the key forcefully, and drive out of the parking lot, not even sparing a glance in my rearview mirror.

Who does he think he is anyway? The greatest gift to mankind? Poor Paige, I dumped her and now she must be miserable without me?

I grip the steering wheel, staring through my windshield wipers that aren't really needed for the tiny drizzle coming down. Idiot. Does he really think he can just waltz back into my life without even a thought to the past?

My apartment is very close to work, and I get there in record time. It seems that fuming makes you drive faster. I gather up all of my birthday gifts and am halfway to my apartment when I realize I forgot to pick up dinner.

Apparently fuming makes you forget important things like eating as well. I stand there in the drizzle, staring at my building, wondering if I should just make do with the cheese stick and rice cakes inside, thinking about how I likely happened on a life-changing discovery in the diet industry and how my soon-to-be bestseller could put my money troubles to rest.

Fume More, Consume Less.

"So, about dinner . . ."

I close my eyes, willing the voice behind me to leave.

"Come on, Paige. You can't avoid me forever."

"Maybe not, but I can try."

"Paige." He draws my name out, a slight teasing tone to his voice. I take a deep breath and turn around, squinting at him through the spitting drizzle.

He looks good. Luke has always looked good. While most boys went through the goofy years where their head, feet, and hands were too big for their bodies, I can't remember Luke ever looking anything less than perfect. I met him when I was a beyond-awkward fifth grader wearing my mom's old stirrup pants and carrying around toothpicks to get food out of my braces. Layla was assigned the desk next to me and we were instant friends. I'll never forget the day she took me to her house and I met Luke.

I thought he was the cutest boy I'd ever seen. And he was way mature because he was already in the seventh grade and had to shave.

I just look at him now, biting the inside of my cheek. The years have been good to Luke. His shoulders have filled out and his jawline has become a man's. His hair is thick and straight and nearly black, eyes dark. He smiles at me then, and I realize how long I've just been staring at him.

"Sorry," I mumble, looking away, blinking the raindrops out of my eyes.

"Look. I recognize I'm not exactly your favorite person on the planet. But I know Layla had something come up for work, I'm assuming the same can be said of the guy you were dancing with at Mom and Dad's party, so rather than sit inside a tiny apartment by yourself on your birthday, will you please just come to dinner with me?" He smiles self-deprecatingly. "I won't even talk to you if that's what you want."

I sigh. The options do not look good either way.

"Fine," I bark, stalking back to my car. "I will drive. We will stay for one hour. *One* hour, Luke." I whip around to face him and find him right on my tail, with a satisfied smile on his face. "And we will not discuss anything in the past." I use my best This Is Nonnegotiable voice I perfected during my many years babysitting.

Kids feared me.

Luke, it would seem, does not. He obviously fights to contain a grin and the battle is painful to watch.

"Yes, ma'am," he chokes out finally, hurrying around to the passenger side of my car, probably worrying I will change my mind.

Which I do six times by the time I open the driver's door. This is not a good idea. I slide into the car and look over at him sitting there so close to me.

This is the worst idea ever.

I check my phone, hoping that by some miracle Tyler's meeting has been canceled and I suddenly have a great excuse not to go out to dinner with Luke.

Nothing. Not even a low-battery warning, which obviously would have sent me back up to the apartment to charge it, therefore canceling my plans.

I start the car, my jaw aching from the sheer stress of sitting sixteen inches away from Luke Prestwick. He is even wearing cologne that is quickly soaking into my car. From the smell of it, some things haven't changed in the past four years.

"Where would you like to go?" he asks. "Didn't you always like that little Italian place over by the—?"

"No talking about the past," I interrupt. "We will go to

the Cheesecake Factory." We never ate there when we were dating. I drive, thankful for its close proximity to my apartment. The quicker we get there, the quicker I can get out of this car and get home and away from Luke forever.

The restaurant is packed, but it always is. I finally find a parking spot and march to the doors, push past a throng of people waiting, and approach the hostess stand. Luke hurries behind me like a little puppy struggling to keep up. "Two, please. Preferably with your fastest server."

The girl gives me a weird look but nods. "Two? Right this way." She picks up two menus, and I give an apologetic look to one of the fathers in the large group who shrugs in a "it's okay" way as he picks up his screaming three-year-old while another child runs around with a toy airplane making engine noises.

With any luck, we'll get seated right beside them and we won't even be able to make conversation.

It is not our luck. The waitress keeps walking farther and farther into the bowels of the restaurant, and we finally end up in some tiny alcove in the back, full of tables of couples holding hands across the tables and smiling into each other's eyes.

"I'm sorry, we don't need a quiet table," I tell her.

"It's the only table I have right now. The others will be about a thirty- to forty-minute wait."

"Here is fine." I sit down and try not to look at the couples around me, sling my purse on my chair, and take the menu.

Luke thanks the hostess and then sits across from me, smiling first at the people around us and then at me. "Nice little spot. I guess I've never been here with just one other person. I always get seated in the big room."

"Mm-hmm. It's great. We should probably know what we want to eat since we only have about forty-five minutes left." I prop up my menu on the table and stare at it, trying to focus, trying to get my brain to stop thinking about the fact that Luke is sitting opposite me in the Cheesecake Factory on my birthday.

I should just mark twenty-three down as the worst birthday of my life.

"Well, I'm going to get their steak. They have great steak."

He would pick something that takes ten years to cook.

He smiles at me and lays his menu on the table. "What is the birthday meal going to be?"

"Chopped salad." I close the menu.

"Salad?" he repeats dubiously. "We are at the Cheesecake Factory and you're getting a salad?"

"It cancels out the cheesecake. You should decide what cheesecake you want too so we can just order them both together."

He gives me a resigned look and then nods. "I'll get the strawberry one."

The waiter comes over. "You guys all set?"

I point to myself. "Sweet tea, the appetizer chopped salad, and the chocolate mousse cheesecake. Thank you."

"And I'd like sweet tea as well." Luke nods, telling the waiter the rest of his order.

The waiter scribbles furiously and then smiles a fake smile at us. "Sounds good. I'll have those right out."

Now comes the awkward part. I look around us. The couple seated right beside us is also waiting for their food, lacing their fingers together across the table and sighing into each other's eyes.

I look back at Luke. He is smiling at me. I bite the inside of my cheek again and cross my arms over my chest. The way this night is going, my cheek innards are going to have permanent nerve damage.

Happy birthday to me.

"It's good to see you, kid," he says in a low voice, and I flinch at the use of his old nickname for me. He smiles in a sad way and weaves his fingers together on the table. "It's been a long time."

I meet his eyes for a brief second, and then he looks down at his hands. My mom always used to sing that "If you can't say something nice" song to me when I was little so I keep my mouth shut.

I look away and then back over at him after a few minutes. He is staring off at something behind my right shoulder, looking so sad I feel the tiniest twinge of guilt.

I blink, willing the feeling away, but it persists, burrowing into my gut.

Seriously, Lord? Do You remember what he said to me?

Somehow I doubt that really matters to God at the moment. I make sure I give heaven a nice eye roll and then clear my throat. "How is work." It is a question. It just doesn't come out sounding like one.

Luke's head pops over to me so fast, I think his ceramic tooth, which he had to have put in after an unfortunate game of freeze tag in the youth group junior year of high school, might come dislodged. "Work?" He's back to grinning at me. "Work is great. I really love it there, Paige. I get up every day excited to go to work."

That makes one of us.

"I'm just so blessed."

Blessed. The word catches me off guard coming from Luke Prestwick's mouth. I narrow my eyes at him, wondering if it is just for my benefit that he said it.

He is off on a work-oriented train though and doesn't show any signs of coming back anytime soon. Which is nice because I am too busy fighting the Holy Spirit to pay very close attention to what I am hearing. Plus, the waiter comes by and brings our food, so I try my best to eat as fast as I can while arguing in my head.

I do not want to be polite.

"So I actually just got promoted about a year ago to be the executive—"

Let all bitterness be put away from you.

"And then I've been doing all this training and learning all these amazing new techniques—"

I wasn't bitter until he came back here. Just please help time go by in double speed so I can leave. He left everything almost five years ago, God, including You. Doesn't that give me a little bit of a license to be angry?

"There are so many cutting-edge technologies available to us right now—"

Restore such a one in a spirit of gentleness and watch yourself that you will not be tempted.

I'm not tempted, Lord. I'm mad.

"Which is why I'm moving here."

I blink at him, not sure if I actually heard what I thought he just said. "Excuse me?" I say, mouth full.

He smiles. "I'm moving here. For good. Permanently. My work is opening a Dallas office and they want me to be the lead on it." His smile grows even wider. "Isn't that great, Paige?"

I open my mouth, but no words are there to respond with.

"And I overheard that it is someone's birthday." Our waiter is suddenly right beside us setting our cheesecakes in front of us. Mine has a little red candle sticking out of it, and the waiter clicks a lighter, and without warning, twelve other waiters and waitresses appear and all start singing.

"Happy birthday to you . . ."

I stare at Luke, at the candle, at the cake, and then at the waitstaff. They finish the song, I blow out the candle, then they clap and leave.

Happy birthday to me.

Chapter
3

My mother, with all her quite loud distaste for organized sports, still somehow managed to end up with my dad, who usually has the TV tuned to ESPN before dinner leftovers have even started the cooling process in the fridge. I remember them arguing about it often during the early years of my childhood, but eventually Mom just gave up. Now she'll sit beside him on the couch with her book and hot tea, and Dad will watch the games with his bottomless glasses of sweet iced tea.

I guess in an effort to sway his oldest daughter to his side, Dad bought me the *Casey at the Bat* book when I turned two. And for the next six years, it was my absolute favorite book, even though the love of baseball didn't stick like Dad had hoped.

But every so often, if I am feeling lonely or homesick for Mom and Dad, I'll turn on the TV to whatever baseball or football game is on and just snuggle up on the couch, listening to the sounds of home.

I didn't say another word to Luke other than "Thank you

for dinner" and "Good-bye" when we got back to my apartment. Then I turned and ran up the steps before he could offer some reason why I should let him inside to keep me company since it was only seven o'clock on a Friday night.

I locked the door behind me, immediately changed into my black yoga pants and an old soft T-shirt my parents got for me on one of their anniversary trips that said *Loo-WOW Luau. Hawaii 1996*, and flounced onto the couch, reaching for the remote.

Last night was a baseball night.

And thankfully, it was right at the start of the season.

"There was no joy in Mudville," I muttered to myself, quoting *Casey*.

* * * * *

I pour my cereal into a bowl, still wearing my pajamas. I stayed up until almost midnight last night watching ESPN and wishing I was at home on my parents' couch, listening to Dad talk about the glory days of baseball and how everything is motivated by money now. Mom called and sang a tearful happy birthday and told me she hated that she couldn't be with me. I read Galatians and don't remember a word of it.

Moving here. Luke is *moving* here.

Permanently, he said.

There are things in my life that I would like to be permanent. Nail polish that permanently stayed on my toenails. Hair that permanently stayed away from my legs. Sweet tea that was permanently in my fridge.

Luke is not one of those things I want permanently in my life. Or even in my city.

I crunch a spoonful of Raisin Bran. I should not take my rage out on my temporomandibular joint.

The doorbell rings and I stop, midcrunch, and just sit there like if I didn't move, whoever is outside will go away. I am wearing a pair of pink plaid pajama shorts, a gray T-shirt, and my hair is in a low sloppy bun. I have mascara smudged all over my face.

Whoever is outside my door does not want to see this.

I creep over to the door all stealth-mode-like and peer through the peephole, half hoping it is a big box from UPS that contains all sorts of birthday gladness, even though my parents' check arrived two days ago and is already finding a happy new home in my savings account and I can't think of anyone else who would send me a birthday gift.

It is a girl about my age. She is wearing sunglasses and standing about three feet away from the door. Her hair is almost halfway down her back in dark brown curls, and she is wearing white shorts and a black fitted shirt, from what I can tell. Peepholes don't always tell the whole truth.

I don't recognize her, which means she likely has the wrong apartment.

I flip my pajama shirttail inside out, swipe it under my eyes to gather up most of the mascara, and open the door. "Hi, sorry, I think you might have the wrong apartment. Jeremy lives in 27C. This is 27B."

"Paige?"

Every single fiber of my being freezes.

I stare at the girl as she pulls her sunglasses off her face and am shocked into complete silence.

It is Preslee.

She is old. That is the first thought that hits me. Four

years ago, the last time I saw her, she was a kid. Now Preslee is a woman.

I don't know what to do. Or say. So I just stand there in my pajamas, gaping at her.

"Can I come in?" Preslee points to my apartment.

I nod mutely at her, feeling mechanical as I step back into my living room to open the door wider to let her in.

She walks into my apartment, looking around. I follow her gaze. The couches that used to be Mom and Dad's. The picture on my wall of our parents and me last year at Christmas, the fourth Christmas in a row that we didn't even get a phone call from Preslee.

I finally look back at her. She is thin. Much thinner than she was when she lived at home. Her hair is a lot longer, too. I knew she'd gotten a tattoo on her shoulder blade when she first was threatening to move out, but there is a small brown bird traced onto her ankle now as well.

Finally we just look at each other.

My stomach feels like I've just finished competing in a hot dog–eating contest. The nerves in the backs of my eyeballs tingle. I keep waiting for her to talk, hoping she will say something and then praying she won't say a word and she'll just leave again, sort of like she did four years ago.

She just looks at me. Half smiling. Half pained.

"Here." She shoves a gift bag I didn't even notice at me. "Happy belated birthday."

Somehow, I speak. "Thank you."

She smiles another sad smile at me and then nods. "Okay. I just wanted to give you your birthday gift. Bye, Paige."

She opens the door and leaves. I watch Preslee walk down the steps and out of sight wordlessly.

Part of me is relieved. Part of me wants her to come back. Most of me is just still in shock.

I look down at the cream-colored gift bag with the brown tissue paper in it. Boring colors. My favorites. I feel a little twinge in my stomach that she remembered.

I sit on the couch and carefully pull out the tissue-wrapped blob. It is a tiny brown jewelry box and I open it, biting the inside of my cheek.

A very delicate silver chain holds a tiny charm that says *Sister*. An even tinier little ring holds my birthstone next to it.

A note card falls out of the tissue paper and I just stare at it.

Then I start getting angry.

Preslee left *us*. There was none of this "let's kick her out of the house and see if that turns her around" business at my house. She willingly and unflinchingly walked out my parents' front door, not even sparing a glance backward. And before she left, she did everything in her power to make my parents' lives a living hell.

The unicorn on her shoulder blade was the beginning.

I missed a lot of the worst of it. I was already here in Dallas going to school. I'd seen the warning signs that it was coming, though. Preslee had never been one to stick to the rules. While I was home five minutes before curfew the few nights I was out, Preslee never got home on time. I got straight As; Preslee flunked out of a few classes and not for lack of intelligence. I worked the newsletter and yearbook staffs; Preslee started a punk rock band and became a drummer.

We lived down the hallway from each other but we were worlds apart.

Then she was gone. Left, claiming she was going to tour the country with her band and she'd just live with her boyfriend in their tour bus.

"Spike." Or whatever fake name he had.

I happened to be home visiting the Friday night she walked out, and I can remember the roller coaster of emotions I felt. Sadness because she was my baby sister. Relief because she wouldn't be there making my parents crazy anymore. And mostly anger because of what she did to my mom and dad.

I look down at the note card, stand up, and walk into my bedroom without reading it. It is time for a shower. A shower and a fun day.

The last eighteen hours have not been great ones.

I get out of the shower twenty minutes later, dry off, pull on a pair of jeans and a gray fitted T-shirt. It isn't raining today, but it is about 90 percent humidity. That means I am not about to spend thirty minutes styling my hair only to have it fall completely flat by the time I get to the bottom of my front steps.

I brush on some eye shadow and mascara and scrunch my wet hair into semiwaves. I have always had issues with the color of my hair, as in, my hair can't pick what color it wants to be. It's red, brown, and blonde. I always have a hard time at the DMV when I'm renewing my driver's license, but I've come to grips with it. I am usually fairly content with my hair, but on days of extreme humidity, I really wish for curls like Layla's.

My phone is buzzing in the living room when I come back out. I purposefully ignore the half-opened gift on the couch and answer the phone.

"Hey, Paige."

I smile. "Hey, Tyler."

"So. I just happen to be about ten minutes away from a beautiful girl's apartment, and I was just calling to see if she might be up for a late breakfast with me."

I grin, feeling a blush on my cheeks even though he isn't even here. Tyler is good with the compliments. "Well, if you're referring to me, I already ate."

"What?"

I speak louder. "I said, if you're referring to me—"

"No, I heard you. What did you eat for breakfast?"

"Oh. Sorry I yelled. Raisin Bran."

"Gross."

"Hey," I say. "I don't call your food choices gross."

"Yes you do."

I think about that one. Well, okay, he is right. "Never mind. Anyway, I'm free for lunch though."

"Why aren't you going to eat lunch?"

I pull the phone away from my head to look at the signal bars on the screen. Full signal. I crank the volume in my voice again. "I said, I'm free for lunch," I say, annunciating everything clearly.

"I heard you, Paige. Can you not hear me? Hello? Calling Paige Alder."

"Tyler."

"Look, all I know is that I took an economics class as a ninth grader, and I definitely was taught that there was no such thing as a free lunch. So if you are planning on being free at lunch, I'm just assuming you're not eating. How much Raisin Bran did you have this morning? Because I can only stomach so much before it starts getting soggy, and there really is nothing nastier than soggy bran flakes all clumping together."

I close my eyes. "It is too early to talk to you."

"Which is why we should eat instead of talk. Come on, Paige. I didn't even get the chance to give you your birthday gift yesterday."

I smile. "I'd like that."

"All right. Ten minutes. See you soon."

The phone clicks in my ear. I go to find a pair of shoes and decide on flip-flops that do not look very good with what I have on but look supercute with a red skirt and white T-shirt. So it is time to change then.

I stare at the jeans and gray shirt after I take them off. This is always a dilemma for me. I have technically worn them. Does that make them clean or dirty? My mother's philosophy is that if it has come off the hanger, it's dirty and should be washed before being hung back up. I think that has something to do with my dad. When Mom met Dad, he was cutting all the tags off his shirts and wearing the front side one day, then flipping them inside out and wearing the other side the next day.

I think he called it "two-timing" his shirts.

I don't think Mom ever recovered from knowing that about my dad.

I end up just leaving the jeans and shirt on the bed, and I'll decide what to do with them whenever I get back. I stick my phone in my purse and am just sliding on a pair of silver dangle earrings when Tyler knocks on the door.

He is standing there grinning at me behind a huge bouquet of yellow roses. "Happy birthday!"

I take the bouquet, trying not to blush again. "Thanks,

Tyler." The flowers are already in a vase, which is a relief.

I'm the worst floral arranger in the history of bouquets. Somehow I always get half of the flowers cut three inches shorter than the others.

I smile at Tyler. Tyler is a software engineer, but you'd never be able to tell it by the way he looks. Most of the time he wears jeans, flannel shirts, and work boots. Right now, he's wearing cargo shorts, a T-shirt, and flip-flops. I am fairly certain this is the first time I've ever seen his feet.

It can be a scarring thing to behold a man's feet.

Tyler's aren't the worst I've ever seen. They aren't the best either, but considering the fact Tyler thinks jeans without holes are "nice" clothes, I am not too shocked.

His blond hair is all curly, like he forgot to run a comb through it after his shower. I smile wider. I like it like this.

"Ready for second breakfast?" he asks me as I set the vase on the kitchen table.

"Depends. Are you ready for first breakfast?"

"I'm starving."

"I bet. It's almost eleven." I pick up my purse and follow him out the door, then lock it behind me. When we get to the base of my stairs, he smiles warmly at me and gives me a side hug.

"I'm sorry I had to work so late yesterday. Where should we go to eat?"

I shrug. "I'm good with whatever."

"Oh great. You're *that* person. I might have to rethink this."

"What person?"

"The 'no, really, whatever you want to do is exactly what I want to do' person. I'm sorry, Paige, but if this is going to work, I'm going to need you making approximately 50 percent of the decisions."

I grin at him and follow him to his blue truck. "Yeah, but you haven't made any decisions yet either."

"I did too. I decided we should go out to eat."

"I am fairly certain that does not count."

He holds the passenger door open. "Well, one of us has to decide."

"How about that pancake place over by that pet store? They've got brunchy stuff."

"Sounds good."

He drives there, talking the whole time about how busy work is and how sorry he is that he missed seeing me on my birthday.

"Really, Paige. I felt terrible. What a way to make a good impression, right?"

I shrug. My birthday wasn't all awful, but it wasn't great. I am not sure Tyler could have changed any of that, though. Odds were that Luke would still have shown up.

And then Preslee this morning.

I rub my forehead.

Tyler looks over at me. "All okay?"

"Hmm? Yeah. Sorry. I'll explain later."

We get to the restaurant and Tyler pulls the truck into a parking space. I first discovered this place when I was in the middle of my first midterms here. It was the only nonscary-looking place open late and it smelled like heaven inside. And another heavenly attribute, it was cheap.

I came here a lot through college. Most of my Freshmen Fifteen was thanks to the peach pancakes with a side of bacon.

Which is why the day after I graduated, I started running.

We get seated at a table in the corner and I look around at the Saturday late-morning customers. Families who are visiting over ice-cold pancake remnants and likely their umpteenth coffee refill while babies and kids play goofy games with each other. Men reading the paper alone. Ladies chatting over some of the lunch options.

"I don't know if I've ever actually eaten here before." Tyler opens the menu. "I think I came in here once with Rick, and it was packed to the rafters so we headed to IHOP instead." He shrugged. "Rick was apparently in a pancake mood."

"Those moods are hard to shake," I say, feeling Rick's pain. The need for pancakes struck often after I vowed to stop coming here. I tried to shut the need up with celery sticks, and it rarely worked.

I will never understand how some people can exist on diets of fruits and vegetables. I have a deep mix of sympathy for them and envy of them.

"So. What's good here?"

"Peach pancakes," I tell him decidedly. I've already eaten my semihealthy breakfast of Raisin Bran, and I am still thinking of ordering the peach pancakes.

I always thought there was no cereal more healthy than Raisin Bran until I was sleepily reading the cereal box one morning and realized that sugar was listed twice in the ingredients.

Now I am not sure, even though in my brain the word *bran* is pretty much synonymous with *lover of all things healthy*.

Tyler makes a noise deep in the back of his throat. "Mmm. Burritos. Ever had the meat-lover's burrito?"

"You do not know me at all."

"Why not?"

"Because, Tyler, there are peach pancakes here. Peach. Pancakes. As in, the best ever. Why would I trade those in for something I could get at any truck stop in the city?"

He shrugs. "I figure this burrito is probably made with real bacon. That's one up on the truck-stop burritos."

I just stare at him. "Please tell me you are joking."

"No, I'm serious. I bet this place uses real pork."

I make a face and the waiter comes over. "Good morning. Can I start you off with some coffee? Or perhaps one of our cinnamon rolls? Are you feeling okay, ma'am?"

I look up at the waiter, and if I have to guess, he is right around my age. And he is calling me *ma'am*.

That doesn't sit well for some reason. Probably because I just turned another year older. "I'm fine, sir."

Tyler smushes his lips together and stares very intensely at his menu.

"Coffee?" the waiter asks again.

"Yes please. With cream for mine."

"You, sir?"

Tyler shakes his head. "Just orange juice for me, thanks."

"Are you ready to order?" he asks, scribbling our drink order on a notepad. We both order our breakfast and Tyler hands the menus to the waiter.

"Happy birthday, *ma'am*." Tyler hands me a small wrapped box across the table.

I didn't see him carrying anything in, so it must have been in his pocket. I smile. "Thanks, Tyler."

I rip off the wrapping paper, a little worried that it's jewelry or something way beyond where I think we probably are in a semirelationship. I mean, we haven't even defined anything yet.

To me, that equals way too early for jewelry.

I get the last of the wrapping paper off. It is a jewelry box. A blue velvety one.

I look up at him and he grins cheekily. "Will you open it, slowpoke?"

I bite the inside of my cheek and squeak the tiny box open.

Two tickets are propped in the box, and I look up and squint at him. "You're not telling me that you sleep on Red Sox sheets, are you?"

"No, but *Fever Pitch* was a great movie. Read the tickets, Paige."

"Frisco RoughRiders," I read slowly and then look up at him. "It's a rodeo?"

"It's baseball, Paige. It's the minor league team near here? Please tell me you've heard of baseball. Batter up? Home runs? Strikeouts? Hot dogs?"

"Easy there, Tyler." I hold up a hand. "I have heard of baseball."

"Ever been to a game?"

I nod. "My dad took me to a few when I was little."

Tyler beams at me. "Great! Then you know it's tons of fun."

I just look at the tickets, at Tyler, and then nod, smiling. "Oh yes," I say, closing the jewelry box. "Thanks, Tyler."

It's not that I have something against baseball. Like I said, my dad is a huge baseball fan. I just like the freedom to wear my pajamas and change the channel to more important things like finding out what color cabinets the *Kitchen Cousins* are going to install on that episode while watching baseball. I'm not a fan of the whole go-to-the-park-and-eat-artificially-flavored-nachos thing.

There is a place for artificial flavors. It is usually in cough drops.

"Well, anyway, the tickets are actually gift certificates so we can go whenever it's a good time for you," Tyler says. "I mean, they play 140 games. I figure, surely we can find a time that works for the two of us *one* of those nights."

I suddenly feel very sorry for all of the wives and girl-friends of those players. That is a major time commitment for something that only serves to be entertainment while eating hot dogs.

"So, Tyler." I drop the box into my purse, preparing to tell him all about Luke and Preslee. The Luke part will likely be awkward. Actually, so will the Preslee part because I haven't shared very much of that with Tyler yet.

Some things just shouldn't be shared in detail for a little while.

The waiter comes right then, and I stop while he situates our drinks and food on the table. "Let me know if you need anything else."

I barely hear him because I am distracted with the plate of steaming hot peaches, pooling peach syrup, and melting whipped cream all piled on top of four of the largest pancakes I've ever seen.

This is much bigger than it was when I came here in college.

Unless it is one of those perspective things like teenage drivers. When you are one, you and everyone else your age look very mature and capable. When you are older, all teen drivers look like they should still be in booster seats.

Tyler whistles at my plate. "Now *those* are pancakes."

I glance up at his burrito and shake my head. The thing

is larger than Tyler's torso. And Tyler is not what I would call small-chested.

"Why don't we pray? I'm worried now for our arteries." Tyler grins.

I fold my hands under the table to avoid the whole awkward "should we hold hands to pray yet?" thing, and Tyler says a quick prayer.

"Thank You, Lord, for this meal, for this day, and for the beautiful company. Please bless this year of Paige's. Amen."

"Amen. And thank you," I say, smiling up at him.

"Okay. Let's eat!" He grabs his fork.

I take a few bites and then decide it is now or never. "So, Tyler, I actually—"

"Hi, Paige."

And there is Luke, standing right next to my chair.

Timing will never be my strong suit.

Chapter 4

I was never the girl in school who always had a string of boys around her. If anything, I was the opposite. I barely went out unless it was to Layla's house, and I didn't even know I was on my first date until it was over, seeing as how a "bunch of us going to the movies" turned into me; Layla; Layla's high school crush, Tim; and Tim's cousin, Daniel.

After the boys left the theater, Layla burst into a happy monologue about how excited she was that our first double date was with each other and how we could just marry Tim and Daniel and be cousins-in-law and have all kinds of cute babies that had the same last name.

Tyler looks up at Luke and smiles a polite smile. "Luke, right?"

"That's right. And you're . . . uh . . ."

"Tyler."

"Right," Luke says, looking back at me.

I, meanwhile, am praying like crazy.

Please, Lord, don't let Luke say something that will ruin this whole breakfast with Tyler.

He must see something because Luke smiles once at me, lays a hand on the back of my chair, and nods to both of us. "Well. Y'all have a great time. I'll see you later, Paige."

I manage one of those "mm-hmm" faces at him and he leaves, picking up a to-go cup off of a table on the other side of the restaurant and waving at a few guys. I recognize their faces but can't remember their names.

"Luke is Layla's brother, right?"

"Right. Listen, Tyler . . ." I say, starting again.

"Paige."

I swear the insides of my cheek are going to be just a mass of overworked flesh in the very near future.

I look at him, at his sweet expression, at his bright blue eyes, and chicken out.

"Never mind," I say quietly, then shovel another bite of peach pancake into my mouth.

He looks at me for a second and then shrugs it off. "Okay then. So I've been meaning to ask you, I heard a rumor you like that awful Chinese place with the three-dollar General Tso's chicken. That can't really be true, right?"

"Oh, of course, no," I say, pulling my best impression of Zorro.

He keeps talking about how he went there one time with some coworkers and three of them got food poisoning. I'm trying really hard to pay attention, I honestly am, but my brain keeps wandering away from the table.

Luke is moving here. Permanently. The running into him at restaurants is going to end up becoming a common thing, I think. We both like the same ones. It always made date night easy because we both liked the same four restaurants.

Preslee was in my apartment today. In my *apartment*.

Mom must've given her the address. I talked very briefly with Mom yesterday when she called to sing happy birthday, but she called last night after the Cheesecake Factory fiasco and I was just too emotionally exhausted to hear Mom's new constant conversation killer.

"Have you talked to your sister yet? She really wants to talk with you, Paige."

Tyler is still talking, and I am sad to realize I didn't hear a word of the last thing he said. He's grinning and talking and obviously enjoying his burrito while my peach pancakes suddenly taste gritty.

I believe that's because they are mixing with a good dose of Frustration and Annoyance.

Not the best of spices.

I swallow a bite, mentally corralling my thoughts. *Focus on Tyler, head. Focus!* Tyler is here. Tyler is sweet. It seems like there could potentially be some sparks with him.

"Anyway, what did you end up doing for your birthday?" Tyler asks. Ah, the segue into the I-got-kidnapped-for-dinner conversation.

I finish another bite and try not to feel guilty over something I probably could have controlled better. "I worked. And then I went to dinner at the Cheesecake Factory with Luke."

Sometimes it's best to just say it. At least, I hope that's the case.

Tyler just looks at me, chewing his burrito, the faintest glint of something — sadness? curiosity? worry? — in his eyes.

I immediately keep talking, waving my hands for emphasis. "It was ridiculous, Tyler. He showed up at my work right when I got off and told me how lame it was that I was going to dinner by myself on my birthday, and he was really persistent, and I was just trying to get him off my back. We sat there for an hour and it was the worst hour of my life."

Tyler smiles then. "It's okay, Paige. You don't have to explain anything."

"Well, I just need you to know that Luke and I dated years ago, but it's over. Okay?"

He stares at me for a minute, searching my eyes. "Does Luke know that?"

"Yes." Especially after last night.

He just nods. "Okay." He looks like he's about to say something else, but then he stops.

"Preslee came by today." We should have asked for a bigger table with how much stuff I'm unloading at the moment. All of these issues aren't going to fit with our huge plates.

"Preslee, your sister?"

"Yeah."

"Cool."

Obviously I haven't shared a lot with Tyler about Preslee yet. But we are still just in the getting-to-know-you stage. We aren't officially dating.

I take that issue back off the table and try to swallow it along with my now-soggy pancakes.

*　*　*　*　*

Eleven o'clock. And Galatians.

I stare at the words swimming on the page in front of me, wishing I were one of those people who could do their devotional times in the morning. I've tried. I end up forgetting everything I've read and focusing on the coffee beside me.

Coffee is a big motivator in the mornings.

I read the same sentence for the third time. *"For through the Law I died to the Law, so that I might live to God."*

It sounds like one of those this-is-my-grandmother's-third-cousin's-son's-wife sentences. I need a pencil to figure the sentence out.

I'm too tired to go get a pencil.

I look at it again. *"For through the . . ."*

I rub my eyes and shake my head. Never mind. I'll try again tomorrow night.

Chapter 5

This is my one week out of the month when I teach the two-year-old Sunday school class. I used to teach it more often, but I'm working on not working too much.

Like Dad told me, "Grace is free, but therapy is expensive."

I never really understood that until recently.

I shower and pull on a pair of faded jeans and a black nicer top. Two-year-old Sunday school is not the time to pull out the fashion stops. Not that I pull out the fashion stops very often. The older I get, the more I cling to comfort.

I never expected that to happen so soon.

I mess with my hair for almost fifteen minutes and finally just pull it back in a sloppy, low bun. I'm teaching. I'll use that as my excuse for everything today. I pour my coffee into a thermos and run for the door. I took too long on my hair today so there is no chance for breakfast.

Maybe someone will bring doughnuts to church and feel sorry for me.

I get to church and into my classroom right as the other teacher arrives with her son, Ben.

"Morning, Paige," Rhonda says all singsongy. "Beautiful day today. Benjamin, how do you say hi to Miss Paige?"

Ben pops the three fingers he was chewing on out of his mouth and the drool crests over his chin. "Gwud mownin, Mwiss Paid."

"Good morning, Ben," I reply, somewhat thankful now that I missed breakfast.

There are weeks when I have definitely sworn off future children of my own after working in here. I just don't have the gag reflex for parenting. Or the grime tolerance. Everything these kids touch is blackened afterward.

"Ben learned a new trick," Rhonda says, her smile proud as she looks at her son. "Want to tell Miss Paige what you learned how to do?"

"Um. I kin count." Ben holds up four fingers.

"Oh yeah? Let me hear it," I say.

"Um. One, two, free, four, one." Then he cheeses at me, eyes squinty. "Yay Bwen!" he yells, applauding himself.

Rhonda smiles as Ben runs off to play with the toys we keep in the corner of the room. "They just change so fast, you know?" She gets all misty-eyed.

This is Rhonda's constant mantra. Every time I see her, she's bemoaning how quickly her son is growing up.

Whenever, or if ever, I have children, I will not be able to wait until they are old enough to blow their own nose and go to the bathroom and wash their hands unassisted.

The kids slowly trickle in, and by nine fifteen, Rhonda and I are surrounded by twenty-one two-year-olds. I do believe it is time for our church to find a third teacher for this classroom.

"All right!" Rhonda yells over the chaos abounding in the

room. "Time to clean up the toys and sit down for our story! Benjamin Wilder Matthews, if you don't let go of that truck *right now*, you have got another thing coming!"

Ben immediately lets go of the truck and goes to sulk in the story corner. A few of our more obedient children head that way as well. It takes some coaxing and finally some demanding before everyone leaves the lure of the toys.

I will never buy my potential future children Duplo blocks either. Too many pieces. Too much mess.

"All righty," Rhonda says again once everyone is seated on the floor, including both of us. "I think Miss Paige has prepared a fantastic Bible story for us today. Everyone needs to be quiet and listen."

Nothing like the pressure of forty-two eyes staring at you, waiting for entertainment that will very likely not measure up to *Sesame Street*, or whatever kids are watching these days. "Today we are going to learn about a blind man," I say, trying to instill some drama into my voice.

One little girl who I think is about the cutest thing in the classroom interrupts. "What's bwind?"

"Blind means they can't see," I say. "All of you can see me, but if you were blind, you wouldn't be able to."

Twenty-one heads start nodding. "Because it was dawk," one little boy says knowingly.

"Oh," three of them chorus, drawing the word out.

"I don't wike the dawk."

"Sometime it get dawk if you hode your hand over your eyes," another one says.

"Yeah . . ." The three hum again.

"It wasn't dark," I say, trying to get the audience back. "It was daylight. He just couldn't see *ever*."

"'Cause he had on his mommy's gwasses?"

I just look at the boy who asked me the question, mashing my lips together, trying not to laugh in the very serious little face six inches away from mine.

Rhonda grins across the sea of children at me. "Add in about ten zillion of those kinds of questions a day, Paige, and you've got life as a mother."

*   *   *   *   *

I used to go to our church's singles class. Then the pastor in charge of the class, Pastor Dan, went on a sabbatical and left four of the single guys in charge of the teaching while he was gone.

After one too many lessons on how Xbox is biblical, seeing as how it doesn't allow for "idle hands," I decided to go back to the regular service and see how things were there.

Things are much better. I've been here for almost six weeks now and I have never once heard Pastor Louis mention the word *Xbox*, much less the other favorite *football*.

I find my new regular row. When I left the singles class, Layla and her fiancé, Peter, came with me. Tyler never went to our Sunday school class, but he always went to service, and he sits with us too.

No one else is there yet, but that's typical on the weeks when I teach the two-year-olds. I always end up here by myself for about fifteen minutes, in the lag time between services, before the others show up.

I set my Bible and purse down to save seats.

Right then I hear a gurgling, spitting noise and I look up

to see Natalie, our youth pastor's wife and my dear friend, standing there holding their new baby, Claire.

"I can't sneak up on anyone anymore," Natalie gripes but smiles adoringly at her daughter. Now that Claire is sleeping better through the nights, everything is all sunshine again.

There were days when I wondered if Natalie was going to make it.

"Hi, cutie patootie!" I have no idea why babies promote such goofy reactions from adults, but I partake in the tradition without much resistance.

"Hi," Natalie says.

I barely spare a glance at Natalie. "Here, let me take that huge burden out of your hands." I make silly faces at Claire. She's still so little that she just looks at me, pacifier bobbing in her mouth, but I do it anyway.

Like I said. Tradition.

"Gosh, she's heavier." I shift her into the crook of my right arm.

"Yep. And I am getting biceps, baby." Natalie flexes for me. "Forget Jillian Michaels. I'm going to start marketing that the best thing for weight loss is to carry a ten-pound baby around for sixteen hours a day."

"I'm not sure very many people could commit to that kind of workout," I say.

"Most likely not. How are you? I haven't seen you in decades."

In all reality, I picked up lunch and brought it over to Natalie's house two weeks ago, but she's right. Ever since Claire was born, we just haven't seen each other as often.

The tiniest people seem to cause the biggest conflicts in scheduling.

"I'm . . ." I think about my answer. "Good" might be an overstatement, considering the current Luke/Preslee drama. "Okay" though will send off warning bells in Natalie's brain, and we'll have to rehash my entire life after the service over lunch at her house while Rick makes sarcastic remarks the whole time.

I end up being saved by the baby, because right then, Claire erupts in a smelly white lava covering the entire front of her dress and my left hand.

"Oh my!" I have never seen so much come from something so little.

Natalie sighs and digs around in the diaper bag hanging off her shoulder, then comes out with a cloth that already looks a little damp. "Sorry," she mumbles. "Something I'm eating this week is not working for her. I should have warned you."

I don't say anything because "Uh, yeah, you should have" sounds mean and I don't mind so much because I've already been snotted on, cried on, slobbered on, and I'm pretty certain I had pee rubbed on my pants during class this morning from a little boy who failed to wash his hands after using the potty.

A shower is in my very-near future. Preferably within the next two hours.

Natalie sops us both up and I shrug, patting Claire's wet stomach. "Sorry, peanut."

"No, she's sorry. There's no call to spit up on Auntie Paige like that."

If Rick and Natalie keep calling every adult "Auntie" and "Uncle," this poor child will believe that everyone everywhere is related to her.

I hand Claire back to Natalie as the band starts to take the stage. "All right, you need to call me," Natalie says. "This is ridiculous that it's been so long since we've seen you. And speaking of that, you can come to dinner. Tomorrow night. I'll make that pot roast you like."

My mother makes an incredible pot roast. Out of this world. She's given me the recipe seven times when I call her completely homesick for her cooking, and each time it turns out terrible. I've kind of decided that she spits in it, since my mother's saliva is the only thing missing from mine.

Natalie, though, also makes an incredible pot roast. Very similar to my mom's. Which is probably why we became such good friends so quickly.

"I will be there."

"Good. See you, love," she says, balancing the baby, the diaper bag, and her Bible as she leaves the sanctuary.

Layla and Peter come skirting in right as the band starts playing. Layla smiles at me, brown eyes sparkling, hair bouncy, and hugs me as she slides by. "Hi, Paige!" Peter smiles slightly at me as he slides past, wearing jeans and a button-up shirt, his short dark hair obviously freshly cut.

Layla is the happiest person I know. I am fairly convinced it could be raining teacup saucers outside, shattering everyone's windows and eardrums, and Layla would still be declaring that it was the most beautiful day and her best day ever.

It can be an annoying trait, especially when I am PMSing. Which I'm not today. That I know of anyway.

Halfway through the second song, Tyler shows up and smiles at me as he sets his Bible on the aisle seat I'd saved for him. "Right on time," he whispers and I shake my head.

Tyler is late 90 percent of the time. The other 10 percent

he shaves so close to the time that he doesn't need to use a razor the rest of the week.

I am on the other extreme. I really like being early. I don't like the getting up and leaving my apartment early, but I do like being on time. My father taught me well. My mother made us both crazy my entire living-at-home life. "I'll be right there, go get in the car" was the code phrase for "I've still got probably twenty minutes in the house."

To this day, I have no idea what would take her so long to get ready to go.

We finish singing, Pastor Louis preaches on 1 John chapter one and says we are going to be starting a new series. "I haven't ever preached through this book and I'm very excited to do so. If you are struggling with how to love your family or your friends, if you are curious how to live in this world without becoming tainted by it, if you are wanting to know how much God loves you, then keep coming back. It will be a great sermon series."

I bite the inside of my cheek and further damage those nerves when Pastor Louis mentions "love your family."

Great.

Never once have I been able to go to church and sit here and just half listen to the sermon since it doesn't apply to me. Just once I'd like to go to church and hear a message on not kicking puppies or something like that.

Then I could just mindlessly listen, agree that is a bad thing, and never do it.

Not that I would anyway.

The band plays another two songs and then dismisses us. Tyler turns to look at me, stretching. "Good morning."

"Hi."

"Hello, Late One," Layla says around me to Tyler. "Your alarm clock break again?"

"I was early!" Tyler protests. "I didn't even know they did music before the sermon."

I laugh. He's kidding. He's usually here right around when the band moves onto the stage.

"So where are we going today?" Layla asks.

She means for lunch, because the four of us have gone out for the last four weeks in a row. It works as long as I budget the money for lunch into my groceries for the week.

Although Tyler has paid for me the last two times.

I've felt horribly guilty both times, seeing as how we aren't official and we certainly weren't on a date then.

Tyler shrugs. "There's that new place just up the street. The Store?"

"The Market." Layla nods. "I was going to suggest that. One of my boss's clients said that it's the bomb."

"That bad?" Tyler grins at Layla.

Tyler and Layla can hardly communicate between all of his sarcastic comments and her miscommunications. I have somewhat decided that they need to just stop talking to each other.

But there's another part of me that is very glad my best friend is getting along with the guy I'm kind of interested in.

Definitely interested in?

I look at Tyler and he's cute today. He doesn't look any different than he normally does and I like that. Jeans. Work boots. A flannel shirt over a T-shirt. Five o'clock shadow. Curly blond hair.

I never in my life would have thought I'd find that look

attractive, though. I used to be all about the clean-cut and put-together look. None of this ratty-hems-on-the-backs-of-the-jeans thing like Tyler currently has going on.

"Hey, guys."

A part of my chest freezes at the voice behind me. Speaking of clean-cut, Luke has apparently decided to join our church this morning.

My church. Layla and I started coming here when we were in college. Right after the Luke phase of my life was officially over.

Or so I thought.

Layla smiles happily at her brother and then drops the expression. "What are you doing here? This is our church."

"I'm trying out churches." He holds a hand out to Tyler. "Tyler, good to see you. And Peter, you as well." The men all shake hands while Layla and I have a little silent chat.

I had no idea, Layla mouths.

It's okay. We were leaving anyway.

"Well," I say, probably louder than I should have. "Shall we?"

"Shall we what?" Luke asks.

Awkwardness. I shouldn't have opened my mouth. Layla gives me a pained expression and then looks at her brother. "We are going to lunch," she says in a quiet voice.

Luke is a bright guy. He got straight As all through school and a hefty scholarship to college. He's obviously moving up in his company. He knows social cues.

He apparently doesn't care today. "Great! Where are we going?"

Layla tells him in an even quieter voice and we all walk out to the parking lot, Luke chattering happily while Layla,

Tyler, and I are uncharacteristically quiet. Peter is silent as well, but that's not that weird. Peter is a quiet sort.

Tyler offers me a ride since it's just up the road, and I climb into his truck. He closes my door and the second he closes his door, I start ranting.

"We! We, we, *we!*"

"Want to go all the way home?" Tyler grins over at me. I guess I am sounding a little too much like the Fifth Little Piggy, but I can't help it.

"It's apparently a very hard word to understand. *We.* I understand it. You understand it. Why doesn't *he* understand it?"

"Well," Tyler says, pulling out of the parking lot. "We can't all be we-ally smart. That would just be we-diculous."

I cover my face. "I don't even like you anymore."

"Ah, come on. It was funny."

"No it wasn't."

"Not even a wee bit?"

I hit him with my purse.

Chapter 6

Rick and Natalie live in a cute little neighborhood on the north side of Richardson. I get to their house a little early, but I brought dessert so Natalie won't make me wait on the porch until it's officially six o'clock.

"Please tell me those are salted caramel brownies," she says, opening the door, not bothering with common courtesies like "hello" and "how are you."

"I got your text." I hold the foil-covered pan out in both hands, bowing my head lightly as I offer it to her.

"I really do like you, you know."

I shrug. "You can say whatever you want. I know the truth. You only like me for my brownies."

"Well, it will make for less-awkward dinner conversations now that you're in the know." She closes the door behind me.

Rick is in the kitchen, Claire in one arm and a cup of coffee in the other hand. Rick is a big, big man with a bald head, which makes him both a cool yet somewhat threatening figure. Perfect for a youth pastor. "Dude, I almost wore that shirt."

I look down at my outfit. This is Rick and Natalie's house. So I wore my most comfortable jeans, which are also full of snags and fades and holes, my favorite T-shirt from youth camp last summer that I chaperoned on, and my slippers.

"Aw, you should have called her." Natalie lifts the lid on the slow cooker on the counter, sending a plume of delicious, meaty-filled steam up into the room.

"I'll just have to do that next time. So. Paigey."

Anytime Rick adds a *y* to my name, it's bad.

"No," I say.

"Come on. You haven't even heard what I was going to say."

"I don't need to. The answer's no. And I've been working really hard to learn how to say that word, so give me points on saying it so well a second ago."

"I thought your diction was perfect," Natalie says.

"Thank you." I nod graciously because no one really likes an overly proud person.

"I need you, Paige."

I sigh and give him a resigned look before pushing him and Claire out of the way so I can get the silverware out of their drawer. "Need me to do what exactly?"

"Intern. At the church. It's a paid position. Probably more than what you are making now answering phones and kicking the copier."

Rick and Natalie know all about my copier issues.

"Intern," I repeat, dubiously, setting the table. "What exactly does that entail?"

"You would be at my beck and call any and every minute."

"No."

"Again. I just can't get over how well you say that word." Natalie pushes a cookie sheet with a store-bought bread loaf on it into the oven.

"I told you, Nat, I've been practicing."

She nods. "It's just amazing."

"Okay, how about only the minutes included in forty hours a week?" Rick bargains.

"Rick."

"Paige."

"Look." I finish setting the table and cross my arms over my chest. "I'm barely back to having time to myself. I've just barely started doing my daily devotions again, and I've got major personal issues at the moment."

"All of my stuff is on the top shelf in the cabinet above the toilet," Natalie tells me, not even looking at me as she pulls plates out. "Help yourself."

"What?"

"Tampons. Pads. I think I even have a couple of panty-liners in there."

I shake my head. "Not those kind of personal issues."

"Oh. Well. You know for future reference."

Rick is waiting for me to continue, sipping his coffee.

"Can't do it, Rick."

"Let me just ask you to think about it, Paige. You'd be perfect for the job. You already teach the high school girls. And it requires a lot of counseling type of work with the girls one-on-one, and *that* would give you the opportunity to use your major that you worked very hard for and don't currently use."

I just sigh at him. "Well played."

"I've been holding that card for a while." He grins all

self-satisfyingly, sipping his coffee, cradling his sleeping daughter, and I just smile at him.

"You look happy," I say. I like seeing Rick and Natalie like this. Content. Settled. The baby is a natural part of their home now. For weeks I'd come over here and all I'd hear about was their fears about parenthood while Natalie's stomach stretched and grew. Then Claire was born and didn't ever sleep, and I came over to find a sobbing girl in the fetal position while Claire looked on.

Natalie finally pulls the bread from the oven and puts the pot roast on a platter. We pray and I start pulling off the tender meat, slicing it onto the plates, and adding scoops of potatoes and carrots.

"Going to set her down to eat?" Natalie asks Rick.

He shrugs. "I can eat one-handed."

Rick is softening and I love it.

"So," Natalie says to me, chewing a bite of bread. "Tell me about your huge personal problems that have nothing to do with monthly visitors."

I growl into my delicious dinner. "Ugh. Don't ask."

"I already did."

I was still dating Luke when I moved here for college, but it ended fairly soon after. I wasn't super close with Rick and Natalie then. They were spared a lot of the drama.

"This guy I used to date is back in town," I say.

"Please tell me it's not Michael the Martian," Rick says around a bite of pot roast.

"That's not very nice, and no." Michael was a little too into space-related things. On our first date, he took me to the planetarium. Which sounds romantic until he made me sit through a four-hour discussion on whether or not some comet's tail was long enough to be considered a comet.

Or something like that. I think I nodded off six times that night.

"Who?" Natalie asks.

"Luke. And uh, I don't know if you remember or not, but he's also Layla's older brother."

Natalie swallows and squints at Rick. "I kind of remember that. Tall guy. Dark hair. Really cute?"

I nod.

"I don't see the big deal," Rick says.

"That's so awkward," Natalie says at the same time. She frowns at Rick. "Seriously?"

"What? They're adults. It was what? Five years ago?"

"Around there." I nod.

"Eh." Rick shrugs. "*Hakuna matata*."

I look at Natalie as she shakes her head while stabbing a carrot. "I'm seeing now why he needs me to counsel the kids," I tell her.

"No sympathy. No sympathy. Want to know what his Bible college professors said would be his biggest weakness?"

"I'm going to assume the no sympathy."

"No sympathy." Natalie is stuck on repeat. "They said, 'Rick, you've got to learn how to have some sympathy as a youth pastor.'"

"Hey," Rick says, rising to his own defense. "I have sympathy. In certain cases."

"Like what?"

"Look." Suddenly Rick changes into Pastoral Rick. You can see the change like it's physical. His shoulders get straighter, his posture gets better, his voice gets deeper and more thoughtful.

It's very weird, honestly. I glance over at Natalie and she's just leveling Rick with a look of annoyance.

"There is a big difference between sympathy and compassion," he states. "I have compassion. I have compassion in abundance. But I do not think sympathy is as much of a biblical character trait as others might think."

"Therefore you don't need it," Natalie says.

"Exactly."

She is quiet for a minute, chewing a bite of potato. "Our kids are so going to favor me."

I'm pretty sure I snorted up some of the carrot.

*   *   *   *   *

I get home late. Typical for a night over at Rick and Natalie's. We always end up getting on some random conversation train, and before I know it, it's way past my bedtime.

I climb the stairs wearily, unlock my apartment door, and then lock it behind me. I'd left a lamp on in the living room so I wouldn't be coming home to a dark house.

That creeps me out to no end.

I hurry through my nighttime routine and climb into bed ten minutes later, yawning. I pull my Bible over and on my way to Galatians, I end up in Psalms. I am a big fan of this book of the Bible. There aren't too many other places where the writer just lashes out about everything to God and then praises Him with the next sentence.

Something about that just really appeals to me right now.

I still haven't read Preslee's note. I moved it to six different places around the apartment, and it finally ended up on my bedside table. I look at it, frowning, and look back at the Bible.

Maybe I need a little preface to tonight's Bible reading.

I bite my bottom lip, take a deep breath, and pull over the cream-colored envelope. She scrawled *Paige* across the front in her distinctive chicken scratch. I can recognize Preslee's handwriting anywhere.

I open the envelope and slide out a little folded note card, taking another deep breath, my lungs tight.

> *Paige,*
> *Happy birthday, sister. I know this is a shock to have me here, to have me this close to home. Honestly, I am shocked as well.*
>
> *I know I made your life and Mom and Dad's lives miserable. I know I wasn't the little sister I could have been. I missed birthdays, I missed Christmases. I missed Mom and Dad's twenty-fifth anniversary. You have no idea how much I wish I could get those back.*
>
> *I'm sorry, Paige. I don't know any other way to say it, but please know I mean this with all my heart. I am so sorry. I hope someday you can forgive me.*
>
> *I love you, sister.*
> *Preslee*

Tears burn the backs of my eyes when I close the card. *Sister.* The word should mean so much more to me. Something along the song in *White Christmas*. Like matching blue dresses and peacock feathers and piano music and tap dancing.

It doesn't bring up any feelings of happiness in me at all.

There was a point when Preslee and I were close. When I was in middle school and she was in elementary school, we did everything together. I was the cool big sister who got to have her ears pierced, and Preslee idolized me.

She started getting mixed up with the wrong crowd in late middle school, and by sophomore year in high school, she was pretty much as far down the path as she could get.

Or so we thought.

I rub my eyes and look back at the Bible verses swimming in front of me. Psalm 27 catches my attention.

"When You said, 'Seek My face,' my heart said to You, 'Your face, O LORD, I shall seek.'"

I could feel it now. The gentle longing. The whisper.

Seek My face, Paige.

I'm trying, Lord. Show me how.

Chapter
7

*W*ednesday morning.

      Eleven o'clock.

I have now answered the phone sixteen times. Eight were potential adoptive parents. Two were potential birth mothers. The other six were all Mark's wife because he apparently left his cell phone at home, and this was just not acceptable.

The phone rings again and I don't recognize the number on the caller ID. Part of me is relieved not to have to talk to Mark's wife again. I like Cindy most of the time. I don't necessarily like her on days when she is feeling clingy and I'm the one standing between her and her husband.

Or sitting, rather.

"Thank you for calling Lawman Adoption Agency, this is Paige, how may I help you?" I say this phrase so often, I've answered my cell phone like this without even realizing it until my mother started laughing.

"Hi, um yes, I'm assuming I'm calling the right place."

I immediately take in the nervousness, the approximate

age, and the way she's phrasing her sentence. Potential adoptive mother.

I grab the appropriate notebook to start writing down notes. Mark likes to have first impressions of both the adoptive and birth parents. "What can I help you with?"

"My husband and I are looking to get some information on adoption."

I smile to myself. Score for me.

"I'd love to give you some info, Mrs. um . . ." Kind of my informal way of saying, "Name please."

"Oh, it's Tammy."

I end up talking to Tammy for over an hour, going over fees, legal questions she has, and then she just starts talking about how long they have been trying and hoping for a baby.

"We've spent thousands and thousands of dollars on very expensive medical treatment to help us get pregnant and nothing worked," she says, tears in her voice. "This is our last hope for having a family, Paige."

My heart hurts for her. What I want to say is "Don't give up hope. God has a plan for you." But this is a place of business and I can't talk to the clients about God. So I just say, "Don't give up hope, Tammy."

It sounds about as reassuring as a five-dollar bill not backed by anything substantial.

I hang up a few minutes later, ready for my later lunch. Peggy comes down the hall, holding a Tupperware dish filled with some kind of bean salad. "Long conversation there, Paige. I've got nothing to teach her at the orientation meeting now." She grins at me, poking a fork into her dish and leaning against my desk.

I shrug. "I just tell everyone the basics."

"You're going to make a good counselor someday."

I sigh. "Not if Mark has anything to say about it." I tell her about the pay raise and she nods.

"I know. He asked me and Candace for opinions on that too."

I pull my lunch out of the drawer with my purse and look at Peggy. "And you said that was a good idea?"

"It's a pay raise, Paige. Most people don't complain about raises."

I dig my peanut butter and jelly sandwich out of the plastic baggie. I'm not sure what I'm upset about. Everyone seems to think this is a good idea.

Except me.

Well and Rick. But he has ulterior motives.

I think Peggy can tell I don't want to talk about it, so she changes the subject, leaning back against my desk while she pokes at her salad with her fork. "So, how's it going with Tyler?"

Peggy and Candace are all for Tyler. According to them, I usually only date needy, weird men so they think Tyler is an angel from heaven.

"It's fine." I think it's fine anyway. It's a little sticky with Luke being back in town, but I'm not going to say a word about Luke to Peggy. Lunch on Sunday was bad enough. I'm not necessarily in the mood to relive it.

Plus, I don't have time for a psychoanalyzation from my friendly counselor coworkers today.

"Fine. Hmm."

"Peggy."

"Paige."

"Stop," I command her, looking her in the eye. "It's fine. No reading into it."

"It's just that —"

"It's *fine*."

She looks at me, takes a bite of her salad, and then nods. "All right then. Whatever you say. I'm heading back to work."

She walks down the hall and I feel incredibly guilty for not wanting to talk about it. Then I feel justified because I had to go through a very long few months to learn how to say no. Then I feel awful again because, dang it, I was born with a very healthy guilt complex.

I stand, slink down the hall, and tap on her door. She's sitting at her desk, looking at a laptop.

"I'm sorry," I say. She looks up and smiles at me.

"You don't have to apologize, Paige. It's your business. Frankly, I'm just glad to see you've started telling people no."

"Well, anyway. I didn't mean to be rude."

"You're fine. I'm glad everything seems to be going well with Tyler. You deserve a good man."

I kind of nod at her, smile, and go back to my desk, thinking about that. A good man. Tyler is definitely a good man. He was even very gracious to Luke at lunch on Sunday, though Luke kept bringing up memories he had of when he and I were dating.

"Oh," he interjected into the conversation, laughing. "Paige, do you remember when we went to that coffee shop, and the waiter gave you the tea latte on accident and you said you didn't think you'd be able to even *chai* to force it down?" He laughed. "Didn't they rename the drink after you because of that response?"

I sigh now, raking my hands back through my hair that is still in desperate need of a cut. I glance at the clock. I still have five minutes in my lunch break. Time to call my regular salon.

"Ramona's," a receptionist answers.

"I need to schedule an appointment with Carla."

"Okay. Her first available is on Monday at five thirty."

"Great, thanks." I tell the girl my name and number and hang up, feeling like I've at least accomplished something for myself today. I haven't had a haircut in six months.

Six months is too long to go between haircuts. If I go any longer, they'll make me go to the new pet salon instead of my stylist.

Five o'clock finally comes and I grab my purse and run for the door. Wednesdays are long days. I only have a few minutes to get from work to home, change, and grab something for dinner, and then head from home to church to teach the ninth-grade girls' small group.

I actually really enjoy it. It's one of the few activities I didn't cut out when I went on my rampage against all my obligations a little while ago.

I drive home, park, run up the stairs to my apartment, replace the skirt and pretty top for jeans and a ragged T-shirt I've had since high school, grab my sneakers in one arm and a Lunchables and my Bible in the other, and run back down the stairs in my socks.

My mother spent years of her life telling me to take better care of my socks. "People will think you have no home," she'd always tell me, pointing to my feet.

"What people, Mom?"

"EMTs. Emergency sorts. Anyone who would be looking through the wreckage to see if the poor girl in the accident has a family who needs to know what hospital she's at."

Mom has a morbid sense of priorities.

My phone buzzes as I slide behind the wheel, and it's my mother. I love when I am thinking or talking about someone and they randomly call. It makes me want to declare myself a superhero, stop sleeping at night, and start wearing glasses during the day to hide my identity.

"Hello, Mother."

"Hello, Daughter."

"I was just thinking of you."

"I guess an angel got its wings then."

I turn the key in the ignition, frowning. "What?"

"Oh no, that's when a phone rings. No. Bells? Whistles? I don't know. Anyway, I was calling for a purpose beyond remembering lines from movies I haven't seen in years."

I tuck the phone between my shoulder and my cheek while I back out. I love my mom.

"Yes, ma'am?"

"Well, as you know, Preslee is staying here."

Something freezes deep down near the base of my esophagus at the mention of my sister's name, but I keep swallowing, hoping I can thaw it out quickly.

"She mentioned that she saw you."

"She did."

"She said it was brief."

"It was."

"Well, that's what I want to fix. I know the past and I just want to remind you that Preslee hurt us as much as she hurt you. But I'm calling a truce. And I'm your mother and it's your duty to listen to me."

I bite the inside of my cheek, knowing what is coming.

"We are having a family dinner on Sunday," Mom says.

"And you are going to be there. At four o'clock sharp because I know you have a long drive home. I don't care if you are mopping yourself up off the floor thanks to the flu. You'll be there. Okay, Paige?"

Mom is pulling out the big guns today. Rarely does she ever ask me to do anything and today she's not asking — she's demanding. I suddenly have a great deal of sympathy for the older brother of the prodigal son. No one ever cares about his side of the story.

"Yes, ma'am," I mutter.

"Paige?"

"Yes, ma'am!" I say louder.

"Good. Now. What would you like me to make for dinner?"

"Traditionally, I believe it's supposed to be a fattened calf."

"Sorry, honey, I lost you for a minute. You must be driving somewhere. What did you say?"

Probably is a good thing she didn't hear my sarcastic response. I clear my throat and put on a fake happy voice. "Whatever, Mom! I like all your meals."

"Well, that's a statement that was born in the Falsehood Tree and hit every branch on its way out."

"Okay, fine. All of your meals except for stroganoff." Even saying the word makes my gag reflex act up a little bit.

"No stroganoff. Got it. I'll let you go. You shouldn't drive and talk on a cell phone anyway. Especially with the kind of socks you wear. Love you, sweetie." She hangs up.

Only my mother can pay me a big, fat insult and then tell me she loves me in the same breath. My socks are fine at the moment, running through the parking lot notwithstanding.

I walk into the church and into the youth room, still carrying my shoes, Bible, and dinner.

"You are late," Rick declares.

"Am not," I say, sitting in one of the folding chairs.

"Are too. I have five thirty and forty two seconds." He waves his phone at me.

I set everything in my lap and pull my phone out. "Five twenty-eight." I wave my phone right back into his face.

Rick garumphs, which means I win. A good thing. Rick is mean to those who are late to the leaders meeting. Last week, he made Tyler walk across a littering of Legos barefoot.

That one hurt to watch.

Typically, Tyler is the only one who is ever late.

Tyler is in the chair beside me, early for once, and he grins at me. "Dinner?" he asks, nudging my arm.

"I always wanted these as a kid and my mother never bought them for me." I push my shoes to the floor and rip open the Lunchables. "We're about to see if all the commercials were correct in that they are fulfilling and nutritious."

"They are fulfilling. If you're five."

Rick claps a hand. "All right. Order of business for tonight. Sam, the junior and senior guys are doing a project on Saturday, yes?"

"Yep."

"Got enough chaperones?"

Sam shrugs. Sam is one of the most laid-back guys I've ever met. "Half of them are eighteen, Rick."

"True point. Trevor, fill us in on the sophomores."

We spend the next few minutes talking details about service projects, studies, and prayer requests the kids have. I eat my crackers, ham, and cheese in silence, trying to make it to the Oreos before it's time to pray and go mingle with the kids before the study officially starts for the night.

Two Oreos. I can't even remember the last time I ate only two Oreos.

Even after I had my wisdom teeth taken out, I still managed to eat three.

That's the reason I never buy packages of Oreos. I will polish them off in two days. I do not trust myself with them. And I don't have the energy to run the hundreds of miles it would take to burn them off. Or the time.

"Paige? Questions? Comments?" Rick looks at me.

"They only put two Oreos in my Lunchable."

"That's because they are meant for children. Anything that applies to this discussion?"

"It's not all it's cracked up to be."

"The Oreos?"

"The Lunchable."

Rick just looks at me and I start on the Oreos. "That's all I had to comment on."

Tyler looks amused.

Rick just rolls his eyes. "And with that, let's pray." He prays something short and sweet and then we head out to the foyer to mingle with the kids already congregating.

I spend the next hour teaching the girls about love. We are starting a new series on the fruit of the Spirit, and I'm going to regret being the teacher for it, seeing as how the opening chapter Rick wrote says this:

People use the word love *to describe many things, but to see what love really, truly means, we have only to look to the Cross and who hung there. Love is sacrifice. Love is*

88 ERYNN MANGUM

being willing to put others first. Love is putting wrongs
behind us and turning to the future.

I am not so fond of that last sentence. Especially with my
mandatory dinner with Preslee and my parents coming up.

One of my girls, Nichole, raises her hand. Nichole and I
still try to meet weekly, though lately it's been more like every
other week. She moved here with her mom after her parents'
divorce.

"So, the whole putting things in the past . . .," she says.

"Yes, Nichole?"

"What does that mean? I mean, my dad left us for his
secretary. So should I just move on like he never did anything
wrong?"

Twelve pairs of eyes stare at me.

I hate teaching the girls. They ask hard questions.

I rub my cheek and pray that God gives me both grace
and wisdom. "No," I say slowly. I squint at the ceiling, trying
to make sense of what is in my head so I can put it into
words.

"I think there is a difference between forgiveness and
forgetting." I pray my interpretation of the Bible is in fact
biblical. "You can forgive someone without forgetting what
he's done."

They all just look at me, and I see no connections
happening.

"For example," I continue. "Nichole, you're right. Your
dad sinned against you. And you should forgive him. You
should give all the hurt and pain and anger to Jesus. But you
will always remember what he did. It's just choosing how
you will react to him now."

Every word I'm saying is turning into a pocketknife the second it leaves my lips, flipping around 180 degrees and slamming right into my chest.

Teaching is painful when you haven't come to grips with the subject.

"What about the whole like, 'forgive and forget'?" Tanya asks.

"*God* forgives and forgets. We forgive and move on. I'll use another example. Let's say you are in an abusive relationship with a boyfriend, so you break up with him. You can forgive him. You should forgive him. But I would never counsel you to forget what he did and start dating him again." I rub my forehead, wincing. "Does that all make sense?"

Twelve heads start nodding like an audience of bobble-head dolls, and I start seeing some pistons firing in their eyes.

"Sooo . . ." Nichole says, drawing the word out, still some confusion in her expression. "I should forgive my dad, but I shouldn't trust him again?"

I sigh. "Here's what I'm saying. Remember that verse, 'Shrewd as serpents and innocent as doves'?"

The bobble heads are back.

"I'm just saying be wise. You might someday be able to trust your dad again. Be gentle with him. Encourage him to turn back to the Lord. But be wise with yourself. Don't put yourself in a situation where you could get hurt again too soon."

She nods. "Okay."

"Okay. I think we're done here." I'm so physically battered and emotionally spent, I couldn't keep teaching even if we weren't done. I take prayer requests, writing them in my teaching binder so I can pray for the girls over the week, pray a blanket prayer for tonight since God knows all anyway, and dismiss them into the youth room for snacks.

I just sit there for a few minutes, thinking over what I said, thinking over what the lesson said, thinking over the list of wrongs longer than my leg done against me by two people in particular.

Tyler pokes his head in the half-open door. "You okay in here?"

"I need EMS."

"Early Morning Syndrome? You don't want it."

"Emergency Medical Services."

"That's only in Canada. We refer to them as EMTs here. Welcome to Texas." He gives me a sympathetic smile. "Tough group?"

"Tough lesson."

"Better that than the other. My guys must have been drinking Red Bulls all day. I finally told them I was going to make them sing karaoke during snack time, singing only songs about love, or they were going to sit down, shut up, listen, and answer the questions."

"You told them to shut up and answer questions? Aren't those mutually exclusive?"

Tyler shakes his head. "You were *that* kid in school."

He holds out a hand and helps me up off the floor. "I think I saw Allison's mom handing her a grocery bag full of Nutter Butters to bring for a snack," he says quietly as we walk out the door. "Make time, Paige."

As a general rule, I prefer Oreos, but Nutter Butters are a very close second when it comes to junk food. Followed by Skittles.

We hurry into the youth room and snag a few cookies before the senior guys' group gets out. They are notorious for walking in this room, breathing in, and leaving the place completely void of edibles. One time I followed them in and one guy had even tried to eat Natalie's pumpkin-scented lotion on a graham cracker.

Boys are gross.

"So when is our next movie night, Paige?" one of the high school girls asks me, crunching a Nutter Butter.

"Yeah!" "Yeah!" "I was wondering that too!"

Suddenly I am surrounded. A few months ago, we started an informal movie night at my apartment every so often. The girls wanted it to be once a week.

I was envisioning more of a once-a-month thing, especially seeing as every time they come over, I have to spend the following Saturday morning cleaning.

"Not sure." I try to be all nonchalant about it. I once asked if anyone else wanted to host it but was quickly assured that having the movie night in a cramped apartment was way more cool.

Ah, to be young and think crappy apartments are cool again.

"Well, we should do it soon. It's been a long time" is met by a bunch more enthusiastic "yeahs."

I finagle my way out of the mob and Rick walks past me, heading for the snack table. "You could be paid for that," he singsongs as he walks.

"Paid for what?"

"And this," he says, drawing the word out in a falsetto that makes the inside of my eardrums ache.

"Listening to you sing?"

"No. Movie nights. Nutter Butter consumption. Bible studies." He crunches a cookie and grins at me. "The ever-changing and joyous company of Yours Truly. All a part of the job I am humbly offering to you."

So not only would I be teaching Bible studies that stab me in the chest, I'd be accepting a paycheck for doing so.

I can't decide if that makes it better or worse. At least I could afford EMS.

Or the EMTs. Whatever.

On *Flashpoint* they call them EMS. Any knowledge I have of emergency services is from movies and TV shows, and I'd prefer to keep it that way. I've never even sat in an emergency room waiting room before. Not for myself. Not for someone else.

I think that is considered a good thing, no matter what country you're in.

"I'll think about it," I say, just to get him to change the subject.

"Yes! Thank You, Jesus, she's thinking about it!" Rick yells, raising his hands in victory fists.

Rick's outbursts are normal. No one even looks in our direction. They just keep talking and eating cookies, chatting with their friends.

"You are obnoxious."

"All a part of my joyous company."

"What's she thinking about?" Tyler asks, coming over, holding a half-empty Nalgene water bottle. I always wished I was sporty enough not to look completely ridiculous holding one of those. Tyler looks good with it. I believe he can suddenly pack up everything he owns into a single backpack and start walking across the mountains, fleeing the Nazis or whatever while a bunch of nuns sing a song for him.

I would just look ridiculous, like when I caught the end of the unfortunate stirrup pant craze in late elementary school.

I have told my mother to burn those pictures.

"She might come work for me, buddy." Rick whacks Tyler with a friendly but painful-looking thump to the shoulder.

Boys are weird. If I greeted a girl like that, I'd get sued. Or written in some awful slam book.

These days, I'm not sure what's worse.

"Are you really?" Tyler asks me.

"Now, now. What's that tone?" Rick says.

"No tone. I'm just surprised. I thought you were hoping to get promoted to counselor someday," Tyler says to me.

"That day is looking bleaker," I say.

"Did they hire someone else?"

"No, but they offered me a raise." I sigh. I still haven't taken it. I just try to avoid the subject when I am talking with Mark.

Part of me thinks that taking the raise is the smart thing to do. I could start building up my savings again. I'd have more spending money, which means I could finally start looking at some of the cute summer clothes in all the stores, and I could stop eating cheese sticks for dinner.

The other part of me is just depressed to think of spending my life answering the phone.

No one prepares you for this stage in life. Someday, very far in the future, I'd ideally like to get married and hopefully have kids. Then I'd fit back into our church. There's youth group. There's college group. There's young marrieds and then the family circles.

Nothing for the out-of-college working single who doesn't quite know what she wants out of life yet. SINGLE AND CONFUSED CLASS. I haven't seen that sign on any of the classroom doors yet.

Which is why I am here. Back in high school.

I look around and grab another Nutter Butter. Might as well enjoy being here.

Chapter
8

Layla calls me at nine o'clock on Saturday morning.

"French Cottage or Sparrow Eggshell?" she asks, not bothering with a hello.

I rub my eyes, having trouble focusing on the coffee-maker in front of me while I'm spooning the dark grounds in, much less what Layla has just asked.

"What?"

"Paint, Paige. Which one?"

"What are you painting?" Layla lives in an apartment. As far as I know, her management would not look kindly on Layla repainting the walls.

"Wake up, Paige! Remember that armoire I found on the side of the road?"

I do not remember Layla ever saying the word *armoire* to me, much less picking one up on the side of the road. I don't have any trouble believing her, though. Ever since she started reading some trash-to-treasure blog a few weeks back, she's been waking up early, going to garage sales, and picking up the weirdest things.

Two weeks ago, she brought home an entire box filled with old, empty Chef Boyardee cans.

"So you are painting the armoire," I say slowly back to her.

She sighs. "Yes, Paige."

"With paint."

"You just got up, huh?"

"Yes."

"Making coffee?"

"Yes."

"Good. It's a beautiful morning and you are missing it."

Says the woman who used to sleep until eleven and tell me that a.m. stood for "absolute morons," as in only absolute morons got up when the clock still said a.m.

"What is the color difference? I don't memorize paint samples, you know," I tell her, turning on the coffeemaker.

"So the French Cottage is more of a rustic, creamy color like what that brown sweater I have looks like on the outside edge of that bleach spot I accidentally got on it. And the Sparrow Eggshell is almost the same color but maybe with a slight bluish tinge to it."

"Sorry about that sweater," I say.

"Yeah. I really wish that blog had mentioned not to wear dark clothing when using bleach. Oh well. I'm repurposing the sweater."

"Repurposing" is going to become my least-favorite word that Layla says. I just know it.

"Um. What are you doing to the sweater?" I ask, a little scared to hear the answer.

"I'm cutting it. Making mittens. Don't worry, I saw a whole thing on how to do it step by step. I've just got to find a sewing machine." She says the last sentence suggestively, and I know what she is hoping I'll offer.

Just solely my opinion, but I don't think Layla should be around anything that involves a fast-moving needle. However, I keep my lips shut and don't mention that she could use mine.

I will not partake in the bloodshed of my best friend.

"I'm going with the French Cottage," she says.

"Okay."

"Thanks for your help, Paige!"

"I didn't do anything."

"That's true. Well, since you haven't helped so far, want to come help me paint it today?"

"Not really," I answer truthfully. Layla is anything but crafty. She tries hard, but she just doesn't have the touch, sort of like me with gardening.

I feel like watching her try to paint this dresser would be like watching a train hurtling right toward a cute little bunny and not having any way to warn the rabbit of approaching danger.

"Oh come on, Paige. It will be fun! And we haven't hung out in ages and I miss you and I'll buy Panda Express for lunch."

Orange chicken suddenly makes the bunny look more like a cockroach and I sigh, pouring myself a cup of coffee and accepting defeat. "Okay."

"Okay! I will see you, Paige Alder, in twenty minutes! Bring paint clothes!"

"I'll just wear your brown sweater."

"I don't want to get paint spatters on my new mittens."

I just laugh.

I drink my coffee and decide that a shower is pointless if I'm going to go watch Layla paint, because watching Layla paint is equal to me painting the dresser while Layla directs.

I really like orange chicken.

I find a pair of old, paint- and Super Glue–flecked shorts in my closet and pull them on. My craft shorts. I dig through to the back of the closet and come out with an old T-shirt from high school and grab my oldest pair of sneakers and a rubber band for my hair.

I dab some mascara on and walk out the door. Painting or not, I always wear mascara.

I find Layla in her assigned parking space of her apartment complex, car moved, staring at a beat-up, oak-colored armoire that looks exactly like one my grandparents had in the sixties.

"Wow," I say, climbing out of my car and walking over.

"I know. Isn't it great? I just can't believe someone left this on the side of the road!"

Right then the right bottom drawer front falls off and clatters with an empty *whomp* that basically shouts, "I am made out of particle board and Super Glue!"

"That keeps happening but I figure we can definitely fix that," Layla says. "They just don't make quality furniture like this nowadays."

"Mm-hmm." It's the safest thing I can think of to say.

"Well!" She looks at me with an excited smile and hands on her hips. She's got her shoulder-length brown curly hair up in a curly mess of a ponytail on the top of her head, faded sweatpants, a white tank top, and gardening gloves.

I love Layla.

"Let's begin!" She grabs the paint can and shakes it.

It would be easier for her to just pop the top open and stir it, and it probably is fairly well mixed already, seeing as how she just came from the paint store, but I don't say anything. This is Layla's project. I will let her craft.

She finally sets the can down and pulls a paint can opener from her pocket, cranking open the lid. The color inside is pretty, but looking at the armoire, I'm going to guess we'll need at least two coats.

Maybe three. That oak is looking awfully thirsty. I would imagine forty-plus years and getting kicked to the side of the road would do that to you, though.

Layla hands me a brand-new brush, grabs another one for herself, and starts swiping the paint on, leaving the drawers and everything still in the dresser. And I highly doubt that she sanded it or prepped it or even cleaned it, but somehow that doesn't seem like the biggest issue at the moment.

"Um . . . Layla?"

"Gosh, this is so fun!"

"You might want to take the drawers out."

"Why?" She swashes a thick and bubble-crested glob of paint along the top of the dresser. "They'll be easier to paint right there." She points with the paint-dripping brush.

I almost hold my tongue. But I decide this is a matter I need to speak up on. "Yeah, but then you'll never be able to open them."

"How come?"

"The paint will dry."

"That's what I want it to do."

Maybe with Layla it's better to let her live and learn. Except I know that I will be the one prying open the paint-sealed drawers with a utility knife, so I take a deep breath and explain it again. "The paint will settle in the cracks, Layla. So you won't be able to open the drawers when it dries."

"Oh. Why didn't you say so?" She plunges the paintbrush up to the handle into the paint, steps back, yanks all six drawers out, and sets them beside the dresser. "I may not use the drawers, but I guess it's better to have them working."

"Probably."

Then she resumes swishing the paint around.

Paint flecks are all over the asphalt at this point. Management may not look kindly on this crafty adventure.

But I keep my mouth shut. And I start on the back of the dresser.

"Use more paint, Paige. I only want to have to go over it once."

"I just don't want it to drip."

"It's supposed to look like that."

I backhand my hair off my forehead and look around the dresser at her. "Drippy?"

"I'm going for a specific look here, Paige."

"Drippy."

"Raw," she says, overannunciating the word. "I'm looking for *raw*."

"Who are you, the next design star?"

She shrugs, totally serious. "I could get into this."

I hide my smirk behind the dresser. This is classic Layla. She's forever going through crushes. A few weeks ago, she was trying to take up cooking.

A pan of gelatinous scalloped potatoes fixed that one.

Then she got caught up in her parents' anniversary party. Now she's restoring furniture.

I am a little scared to see what happens next.

At twelve thirty, Layla declares it's time to let the paint continue to drip dry and we should go get Panda Express.

"What about the dresser?" I ask.

"What about it?"

"Are we just going to leave it in the parking lot?"

She shrugs. "It's in my space."

"You don't think anyone will mess with it?" This is Layla's apartment complex we are talking about here. I've seen three sketchy-looking men walk by in the last twenty minutes, two who had huge tattoos covering their entire visible flesh.

Say what you will about tattoos being the new in thing, I was raised to irrationally fear all people who had one.

Which now includes my sister, apparently.

My fear of her is officially justified.

"Hmm," Layla says. "Good point. Okay. I'll go get Panda. You stay here and guard the dresser. And no fixing the drips, Miss Perfectionist. It's supposed to be —"

"Raw," I say along with her. "Yeah. I get it."

"Okay. I'll be back." She jogs across the parking lot to her car and leaves a minute later, waving at me as I sit on the curb next to her parking space.

Another man wearing a sleeveless shirt showcasing a huge dragon crawling up his arm and eating his shoulder walks by, glancing at me.

Forget the dresser. Now I'm worried about my personal safety.

Layla really needs to move.

My dad once told me that when I'm in a situation where things could get dicey, I need to be paying 112 percent attention to my surroundings. "Nothing should distract you,"

Dad always said. "You live in a constant state of caution, you understand?"

I happen to disagree on one thing. I think a girl on a cell phone is a lot more intimidating because then at least someone, even though the person isn't physically there, knows that I've been kidnapped and sold to Russian carpet thieves.

"Hey, Paige."

"Hi," I say into my phone, looking furtively around me, trying to watch out for potential kidnappers. A girl walking her dog gives me a weird look.

"You okay?" Tyler asks.

"Fine. Why? Do you think I'm not okay?"

"What?"

"What?" I ask back.

"You're just talking weird, like you're standing in line to rob a bank or something. Are you sure you're okay?"

"I'm fine. I'm at Layla's. Babysitting a dresser. In the parking lot."

"Where's Layla?"

"She went to get Panda Express for us."

"There's a shock." I can hear the smile in his voice. "So correct me if I'm wrong, but you're sitting in the parking lot with a dresser?"

"Next to it, if you want to be precise."

"You're just sitting there?"

"No, I'm trying very hard not to get kidnapped."

He snorts. "In broad daylight?"

"I'm sure it's happened before."

"Well, what's the dresser look like?"

"It's raw," I tell him.

"Raw," he repeats.

"Right."

"Like rah, rah, sis boom bah?"

"No, like, hey these carrots in this salad are raw."

He laughs. "What on earth does that mean? It's bare? It's a naked dresser?"

"No, but that makes more sense. Apparently it means that it dries in drips all over the place."

"Huh. Do you sand them off?"

"I'm afraid to ask Layla." The guy with the dragon gnawing on his shoulder is back. He strolls by, looking at the speckled-with-drips dresser, then at me, then at my phone, and climbs into a greasy-looking sedan.

I grip the phone tightly. "Tyler," I whisper. "I am in danger."

"What?"

"There is a man with a dragon tattoo eating his shoulder who keeps walking by and looking at me and the dresser."

"Where are you?"

"In the parking lot," I annunciate it carefully. "Space number sixty-three. I am wearing my paint-splattered denim shorts and a T-shirt. I have my hair in a—"

"Paige, chill. I was only asking to clarify. You have to admit you probably look ridiculous sitting beside a dresser in the middle of the parking lot. I don't think the dragon guy is out to get you."

"Everyone knows that dragons equal danger, Tyler. Have you never watched *Flashpoint*? Or *NCIS*?"

"No, but I've watched ESPN, and I'm pretty sure that five out of every ten football players has a dragon tattoo. And I don't think they are dangerous. Except maybe to other football players."

"You can even basically spell *danger* from *dragon*," I say, ignoring him.

"Dangor? That's not a word, Paige."

"Whatever. If someone was running toward me yelling 'dangor,' I would still run for my life."

He starts laughing. "Oh, Paige."

Layla's back, waving cheerfully at me from behind the wheel as she passes me and the dresser to find a parking place.

"Layla's back."

"I'm glad you lived long enough to eat your orange chicken," Tyler says.

"Me too."

"I'll talk to you soon. Maybe we can watch a movie or something tonight."

"That would be fun. Bye, Tyler."

"Bye, Paige." I hang up and take one of the paper sacks from Layla. She pulls her sunglasses off and frowns at the dresser.

"It's really drippy, isn't it?"

Another trip to Lowe's for sandpaper and another gallon of paint is in my future. I force back the sigh, put on a smile, and nod to the bags. "Lunch first."

Chapter 9

"So, what's it going to be?" Tyler taps the stack of "acceptable" DVDs he found in my TV cabinet.

I glance over. I'm in the middle of doing the dishes. Tyler surprised me at five thirty by showing up to my apartment with pizza and enough paper plates, plastic forks, and napkins to give each of the Duggars their own family-sized set.

In light of that courtesy, I figured I should probably make him some homemade cookies, plus I still have to do dishes tonight.

I am a glutton for punishment, so it would seem.

"And I purposefully grabbed nineteen million plates and forks so you wouldn't have to do those tonight." Tyler points at my hands in the sink.

"What can I say? I love doing dishes."

"Thanks for making cookies."

"Thanks for bringing over pizza."

He's smiling at me from across the high counter separating my kitchen from my living room and my stomach flips a little. His eyes soften as he looks at me and now there are a hundred tiny gnats all trying to showcase their break-dancing moves in my stomach. The smell of freshly baking cookies surrounds us, and I suddenly get that *feeling*. You know, the one where it feels like your heart and lungs are stapled together.

I really like this guy.

Finally he taps the DVDs again, breaking eye contact, and I catch a breath.

"So?" he asks.

"What are the choices?"

"*Iron Man, Count of Monte Cristo, Rocky*, or *Indiana Jones*."

"I don't remember owning any of those movies."

"Thankfully, I brought some of my own tonight."

"Hey!" I say, rinsing the mixing bowl. "I have good DVDs. I thought for sure you'd pick *The Parent Trap* for tonight."

He sighs sadly. "Is that what you want to watch?"

I grin. "We can watch one of your movies." The poor man has watched about ten of mine in the last month. It's probably about time for me to let him have a turn.

I pull the cookies out of the oven, slide them onto a paper plate, and join him on the couch. "What won out?"

"*Indiana Jones*. I haven't seen it in forever."

"Me either." A very young Harrison Ford fills the screen, and I start to wonder why I haven't watched it in so long.

Tyler pauses the movie.

"What's wrong?" I look over at him. We have the cookies on the coffee table, our glasses of water, and I even brought over some napkins.

"I just felt the need to remind you that Harrison Ford is now like eighty."

"What?"

"Maybe older."

I start laughing. "Play the movie, Tyler."

"I'm just saying. And Indiana Jones is fictional." He presses the Play button.

I pick up a cookie and start munching. "Doesn't make him less attractive."

"I knew I should have chosen *Rocky*."

I laugh.

About halfway through the movie, I glance over. Tyler is sitting about a foot or two away, totally engrossed in the movie.

It's different. Tyler is not really a touchy guy. And I'm not sure why. Maybe he's more into the friend side of this relationship? Maybe we aren't really in a relationship?

What if any chemistry I'm sensing is just on my side of things?

I chew on my bottom lip, watching a youthful Harrison Ford dodge all manner of weapons, and try not to worry.

"Try" is such a relative term.

* * * * *

I climb into bed at eleven thirty and bemoan the fact that I chose a book written by Paul for my devotional time at night. Paul needed a copyeditor, because I have to read every sentence eleven times to understand anything.

Tonight's no different.

"I do not nullify the grace of God, for if righteousness comes through the Law, then Christ died needlessly."

I lean back on my pillow, thinking. So basically Paul is

saying that if me being a good person will get me into heaven, then there was no point to Christ's death.

I think. It's late.

I turn off the light and I'm asleep before my eyes fully adjust to the darkness.

* * * * *

Sunday.

A word that has recently become a very stressful word. I stand in the parking lot after church, holding my keys with both hands like I might accidentally ignite a hay bale into sudden and horrifically large flames like in *Oklahoma* if I let go.

Amazing how quickly that hay bale caught fire in *Oklahoma*.

And how no one seemed to feel any financial burden from all the hay bales burning up afterward.

"Are you okay?"

Rick is suddenly standing right in front of me, squinting in the bright sun, looking at me like I'm two red shoes shy of Munchkin Land.

"I am going to have dinner with my family."

"Where? The county prison?"

"Preslee is going to be there."

"Ah." He nods at me, crossing his arms over his chest. "Preslee strikes again, huh?"

"Actually, Mom's making me do it."

"Good."

"Good?" I glare up at him. "You don't know the whole story, so you don't get to have any opinions."

"I am a human being and an opinionated one at that, so I can have all the opinions I want, thank you. Look, try not to stress, okay? It's only awkward if you make it awkward."

I hate that saying. It puts all the pressure of how the evening goes on my shoulders. Plus, just because I don't act awkward doesn't mean she isn't going to. Or my mom. Or my dad.

This is the first whole family dinner we've had in years. I think I'm allowed to feel this sense of concern.

Or foreboding.

Potato, Po-tah-to.

"Well." Rick shrugs. "If it's any consolation, I'll be praying."

"Rick," I say apologetically as he starts to walk away.

"It's okay, Paige." He waves, smiles, and all is well as he leaves. I climb into my car, turn the key in the ignition, and just sit there.

I have a three-and-a-half-hour drive ahead of me. Both ways. Seven hours in the car for this dinner.

You'd think we could have met halfway. Surely there's a McDonald's or something two hours outside of town I could have just pulled in, ordered fast food, stuffed my face, and left. I could have been home and recovering by five.

There's a tap on my window, and it's the second-to-last person I want to see.

I sigh and roll down my window. "Hello, Luke."

"You okay? You're not moving."

"I'm about to leave for Austin."

Luke flashes his cover smile and nods. "Say hi to your parents for me."

I think not. "Well, see you." I reach to roll up the window.

"Oh hey, since I've got you here, Paige," Luke says, keeping his hands on top of the lowered window. "How about coffee sometime this week?"

"I'm pretty busy this week, Luke."

"Next week then."

"Luke."

"Paige." He ducks his head so he can see me better. "I promise, it will be nothing. Just two old friends having coffee."

"Friends." I repeat the word, hearing a different meaning than Luke does, so it would seem.

"Right. I'll call you."

There is no sense in arguing anymore. I have to save my arguing allotment for dinner tonight. "Good-bye, Luke."

"See you soon, Paige!" He waves at my closing window.

Seriously. Get a clue.

I merge onto I-35 southbound and mash around on the stereo, trying to find a station that might carry me the whole way. Country. Somehow, those stations always seem to broadcast across the state.

Plus, it works for my current mood. My devotional time this whole last week was spent in a concordance, trying to find biblical reasoning for not having to go to this dinner.

The closest I'd gotten was Proverbs 23:3: *"Do not desire his delicacies, for it is deceptive food."*

Somehow I'm thinking a concordance should not be used for devotional studies too often.

Regardless, I'm not in the mood to listen to my usual Christian music station. Or even my oldies station. Elvis just reminds me more of Preslee recently.

I glance down at my outfit about halfway to Austin.

Should I have gone with a different look? Preslee seemed so mature and sophisticated when she dropped by my apartment with my birthday present. I decided on denim capris and a gray gauzy top with red ballet flats after trying on nearly every single outfit I own. If someone breaks into my apartment while I am gone today, they will likely assume I've already been robbed since my entire closet is currently piled on my bed.

I chew my bottom lip, then decide to break into the jar of nuts I brought with me to save my lip nerve endings. I never eat nuts except on road trips home. They are my car food. When I was little, my parents would mix Goldfish and pretzels in a big, empty Christmas butter cookie tin for when we would drive fourteen hours to see my grandmother. Inevitably, I would get carsick somewhere between Austin and Omaha.

I still can't handle the sight or smell of Goldfish crackers.

I'm approaching Waco, and there's a Dairy Queen right off the interstate when you first enter the city limits. I have to stop every time on my way to Austin to get a Blizzard. We have about forty-three Dairy Queens in Dallas, but I have never been to any of them.

I've been to this Dairy Queen a least twenty times. If not more.

As a general rule, I find Dairy Queens disgusting, but there is something about a Blizzard on a road trip that just makes everything seem like all is right in the world.

Today, I need that Blizzard like I need a real one preventing me from continuing my trip.

I pull into a parking space, walk into the dingy

restaurant, and leave a few minutes later holding my ice cream and praying that there are no communicable diseases contained therein. I get back on the interstate.

Another hour and a half of sad, bluesy country music that makes me feel like I should sell my car, get a truck and a dog, and never fall in love, and I'm pulling onto my parents' street with a knot the size of Lake Texarkana choking my esophagus.

I remember when I drove back for the first time and didn't refer to Austin or my parents' house as "home." It took me three years. I was a senior in college, and I was very involved at church, very happy with my friends, very settled, thanks to Rick, Natalie, and Layla. Someone asked me what I was going to be doing for Labor Day weekend, and I told them going to Austin and about cried that it didn't feel like home anymore. First out of sadness and then out of relief.

The first year of college had been brutal as far as homesickness went.

My parents live outside the city on a couple of grassy acres. There are a couple of huge old trees and an old farmhouse that my parents bought when I was in the second grade. They've been remodeling and updating it ever since then.

The garage is open and Mom's Tahoe is parked inside. Dad's truck is in the driveway. There's a small silver sedan parked behind Dad. I'm assuming that's Preslee's, which is just weird because Preslee was always all about flashy cars. When she started driving, she talked Dad into helping her buy this lime-green VW Bug that sounded like it had a fatal case of bronchitis. That car broke down more times than Preslee snuck out of the house, and that was often.

I park next to the sedan and sit in my car, gripping my steering wheel with both hands, fighting the urge to put it in reverse and head home.

God. Help.

It might have been the shortest prayer I've ever prayed. Sometimes there are just no words.

I finally take four deep breaths and open my door.

I climb out, trying to smooth out the road-trip wrinkles and instill some fresh air into my stale-smelling clothes and hair. I actually blow-dried and curled my hair this morning. I fish my purse out of the passenger seat, making sure my phone is on loud.

Layla has strict instructions to call me at four with a life-and-death emergency. That gives me an hour and a half to soothe my mother with my presence and wish Preslee a happy and healthy life away from ours.

Really, I probably only need ten minutes.

I unlock the phone and start to text Layla to tell her to call sooner.

Right then the front door opens and my parents' dog, Honey, runs out, all happy and tail-waggy and cheerful. Mom got Honey a couple of months after Preslee left because the empty house was just killing her. She's a sweet, if not horribly ugly, dog. I'm not even sure what breed she is. Some sort of a collie, Lab, cocker spaniel something.

I rub Honey's ears and look up to see my dad standing there. I love my dad. "Hi there, Pip," Dad says, all smiles.

When I was a little girl, my favorite way to wear my hair was in pigtails. Dad called me Pippi because of that for a long time, and then it got shortened to Pip. I don't think he's ever said my real name since.

"Hi, Dad." I give him a big hug and try to relax.

"Glad you could make it."

"I didn't really have a choice."

Dad smiles at me sympathetically.

I follow him into the house. Mom's making her famous honey-glazed ham and sweet potatoes. I can smell the sugary sweetness all through the house. That means Dad's going to make his rolls.

The only thing in the entire world that my dad can make are dinner rolls. But if you're going to only be able to make one thing, Dad's dinner rolls are a good one to make. They are insanely delicious. A couple of years ago, he started making extras and giving them to widows in the church for Thanksgiving. Mom's always telling me how she has to fight off all the old ladies around Dad now.

The house looks identical to when I lived here. A huge river-rock fireplace. Two large couches. Lots of throw pillows. When Preslee and I were both in high school, we would have friends over almost every weekend to watch baseball, football, and just hang out. Some weeks, we had to use the throw pillows for extra seating.

Mom is in the kitchen slicing up a bunch of carrots into a bowl of shredded lettuce on the island. "Hi, sweetheart." She smiles brightly at me. I can see the excitement in her eyes about today and try to force some of my own.

Dinner with my sister who broke our hearts and abandoned us. Yay.

"Hi, Mom."

"How was the drive?"

"Long."

"How was the Blizzard?" Dad grins at me, leaning back

against the counter behind Mom.

"I tried the Snickers. I won't be doing that again." I am an Oreo Blizzard person all the way. A part of me has just always been curious about the Snickers Blizzard.

I hate when I give up something I love to try something new and get disappointed. It's why I consistently order the exact same thing at every restaurant I ever go to.

"How's Tyler?" Mom asks, pretending to be all interested in the carrots.

I roll my eyes at Dad, who is smirking. "He's fine."

"Is it official?"

"Officially what?"

"I don't know. Official. Whatever you guys call it these days. Going steady. In a relationship. I don't know."

I just laugh a short laugh and sit at one of the stools at the island. "I don't know either, Mom."

Right then Preslee walks in.

"Hi, Paige."

"Hi, Preslee."

Then we just look at each other.

I'm still shocked by how old Preslee is. I guess when you haven't seen someone in a while, you just naturally assume she is going to stay the way she was. She's wearing jeans and a loose, vintage-style cream-colored sleeveless top. Her dark hair is long and straight today.

She looks like she needs a few of Dad's rolls. She's too thin.

"Well, isn't this just wonderful?" Mom sighs and leans back into Dad's chest. "Both of our girls under the same roof!"

Yes. Just peachy.

"Preslee was telling us that she's been living in Kansas City, Paige," Mom says all cheery, like Preslee has been keeping in touch with her for the last several years.

"Really."

"Yes. Oh, why don't you tell Paige about it, sweetie?"

Sweetie. The word leaves a sting somewhere on the back of my shoulders.

Preslee, to her credit, looks like she feels awkward. She meets my gaze briefly and then pulls the other stool out, a couple of yards away from me, and sits. She folds her hands in her lap. "There's not much to tell. I've been living there about two years." She seems quieter, more reserved, sorrowful almost.

I fight the pity. I didn't march out of here leaving my mother sobbing, my dad angry. She *should* feel sad.

"How's Spike?" I am pretty certain that was his name, the final nail in the coffin that was Preslee's former good-church-girl life.

Once he entered the picture, things went downhill fast.

"We broke up," she says quietly. "A while ago."

Good. I don't say it. Anyone named Spike should just be steered clear of, I'm pretty sure.

Mom and Dad are looking at each other, then looking at me and Preslee, then looking back at each other, pensive.

"What?" I ask them.

"Paige," Preslee says, quietly. "I came back for a reason."

I look at her, biting my tongue, a sudden rush of panic flooding into my stomach. She has cancer. She's pregnant. She's got seven days to live and I wasted four of them.

Her eyes are dark, concerned. She finally takes a deep breath and then twists a ring on her left hand.

"I'm getting married." She folds her hands together. I can see the huge glittering diamond she'd turned into her palm.

I just look at her.

Preslee's story falls out in a rush. "After Spike, I was just there, stuck in Chicago. I had no money, no job, I lived in a women's shelter. The people that ran it ended up becoming good friends of mine, and they took me to church with them." Her eyes get all teary. "I became a Christian, Paige."

Mom is sobbing softly.

"I started going to church with them every Sunday, got involved in as many Bible studies as I could find, and the pastor of the church introduced me to his son, Wes, who just started up his own realty company." She touches the ring on her finger absently, and I know before she says it that Wes is now her fiancé.

"Anyway, Wes gave me a job, I started working and got an apartment and a car and Wes . . . Oh Paige, he's so wonderful. He wants to move here. We're actually going to be opening a branch of his company in Waco and moving right after the wedding. We're getting married in six months."

I don't know what to think. What to feel. I'm staring at her and I feel like I should be happy.

Or at least happy for her.

Instead, all I feel is this sinking feeling deep in my stomach. It sounds like everything has just worked out great for Preslee, despite the pain she put us through.

"That's great," I say, trying to force the smile. I push myself off my stool, walk over, and give Preslee the most awkward hug in the world.

She latches on to me, though, like I'm Leo DiCaprio and about to drown in icy waters. "Oh, Paige, the second I met

Wes, the first thing I thought was how much I just wanted to tell you about him. He's wonderful. Really, really wonderful." She lets go and looks at me and then Mom and Dad. "I told him we were having a family dinner tonight. Mom, this is so last minute and I know you want it to be the four of us, but seeing as how we're getting married and he's in Waco right now on business . . ."

"Oh my gosh!" Mom says, a blubbering mess. "Invite him! Can he make it here in time?"

Preslee smiles a mischievous smile that sends me right back to elementary school when she and I would conspire to stay up past our bedtimes. "He's actually on his way. I figured you'd say yes."

"Oh my goodness and just look at me," Mom says, sniffling, swiping at her running mascara. "Lyle, take over chopping the salad. I'm going to touch up my makeup." She hands Dad the knife and then squeezes my shoulders as I sit back on my stool. "Isn't this just the most wonderful news?" she whispers in my ear.

"Mm-hmm," I hum.

Thirty minutes pass very slowly. We move to the living room and I try to rub Honey's ears and stuff down the growing sense of frustration as I listen to Preslee tell us all about Wes, how he's so gentle, so sweet, so compassionate, so every other desirable trait.

"Oh, and he's a big coffee drinker, Paige," Preslee says to me from the opposite couch, all smiles, like somehow this will make me and him best friends.

For the record, I like lots of people who don't like coffee.

"That's great," I say for the fortieth time.

The doorbell chimes at four, right as my phone starts ringing. It's Layla and thank God, she's prompt for the first time ever in her whole life.

I mumble something about needing to take it, but no one hears me because Mom is excitedly squealing over the door, Dad's smiling, and Preslee is throwing her arms around someone still standing on the porch. I duck down the hallway and into my old room that Mom left exactly as I left it the day I moved to Dallas.

I cried the whole drive there.

I take a deep breath and answer the phone. "Hey."

"So I hate to tell you this, but we've been under attack from aliens and one of the missiles hit your apartment building. I think you've lost everything." Layla's voice is monotone.

"Watching *Independence Day*?"

"For like the eightieth time. I do not see the appeal of this movie, Paige. How's it going?"

I sigh and rub my forehead, looking at my reflection in the mirror over my dresser. I look old.

Not something I want to look like as a twenty-three-year-old.

"That wonderful, huh?" Layla says to my silence. "Well. Feel free to use the missile excuse."

"Somehow, I don't think they'll buy that."

"How's Preslee?"

"Oh, she's great. She's a Christian now. Got a great job. She's getting married to the perfect man."

"Huh. Times are a-changing. His name isn't Spike, is it?"

"Wes."

"As in 'as you wish'? Wow. Good for her!"

"Yeah."

"You don't sound so happy."

I don't want to get into a discussion of my current feelings over the phone. "I'm fine. He just got here. I should probably go meet him."

"Well, don't go like that. You might scare him off with your enthusiasm."

"Bye, Layla. Thanks for calling."

"Love you, friend."

I hang up, look at myself once more in the mirror, and then plead another quick prayer.

Seriously, God. Help!

The living room is full of happiness when I walk out. A tall, very cute blond guy is standing with his arm around Preslee's shoulders, a smile wider than a long-bed truck covering his face.

I need to not listen to country the three-and-a-half hours home.

"Paige!" Preslee says. The sad, sorrowful girl of forty-five minutes ago is gone, replaced with a bright, glowing, all-smiles woman.

A knot hardens in my stomach.

"Paige, this is my fiancé, Wes Millerman." Preslee is shining, her eyes never leaving Wes's face.

"Hi there." Wes smiles a friendly smile at me. "I've heard a lot about you, Paige."

Here's what I want to say: "I wish I could say the same, Wes."

Here's what I do say: "It's nice to meet you." Then I paste the fakest smile ever on my face, sit on the couch, rub Honey's ears, and listen to the love story and the proposal story and the what-we-hope-our-wedding-will-be story for the next two hours.

Mom's honey ham and sweet potatoes look and smell delicious but taste like a peach that isn't quite ripe — bland and grainy. Everyone else is praising the meal to the skies, though, so I'm assuming it's just the knot in my stomach making everything taste weird. Even Dad's rolls have a funny texture they've never had before.

Wes is adorable and charming and Preslee is all smiles and flirtation. It's odd to see my sister like this. The last time I saw her, she was sullen and angry, ready with a biting response to anything anyone said.

This is like Preslee from elementary school. Carefree. Happy.

Mom and Dad spend the evening enraptured by everything Wes and Preslee say. They laugh, Mom cries at sad parts, and then they laugh some more. In light of their obvious joy at their youngest being home, I feel even worse.

At six o'clock, right as I'm about to say my good-byes, Wes stops laughing and looks over at me. "We are being so rude," he says to Preslee. "We've dominated the whole conversation. Paige, I really do want to hear more about you."

I wave a hand. It is far better that I didn't have the chance to get a word in edgewise, not that I would have taken the chance anyway. "No big deal. I'm actually about to head out. I've got a long drive home."

"Oh, not already, Paige," Preslee says, her face falling. "Mom made dessert. We haven't even pulled it out yet."

I stand and shrug. "That's okay. Some other time. Wes, it was nice to meet you. Good to see you, Preslee." I give Mom and Dad a hug.

"I made cinnamon cake though, honey," Mom says as I hug her. "Are you sure you can't stay? Just thirty more minutes?"

I shake my head and slip my purse over my shoulder. I have reached the limit. If I don't leave now, I will say a lot of things I'll wish I hadn't tomorrow. Besides, cinnamon cake is Preslee's favorite.

Not mine.

"Next time. I'll see you guys soon." I pat Honey on the head and run out the door before they have a chance to formulate another excuse for me to stay.

I hurry to my car, unlock it, slide in, turn the key, and back out. I'm halfway to the interstate before the tears come.

They slide out one at a time at first. Hot and heavy, tracing down my face before dropping into my lap.

I stayed. I was here. I was the one who followed all the rules, heard all the complaints, and dealt with the aftermath of Preslee's behavior. It was *me* who held Mom the years that Preslee hadn't even bothered to call on Christmas or Mother's Day.

And now she is back. Happy. Healthy. Beautiful. Engaged. Right back to living in her old bedroom like nothing ever happened.

And somehow, I suddenly feel like the outsider.

I get home a little before ten, completely physically and emotionally exhausted. I climb the stairs, unlock my door, lock it behind me, and walk through the dark apartment to my bedroom. I put on my pajamas, brush my teeth, and climb into bed.

I look at my Bible but don't pick it up. I just know it will have some verse about loving your enemies or praying for those who hurt you, and I just can't read that tonight.

Then I cry myself to sleep.

Chapter
10

onday and Tuesday are rough days. By Wednesday, I'm wound so tight I'm worried about sitting in my swivel chair at work.

Peggy stops by my desk on her way in. "You okay, Paige?" She's carrying a coffee thermos that most likely has green tea in it by the acrid smell wafting from the open lid.

"Fine."

"Well, you don't seem fine. Are you sure you're—?"

"I'm *fine*, Peggy."

She holds her free hand up. "Okay, okay. I won't push." She leaves to go to her office.

"Peggy . . ." I sigh, rubbing my forehead.

She smiles and shrugs it off. "No harm, no foul, Paige. I'll be in my office."

My phone buzzes then and I look at the text from Tyler.

WHAT ARE YOU UP TO AFTER YOUTH GROUP TONIGHT? WANT TO GO GET DESSERT?

The last in a long string of texts from him. He sent me a message right after I got home Sunday night asking how it went, he asked if we could do dinner on Monday, then dinner on Tuesday . . .

I don't like this side of me that I am seeing. And I like Tyler.

A lot, if I have to be completely honest.

It's best that I work through these emotions without putting him through the wringer while I am doing it.

I type a quick one word reply. MAYBE.

Somehow I get through the day without injuring anyone. I run home, change clothes, consider calling Rick to tell him I'm not coming tonight, and then decide to just go.

Better that than Natalie showing up at the house with baby Claire demanding what's wrong and not leaving until I tell her.

I am jealous of my sister.

Not a pretty thing to say to anyone. Even just putting it into thought form makes me wince.

And here I think I am such a strong, sensible Christian.

I walk into the youth room at 5:34, but one look at my face and Rick doesn't shoot the marshmallow gun he has aimed at the door to fire on latecomers. Tyler walks in and looks at me, concern spreading over his whole face.

Rick prays, says a few things about the lessons that I don't hear, and then everyone stands. I start for the door as well.

"Wait for a second, Paige," Rick says, not moving from where he's straddling his chair. He leans over, tucks the gun on the floor under the chair, and then sits back up, leaning forward to rest his arms on the chair back, just looking at me.

The door closes behind Tyler and Rick nods to my chair. "Have a seat."

I sit, making sure Rick hears my sigh.

"Theatrics aren't going to help here, Paige. What's up? I don't think I've ever seen you so mellow."

"I'm tired," I say. And I am. I've spent the past three nights tossing and turning half the time.

This should not be upsetting me as much as it is.

Rick just looks at me. "And?"

"And what?"

"That's what I just asked. I know you, Paige Alder. You are not just tired."

I sigh again and rub my face. "I don't know, Rick. I don't want to talk about it. I feel petty."

"Someone steal your favorite parking space?"

"Preslee is back to stay."

Rick and Natalie know how much Preslee hurt me. Right after everything happened with her, I spent about three days crying on their sofa. They've had to hear me gripe every year about how Preslee didn't come home for Christmas or whatever the major event was.

"I remember," Rick says.

"She's back and she's completely changed and she's engaged." He already knows some of this, but I can't help the repeat. "She's a Christian, she's beautiful and stylish, she's marrying this guy who's equally beautiful and stylish, and she's happy and I just feel . . ." I let my voice trail off, covering my eyes.

"Sympathy for the older brother of the prodigal son?"

"Lots of sympathy."

He watches me for a second, pursing his lips. "Are you jealous?"

Rick asks the worst questions sometimes. I stand and

start pacing. "She did everything wrong, Rick. She broke the law over and over again and not only that, she broke my parents' hearts over and over again."

He nods. "I know."

"She didn't even come to my graduation, did you know that? Or my twenty-first birthday. She wasn't there when I got my first real job or when I bought my first car."

"I know."

"She did everything wrong," I say again.

"So you feel guilty for feeling jealous of her."

I sit down and try not to cry.

"Paige," Rick says, and there's about nine hundred pounds of compassion in his tone. I don't see this side of Rick very often. He's usually the goofy guy, the one who makes jokes and has fun and causes the kids to laugh.

I shake my head, will the lump in my throat to go down, and mash the corners of my eyes. The last thing I need is to go to my class of freshmen girls and have them all asking questions too.

"Look, I'm not going to tell you what's right or wrong here, because it seems to me that you're already under enough conviction, but I just want you to remember something. God's plan for Preslee is not His plan for you."

I just look at him. "He planned for me to do everything right and her to do everything wrong?"

"Maybe on the surface."

The word *surface* pricks at my conscience. Rick looks at the clock on the wall. "It's time for small groups to start. We're not done talking. I'll see you after you get off work on Friday. Just come on to the house for dinner."

"I'll be fine, Rick."

"I wasn't asking, Paige." He gets up and leaves. I sit there for another second.

There's a soft knock on the door and Tyler sticks his head in. "You okay?" he asks sweetly.

I'm not sure I know anymore.

* * * * *

Cracker Barrel is not crowded at eight thirty on Wednesday nights. I follow the hostess to a table and sit down, Tyler sits opposite me. This is becoming something of a habit.

Tyler's a big Cracker Barrel fan. He's like a seventy-year-old living in a twenty-five-year-old's body.

"Cobbler time," he says, not even looking at the menu. He looks across the table at me and smiles. "How was small group?"

"Fine," I say. And it was. The girls were distracted with school coming to a close in a few weeks and summer starting, but it was nice in a way because I didn't have to focus too much on what I was doing.

A waitress comes by and takes our order. Tyler gets peach cobbler with ice cream and coffee. I just get a cup of decaf. I don't need anything else keeping me up tonight.

"So, you okay, Paige?" Tyler reaches across the table for my hand. He's only held my hand once before. He holds it carefully now, gently.

Suddenly, I'm very jittery and very thankful I didn't order anything caffeinated or sugary. And that old worry about him just being a sweet friend resurfaces.

Why *hasn't* he made anything official yet? And is it way lame to ask?

"I'm fine," I say for what feels like the 547th time this week.

He just looks at me, blue eyes probing, and I sigh.

So much for not dragging him through this with me.

"My sister? Preslee? She's back in the area."

Tyler doesn't know a lot of the history there. I didn't tell him very much, simply because I didn't like talking about her.

I still don't.

"Okay." Tyler nods. "You're not happy about this."

"Honestly? I don't know what I am." The waitress comes over and sets two cups of coffee in between us. Tyler reluctantly lets go of my hand and I rip open a packet of sugar and eye the bowl of creamers that have likely been sitting there unrefrigerated on the table all day.

"Well, you don't have to tell me details," he says, gently. "I just want you to know that I'm here if you need to talk." His eyes are soft, his smile reassuring. He looks adorable today, not that he looks that different than other days. Jeans. T-shirt. His hair is curly despite his obvious efforts to tame it down for work earlier, and that makes me smile.

I really do like this guy.

We end up talking about everything except Preslee until almost ten, and then Tyler drives me back to my car, which is now the only car in the church parking lot.

"Thank you, Tyler." I feel content for the first time since Sunday.

"Thanks for coming with me, Paige."

I sit there in the passenger seat of his truck, not making any moves to leave. He doesn't seem too sad about it. He puts the truck into park and leans back in his seat. The radio is playing some Chris Tomlin song very quietly, and everything feels peaceful.

"Preslee ran away from home when she was seventeen," I say into the silence. I hadn't even known I was about to start telling the story.

Tyler looks over at me and nods.

"We knew it was coming." I rub my temples. "I had already left home to come here for school, so I missed a lot of the end of it, but even when I lived at home, things weren't good. Preslee was always the one to push the rules to the breaking point." She spent a great majority of her junior-high years being grounded.

I skip a lot of the things that led up to it. "Anyway, right before she left, she got a tattoo and decided to move in with her boyfriend, who was in her band and I'm pretty sure he lived in a van." I take a deep breath, remembering those days. "It was awful, Tyler. She just left. Slammed out the door one day and we didn't see her again for months. Mom and Dad looked everywhere. I missed a week of classes and we drove up to Oklahoma where Spike's mom said his band just got a gig. We couldn't find her."

Tyler reaches for my hand.

"Anyway, about three months after she left, Mom got a call from her. Preslee said she was fine, she was happier without them, and she would prefer if they would just stop looking for her because there was no way she was ever going home again." I close my eyes, remembering when Mom called me in tears. I drove home that same day after classes, spent the night crying with Mom and Dad, got up at three in the morning, and drove back in time for my seven o'clock class the next day.

Tyler squeezes my hand.

"Anyway, we didn't see or hear from her for a long time after that. Bits and pieces would come through. Then she texted me the night of Layla's parents' anniversary and told me she was back in Austin."

"She's been in Texas that long?"

I nod. "I just haven't seen her except once. She came by my apartment and dropped off a birthday present. And then Mom told me that we were having a family dinner on Sunday because it was ridiculous that Preslee and I still hadn't talked."

Tyler sighs. "I'm sorry, Paige. How did Sunday go?"

And now the fun part, where he gets to find out what a self-centered, awful person I am. "Preslee broke up with Spike, became a Christian, got a job, and is now engaged to this really nice guy."

Tyler squeezes my hand again, looking at me, lips pursed at my monotone. "And all of this is not good news?"

"Yes. No . . . I don't know." I pull my hand away. "Anyway. That's what's going on."

Tyler just looks at me for a minute. "Have you considered . . . ?" He stops.

"What?" Might as well hear it now.

"I was just going to say that maybe the problem with Preslee isn't so much what happened in the past."

I just look at him.

"Of course it's a problem with the past. Didn't you just hear that whole story?"

"I think you should just find time to talk to her. Let her tell her side of things."

I just nod, smile a tight close-mouthed smile at him, and

climb out of the truck. "Thanks for listening, Tyler." I don't thank him for the unsolicited advice.

I climb into my car and Tyler waits to follow me out of the parking lot. I drive home, park in my assigned space, and climb out of my car, holding my purse and my Bible.

Once I'm inside, I change into my pajamas, turn on the lamp in the living room, and sit down in the rocking chair, still holding my Bible.

This has not been my finest week.

I feel like I've had several of those weeks lately.

I look at my Bible and smooth my hand over the brown leather. Rick's comment about the prodigal son comes back to my mind, and I open the Bible to the Gospels, trying to find the story Jesus told.

John? Matthew? I finally find it in Luke 15.

I read the story once, then twice, then three times, my heart getting heavier with each time I read it. I am like the older brother. I am angry. Part of me wants Preslee to suffer for what she did to us. Part of me wants her to just say her apologies and quietly stay out of our lives.

A lot of me is scared she'll do it again.

I close my eyes and lean my head back on the chair.

What am I supposed to do, Lord? If I forgive her and move on, what if she hurts me again?

I rock back and forth slowly in the rocking chair. The verses about forgiving someone seventy times seven float through my head and I do the math.

Four hundred and ninety.

But what about the memories, Lord? Or everything she missed? I can't just pretend everything didn't happen.

I open my eyes and look over at the clock on my

microwave in the kitchen. It's almost eleven o'clock. I'm tired. I'm too tired to think through theological questions right now.

Maybe in the morning.

Or maybe, if I'm lucky, I'll wake up to a text from Mom that says something along the lines of PRESLEE AND WES DECIDING TO MOVE TO FAR EAST RUSSIA INSTEAD.

Then everything can go back to the way it has been. The way I'm used to.

The safest way.

Chapter
11

Friday evening I turn off my computer at work and just look at the black screen for a few minutes.

I just spent the entire day doing meaningless tasks. I didn't even talk to anyone on the phone about adoption. Just spent the whole day doing paychecks, bills, and writing e-mails to people who don't live anywhere close to Dallas.

I'm sorry, we are not staffed to do a home study in Connecticut.

Apparently, we need to make the words *Dallas Area Only* larger on our website.

Peggy walks over, pulling her purse over her shoulder and smiling at me. "And it's officially the weekend, my dear."

I nod. "So it is."

"You have never seemed happier."

I smile at her. "I'm happy it's the weekend." I'm not so excited about the dinner coming up tonight at Rick and Natalie's. Rick has a way of asking hard questions I don't want to give answers to.

Candace comes walking out of her office as well. "And

I'm off. I don't want to hear another complaint from anyone ever again."

"I hate spinach in between my teeth," Peggy says to her. Candace just sticks her tongue out at her.

"Long day?" I ask Candace.

"Long week. I need a good weekend. Bob and I are going to a wedding, though, so it won't be relaxing."

"Aren't weddings supposed to be fun?" Peggy asks. "Whose is it?"

"My cousin's daughter. And yes, weddings are supposed to be fun." She sighs and rubs her temple. "This particular cousin though is very antimusic and all things fun, so I'm not expecting too much."

I laugh. "Sorry about that."

Candace shrugs. "It's family. What can you do?"

We all leave and go to our separate cars. Mark is working late, so I'll let him lock up. I climb into my Camry and try to stir up some enthusiasm for dinner with Rick and Natalie.

I don't usually have problems with this.

I drive to their house and park. Since I'm coming straight from work, I look a lot nicer than I ever have for dinner at their house.

Natalie opens the door with Claire in a Jedi Knight–looking contraption. Fabric twists around Natalie's shoulders and waist and somehow, Claire is suspended in the middle of it. "Hey, Paige."

I just look at the baby, puzzled. "How is she in there?"

"Amazing these wraps, huh? Come on in. Rick is making some sort of barbecue." She closes the door behind me and lowers her voice. "Honestly, I'm a little scared of food poisoning. I've got a bottle of Tums on standby."

"Tums stop food poisoning?"

She shrugs. "I don't know. Seems like they should."

It's probably a good thing Natalie is not a nurse.

Rick is in the kitchen wearing an apron that says "It's All Fun and Games Until Someone Loses a Pinkie" with a picture of one of those little smokey sausages on it, and he's stirring something in a bowl.

"There's my next employee!" He grins at me.

I sigh, though not as deeply as I probably would have before. After a meaningless day like today, I am maybe even potentially open to a job with Rick.

That should show right there how much I fear a meaningless life.

I watch Rick flick a jar of garlic powder behind his back and over his shoulder and catch it with his right hand.

"You scare me."

"This? This isn't scary," Rick says.

"No, you should watch him do that with eggs. *That's* scary." Natalie pats Claire's back and turns to get into the fridge. "All right, Paige, spill the beans. Rick said Preslee is back in town?"

I sit down at the table and watch Natalie pull salad ingredients from the fridge. I would offer to help, but I would be turned down flat. After so many years of eating dinner at this house, I know when I'm not needed.

"There's not a ton to tell. She texted me that she was in Austin the night of Layla's parents' anniversary party."

Natalie squints at me. "She's been in Austin for almost two months and you failed to mention this to us?"

I shrug. "I've only seen her once before Sunday. She came over with a birthday present for me." I think of the necklace she gave me that is still sitting in the jewelry box, shoved into my bathroom drawer. I see it every morning when I pull my toothpaste out and just try to ignore it.

I need to find a new place to store that.

"How's the jealous thing going?" Rick asks, being his typically blunt self.

I shrug. Yesterday, I'd gone for a very long walk when I got home from work and just thought and tried to pray.

Then I got tired and hungry. So I went home, made dinner, and watched HGTV until I fell asleep on the sofa.

Sometimes, the best use an apartment renter has for HGTV is to avoid the Holy Spirit.

"I do not recognize body language as an acceptable answer." Rick digs around in a drawer and comes out with a baster.

"It's okay," I say.

"I do not recognize *okay* as an acceptable answer," he says.

I roll my eyes. "What do you recognize?"

"Lots of things. My smoking-hot wife carrying my precious daughter in that weird wrap thing. My fantastic barbecue sauce that is about to cover the most succulent pieces of chicken you've ever seen. You sitting there, all forlorn. I recognize a lot of things, Paige."

Natalie grins at her husband. "Back atcha, babe."

"I do make this apron look good, huh?"

"Okay, pause there, please." I wave my hands before marital happiness dulls the memory of me sitting at their kitchen table.

"Anyway, Paige, here's my point." Rick pulls a tray of raw chicken covered in plastic wrap out of the fridge. "You want to make a difference in people's lives, which is why you should come work for me, by the way, but you need to see that *people* includes your sister." He grins cheekily at me. "Now, no more talk of things such as these. You're going to depress my chicken."

"Thanks, Rick." I roll my eyes. Nothing like being invited over for dinner and then being told to shut up before you cause emotional havoc on the animal you're about to eat.

We spend the rest of dinner talking about everything except Preslee. Layla and her upcoming wedding, Natalie's mom coming to visit, and Rick's excitement over the new youth group curriculum. Every twelve seconds, he makes a mini sales pitch.

"And speaking of mothers-in-law, you know where a great place to meet a great guy is? Working in the youth group. Oh wait, you've already met one there." Rick grins at me as he stabs a piece of barbecue-slathered chicken.

"How are things going with Tyler?" Natalie asks, taking a drink of her decaffeinated iced tea. She stripped out of the wrap thing and Claire is nestled happily in a little bouncer by the table.

I shrug, chewing a bite of chicken. The last time I saw him was Wednesday night.

"He's nice," I say once I swallow.

"So is Mr. Rogers, but that doesn't mean I want to date him," Natalie says.

"I should hope not," Rick says to her. "If you were into sweaters, you married the wrong man." He looks thoughtfully at me. "Tyler doesn't really strike me as a sweater guy either."

Not really. If anything, he looks like he needs his own show on some Wilderness Channel.

Flanneled Man Versus The Concrete Jungle.

I'll never be able to picture Tyler as a computer guy. Ever. Even though that's what he does every day from seven in the morning until six at night. He even wears slacks and a button-down shirt every day.

Just an odd mental picture.

"Not really," I say to Rick.

"Are you attracted to him?" Natalie persists. Rick looks expectantly at me as well, chewing a bite of green beans.

This is why I have a love-hate relationship with dinners at their house. I love coming over here when everything is just fantastic in my life and I have no issues going on. Insert one complexity into my life, and I'd prefer to be anywhere but here.

Rick and Natalie don't believe in privacy.

"I don't know," I say, trying to keep a blush from showing up on my cheeks. I really like Tyler. He's sweet. He's only held my hand a couple of times, though, and has only kissed me on the cheek.

I frown. What if Tyler is somewhere at some equally nosy people's house and they ask him this question and he realizes that no, he's not attracted to me at all and that's why he's never gone beyond hand-holding?

I hate coming here.

"You look concerned," Natalie says.

"Did you just get a taste of that cumin I threw in the sauce? It's puzzling at first to the taste buds, isn't it? Eventually it will make sense." Rick pats my hand.

* * * * *

I get home at nine thirty, which might be the earliest I've ever left Rick and Natalie's house. But after spending the rest of dinner depressed that Tyler only likes me as a friend, I didn't really have the morale to stay longer.

"You sure you need to leave?" Natalie asked me about eight times as I slung my purse over my shoulder.

"I'm sure. I'm tired."

I am tired. I fall onto my couch and click the TV on to HGTV.

What a wonderful Friday night.

My phone buzzes and I reach for it in my purse. It's a text.

HOPE YOU ARE HAVING FUN AT RICK AND NATALIE'S! It's from Tyler.

I write him back. HOME NOW. IT WAS FINE. I struggle with typing the word *bearable* instead, but I refrain.

WHAT ARE YOU DOING NOW?

WATCHING HGTV.

THERE IS A SHOCK.

Two rather good-looking cousins are remodeling a restaurant kitchen. I squash farther into the couch. This is one of my favorite shows. Mostly because of the guys.

Like I said. Good looking.

I go into the bedroom during the next commercial break and change into sweatpants from college and a T-shirt that says *And we wonder why Charlie Brown never went pro*, which has a picture of Lucy yanking the football away from a flailing-in-the-air Charlie Brown. It's one of my favorite shirts and it shows. It's nearly threadbare. I pull on a pair of thick white socks and knot my hair into a sloppy bun.

Relaxation time.

I sit back down on the couch and grab the blanket I keep there and that's when a soft knock sounds on the door.

I pause, thinking, my heart racing.

No one I know of is coming over. Layla always calls and it's too late for solicitors.

The only other logical answer is a man in a mask here to kill me and make it look like an accident.

I have got to stop watching crime shows.

I creep all ninja-style over to the door, like maybe the person on my porch can see me through the walls, and peek through the peephole.

It's a man. He's holding a paper grocery bag and wearing a knit winter hat. He's looking down into his bag so I can't see who it is.

It is May. It's a little warm in Dallas to be wearing a winter hat. Obviously, this person is a murderer.

I've never had this happen before. What do I do? Call the cops? Call the apartment security? Run? Go get something to protect myself?

The last one seems to be the most prudent, so I run to get the only thing I own that somewhat resembles a weapon and creep back over to the door, holding for dear life to my phone and staring out the peephole.

He knocks again and looks up and I gasp in relief.

"Tyler!" I yank open the door, breathing in the cooler night air. "You gave me a heart attack! I thought you were here to kill me!"

He grins at me, looking adorable in gray sweatpants and a black UT T-shirt. His blond hair is poking out in curls from under his cap. He nods to the grocery sack. "Maybe with chocolate. Can I come in?"

I open the door wider.

"What's with the flyswatter?" He nods to my hand.

I look at it, debating on whether or not I should tell him that this is my weapon of choice for a knitted-cap invader.

"Mm, nothing. Thought I saw something," I say quickly, setting it back under the kitchen cabinet.

"Like a fly?"

"Right. Exactly. Just like a fly."

"Paige?"

"Mm-hmm? Yes, Tyler?"

"You weren't holding that for self-defense, were you?"

I decide silence is better than lies, so I just peek into the bag he's holding instead of answering him. "Hey! Junior Mints!"

"You were. Oh, Paige, I don't know whether to laugh or drive to Walmart and go get you a can of Mace."

I smile at him. "I'll be fine. What are you doing here?"

He shrugs and sets the bag on the couch. "I just thought maybe you'd want some company. And some Oreos." He pulls out a bag of Oreos, a box of Junior Mints, and a half-gallon of Blue Bell ice cream.

He is my favorite person on the whole planet.

"You even bought the good ice cream," I say, feeling myself get all sappy.

"Well, sure. I'm not the type to show up, scare you half to death, and then feed you some crappy ice milk." He grins at me.

Any worries I had about Tyler not being especially attracted to me are melting away like the ice cream is. I hurry to get an ice cream scoop and a few minutes later, we both settle on the couch with our bowls full of ice cream, the

Oreos and Junior Mints in between us on the couch.

I cross my legs Indian-style and point to the TV with my spoon. "So those guys are cousins. They remodel kitchens."

"I didn't know you were into kitchen remodeling," Tyler says.

I just eat a bite of ice cream off my spoon and look at the TV. "Uh, sure. Sure, I'm into kitchen remodeling."

"Uh-huh. You're not the best of liars, Paige."

"You aren't the best at asking questions that don't make me have to lie, Tyler."

"And you might need to work on your grammar."

"Aren't you just full of compliments?"

He nods and shrugs, faking humility. "I was raised right."

We watch the show in silence for a few minutes. Tyler finishes his bowl of ice cream, takes my empty bowl, stacks his on top of it, and sets them on the end table beside him, scooting the Oreos and the Junior Mints to the coffee table and wrapping an arm around the back of my couch so his fingers graze my right shoulder.

I look at him and he smiles at me. "What?" he asks.

"Nothing."

"Liar. Geez, Paige."

"Thanks for the ice cream, Tyler."

"Thanks for letting me crash your evening." He tugs on my right shoulder shirt seam. "You look cute."

"And now look who has become the liar," I say, but I fight to control the blush jumping up my cheeks like those salmon fish that skip up the rivers.

"Like I said," he fiddles with a stray strand of hair that somehow missed my bun, "I was raised right. I don't lie, Paige."

Cue my stomach dropping into my toes. I am suddenly sorry I'd eaten the bowl of ice cream.

I never imagined that thought would ever cross my mind.

He smiles gently, eyes softening as he looks at me. He finally turns back to the TV, which is a relief because breathing has suddenly become very difficult for me. I try to be as inconspicuous as I can be gasping for air.

"You okay?" He's still fiddling with that strand of hair. I don't know if I am thankful that it evaded my bun or not. On the one hand, it is sending little shivers up and down my arms.

On the other hand, I have no feeling left in my toes because I'm so focused on not moving a muscle so he won't move his arm.

I am not cut out for a relationship. Maybe this is why it's never worked out with any of the guys I've dated. I can't handle the pressure. Not that there were these kinds of creepy crawlies in my stomach with all of the other guys.

Particularly recently.

Luke's face fills my mind and I blink it away.

Tyler and I sit like that, watching HGTV and then switching over to the Food Network, until almost midnight. He finally stretches, looks over at the clock on my microwave, and declares it's time for him to go.

"Thanks again for letting me join you tonight," he says, standing.

"I don't remember having a lot of say in it." I stand as well.

He grins. "Thanks for not kicking me out then."

"You brought ice cream." I shrug. "I can't kick out a man holding ice cream."

"I figured." He walks over to the door and smiles at me, rubbing the curls poking out of his hat at the back of his head. "Sweet dreams, Paige." He reaches over for my left hand, pulls me a tad closer to him, leans down, and kisses my cheek, lightly cupping the back of my head with his other hand.

I focus on taking tiny, short breaths. My lungs are suddenly having trouble carrying out their only duty of bringing oxygen into my body.

He smiles at me, an inch from my face, then flicks my nose with his finger. "Night, Paige."

He leaves and I watch him stroll down the steps, wave once at the sidewalk, and then walk out of sight.

That's when I realize I didn't ever say good-bye to him.

I whack my hand on my forehead and close the door, deciding that it might seem a little weird to run after him shouting good-bye.

Oxygen. That's all my lungs were supposed to provide. Without oxygen, my heart started racing, my head got fuzzy, and my good, rational sense vanished.

Not to mention my sense of balance.

I sit down sharply on the edge of the couch and just focus on breathing for a minute or two. Then I turn off the TV, lock the door, turn off the lights in the apartment, brush my teeth, and snuggle under the covers.

I just sit there for a minute.

It would seem that I have nothing to worry about as far as Tyler is concerned.

Relief makes me smile as I pull my Bible over.

Paul is still talking about his favorite word in Galatians. Law.

"But when the fullness of the time came, God sent forth His Son, born of a woman, born under the Law, so that He might

redeem those who were under the Law, that we might receive the adoption as sons."

I think about those words for a few minutes and my smile slowly fades. Nothing I did gave God any reason to love me as His own. If anything, I was and am like Preslee used to be.

And God still loves me.

I slowly turn off my light and close my eyes, but it takes me a long time to go to sleep.

Chapter 12

I'm just pouring my first cup of coffee the next morning when there's a knock at my door.

Maybe Tyler decided to come back with cinnamon rolls.

I smile, half hoping I'm right, half hoping I'm wrong, seeing as how I look like someone in *Grey's Anatomy*, and not one of the beautiful doctors, but one of the near-death patients.

I never leave my house without makeup on.

I peek through the peephole and it's a guy, but it's not the right one.

"Good morning, Paige!" Luke singsongs, holding up a box of Krispy Kreme doughnuts.

Maybe I should look like crap more often. It seems to bring attractive men to my door holding sugary foods. I open the door.

"Luke. Did I know you were coming over?"

"Nope. Saturday morning surprise. I woke up this morning, went for a run, and while I was on my run, I thought, I wonder if Paige has had breakfast?" He waves the fragrant doughnut box under my nose. "I hope not."

I rub my cheek, feeling ugly. Even if I don't have any of those kinds of feelings about Luke anymore, I still want to look nice around him. It's that whole revenge thing after someone breaks up with you.

"Hmm," I say, because I can't think of anything else to say.

"You haven't eaten breakfast?"

"No."

"Great!" He marches into my apartment, sets the box on the table, and then sits down in a chair.

I close the door, fighting the urge to walk out and leave him in my apartment by himself with the doughnuts. It looks like he's planning on joining me for breakfast.

I look at him sitting there, looking all freshly showered and perfect, and feel even grosser.

"This is so great." He grins all big at me. "I really have been wanting to catch up with you again. We have hardly talked and I've been here almost two months now."

I go into the kitchen, pour him a cup of black coffee, add sugar and cream to my cup, and then carry both mugs over to the table.

"Thanks Paige!" he says, like I just gave him the gift of never needing deodorant again.

I sit at the table and rub at my sleep-matted hair. I am wearing my sweatpants from last night and another old T-shirt. At least I brushed my teeth. I guess I could look worse.

Not much, but a little.

Luke opens the doughnut box and the smell of sugar and dough takes over my apartment. The smell of these things has to be a huge reason Krispy Kreme is still in business, because everyone knows they are made of entirely terrible things for you, yet people continue to eat them.

Luke starts chatting happily about how this is so wonderful, he's so thankful for such great friends like me, and how we should do things as friends more often. It's like he had the channel tuned to watching Rachel and Ross all night while he was sleeping and now the word *friends* is on repeat in his head.

I'm half expecting him to burst into the theme song at any moment.

"But enough of the sappiness, friend," he says. "How's life going?"

I hate this question. How am I ever supposed to answer that? If I answer it truthfully and tell him I'm eating a delicious doughnut in the company of an annoying man, that just seems rude. If I complain about having company when I look like my face should be on the cover of a magazine with the headline *NO MAKEUP HORROR SHOW*, that just seems pitiful. And if I delve into the whole topic that is Preslee and what I've been worrying over in the last week, that just seems too raw and honest for a guy who crushed my heart under his designer shoe and left over four years ago.

Too many things to think about when it's still coffee cup number one. I usually try to save topics like this for my brain once I get to number three.

Sometimes number five. That is for particularly rough days, though.

It doesn't help that there is a coffeepot at the adoption agency and that one of Candace's many nieces works at Starbucks and routinely gives Candace free pounds of coffee.

Luke is looking expectantly at me, and I realize my brain has rabbit trailed into Starbucks. "Sorry about that," I say, lightly shaking my head. "What were we talking about?"

"You." Luke shrugs. "You've heard about me. I started my new job. Love it. I found an apartment. It's actually just up the street. And I really like Layla's and your church, so I'll probably keep going there."

There's a shock.

Lord. I really wasn't joking when I mentioned to You four years ago in the middle of that massive post-breakup cake consumption that I never wanted to see Luke again. Just so You know.

And yet here he is. Licking icing off his fingers at my kitchen table.

The irony is killing me.

"I don't have much to say, Luke. I need a shower and I'm planning on drinking about six more of these." I point to my coffee mug. "I didn't plan very much else for the weekend, other than dinner tonight." Assuming Tyler and I are still on for a double date with Layla and Peter.

Layla called me earlier in the week and asked if we could do the double date. "I need to talk wedding details!" she told me.

"Why do the guys need to be there?"

"Because," she said, her voice hitting the *duh*-tone. "Peter is so covered in wedding details that he can barely see straight. He needs male company, Paige. Badly. The other day, he told me we should consider an eyelet lace for our end table. No man should ever use the word *eyelet*."

I just laughed.

Luke is just looking at me, eyes intent, totally focused on me. When we were dating, one of my most favorite qualities about him was that he listened wholeheartedly to whoever he was talking to. When you spoke to Luke, you

felt like you were the only person in the entire universe right then.

It's a little disconcerting now.

I eat three bites of my doughnut. Luke nods and then stares at the three pictures I have framed on the wall. One of my family when Preslee and I were little kids, one of Layla and me at her parents' anniversary party, and one of my parents and me at my college graduation.

"Paige," he says slowly. "Can I ask a question?"

With that tone of voice, I'm fairly certain he's not about to ask me if I feel like boy bands might be making a comeback.

"What happened to us?" he asks in a quiet voice.

"I'm sorry?" I am incredulous. Surely he remembers this.

"I mean, I know things got weird when I got to college."

I don't remember things getting weird then. We were all living in Austin. Luke went to UT and lived at home. In a lot of ways, we saw each other more after he graduated high school because he wasn't so busy with all the extracurricular stuff he had before, like football and track.

We started dating when I was sixteen. I was a sophomore; Luke was a senior. My parents had 812 rules for us about dating. *No being out past ten. No being anywhere by yourselves. No being in a car alone. No being in a house alone.*

Mom and Dad liked to emphasize points they found to be important.

Honestly, if Luke hadn't been Layla's brother and they hadn't already known him so well, I really doubt if I would ever have been allowed to date him. But Luke was the perfect gentleman. He followed every single rule my parents had down to the punctuation. At first, anyway.

It was part of why I fell so hard for him, I think.

After he graduated and started going to UT, I got busier at school, but we still saw each other often. Some of the time, Layla was with us. A lot of the time, she wasn't. We did group things at the church, we ate out at restaurants, we hung out at my house with Preslee and Mom and Dad.

It wasn't until after I graduated high school and moved here that things started getting weird.

"And I know I got mixed up on my priorities," Luke says now, raking a hand back through his dark hair.

Half of what happened to us was just long-distance problems. That's always what I've assumed, anyway. We were making new friends, going different places. I was getting super involved at church and hanging out all the time with Layla. And Luke was being courted by his current employer and being offered lots of money and a great position, and if he could graduate with honors, he could go work for them.

Suddenly, Luke never seemed to go to church anymore. When I asked why he didn't go one Sunday, he told me he had homework. Then he had a party the next week and slept in on Sunday. Then he had more homework. And papers to write and books to read and parties to recover from.

I finally stopped asking him if he saw my parents at church and if they mentioned anything about Preslee.

Then he stopped calling as much. Our nightly routine of calling each other became a three-times-a-week routine. Then a once-a-week thing. Text messages became less frequent and less meaningful.

Luke rubs his eyes. "And then that awful visit . . ." he mutters.

I was nineteen. I had just gone back to school after the worst Christmas break ever, because Preslee made it completely miserable. Luke called me that Friday and asked if he could come for the weekend. I was so excited. I'd barely seen him over the break.

When he got here, he walked in with a duffel bag and I just looked at him. "You know you can't stay here," I said, shocked that he would even think he could.

He gave me a look that made me feel like the twelve-year-old dweeb I'd been when we first met. "So you're still a prude, huh? I figured college would have fixed that part of you real fast."

I just stared at him in open-mouthed shock.

Luke looks at me now, pain filling his expression. "I am so sorry, Paige. I am so very sorry. I know that nothing I can say will ever fix what happened, but I can't tell you how many times I've had that whole conversation replay in my brain. The expression on your face tortured me."

He left that very same night, less than an hour later, spouting something about how if God really existed and really cared about us, He wouldn't have forced us to have such ridiculous standards. "It's not biological," he told me right before I closed the door on him. I opened it once, only to tell him to stop ringing my doorbell, get off my front porch, and take the promise ring he'd given me two years before with him.

The contrast to Tyler—who barely kisses my cheek—is startling.

I lean back in my kitchen chair, looking at Luke now. In appearance, he hasn't changed too much. Luke has always looked like he belonged in some kind of soap opera. I was always amazed he ever was attracted to me.

We never belonged together.

Lord. I know that now.

"Luke," I say quietly.

He looks at me, eyes bleak.

I take a deep breath. "You're right. You can't change it." Somehow, though, his apology soothes a wound that stretched deep in my heart. "But thank you for saying you're sorry."

"I was an idiot."

I shrug. "It wasn't meant to be."

"Then."

"What?"

He shakes his head. "It wasn't meant to be *then*," he emphasizes.

I narrow my eyes at him, open my mouth to talk, and he slaps the table lightly with his hands and stands.

"All right. I'm going to head out. Keep the rest of the doughnuts. They reheat well. I'm glad I was finally able to apologize."

"Luke." I stand and follow him to the front door.

"Bye, Paige." He leaves without giving me a chance to tell him that there doesn't need to be a *then* attached to the sentence as much as an *ever*.

I watch him walk down the stairs and out of sight and I go back inside, shut the door, and let out a big huff.

So much for my uncomplicated morning.

My phone rings at eleven right as I'm getting out of the shower. Lazy Saturday mornings like this were never a part of my week even six weeks ago. But I've gotten very attached to them since then.

"Hi, sweetie."

"Hi, Mom."

"So."

I wait but Mom doesn't keep talking. "So what?" I ask, swiping at the wrinkles that are starting to form beside my eyes. I always hope that it's just extra makeup that somehow didn't get washed off in the shower that leaves me looking wrinkly, but it never is.

It's a sad day when I need wrinkle cream and acne solution at twenty-three.

"So. How do you think last weekend went?" I can tell by the excitement hiding in Mom's blasé tone that she's been waiting for me to call all week.

I haven't wanted to tell her that I wish Preslee would just move back to Ohio or Idaho or wherever she was living.

"Yeah, uh, it was fine," I say, lying through my teeth. Some lies should be allowed, though. That's what I tell the Jiminy Cricket who is poking me in the heart, anyway. "How did *you* think it went?" This is a very smart question to ask because the focus will be off me and Mom can carry on the conversation by herself.

And it totally works.

I end up putting her on speakerphone and propping my phone on the bathroom counter so I can do my makeup while I'm listening to her talk.

She goes on and on while I try to decide whether the smoky eye-shadow look would be overkill for a double date at a steak house where people throw peanut shells on the floor.

My mother thinks that's the grossest thing in the world.

The lighting isn't fabulous at the steak house, though, so maybe I'll want the extra attention on my eyes. It will definitely be overkill for the six hours before the date, especially since I'm planning on spending a couple minutes of that at the grocery store. I'm not taking another shower before tonight, so I've got to do my makeup now.

"I just love, love, *love* Wes!" Mom gushes. "He is *just* the sweetest thing! He ended up driving back down for dinner on Wednesday night again, and he brought me this bouquet of daisies. Isn't that the sweetest thing?"

She doesn't wait for an answer.

"And Preslee, oh Preslee just *lights up* whenever he's around. It's like watching a strand of Christmas lights or something. It's just amazing." Now Mom is getting teary. "I just never thought this day would happen for Preslee, Paige. I always knew that God had a plan for her life, but I always feared it was not the one we prayed for over her when she was little. And oh, I'm so happy God answered our prayers! My baby girl has finally come home!"

I think I'm going to go with the brown-toned smoky eye. Apparently it works nicely on people with brown eyes. I listen to Mom choke back sobs as I dab on the first layer of a metallic tan shadow.

Part of me feels bad that I don't feel overjoyed that my sister is home. The rest of me just wants to achieve the perfect smoky eye for my double date tonight.

"Aren't you just amazed at the goodness of God?" Mom asks me, voice full.

"Yeah, Mom," I say when she actually waits for an answer this time.

"And that He provided a man like Wes for her! I am overwhelmed. We are having another family dinner, by the way. Tomorrow. In Waco."

I gape at the phone on my bathroom counter. "Tomorrow?"

"I knew if I gave you enough notice, you'd come up with some reason why you couldn't go." Apparently my amazement at God's goodness didn't come across very strongly. "Preslee wants to make amends, Paige. And it's only to Waco. They found a house they want to show us and then we're going out to eat."

Waco is still almost two hours. I don't see why Preslee wants to show me this house anyway. I'm sure she mostly just wants Mom and Dad's approval. Now I'll have to go and pretend to be stoked about whatever beautiful house Preslee is about to buy and then go home to my old apartment.

I sigh at myself in the mirror.

"I heard that."

"Fine," I grumble.

"I'm glad you're so excited about it!" Mom says, all sarcastic and cheery. "We're going to meet at the house at two thirty. I'll text you directions. Have a lovely day, honey!"

She hangs up.

I bite my bottom lip and look at my one made-up eye and my one not. The difference is striking. Probably a sign I did the shadow correctly.

Another dinner with the glowing Preslee and the ever-popular Wes.

Hip hip hooray.

I finish my makeup, pull on jeans and a fitted white T-shirt and flip-flops. This is my typical weekend summer outfit. I used to be all into shorts back when I was in school, but that's mostly because I had more time to make sure I had a decent tan on my legs.

Those days ended the moment I graduated.

I drive to the grocery store, park, get a cart, and go straight for my normal haunt, aka the frozen section.

I have a very hard time cooking for just myself. Which typically means I survive on frozen pizza and bagged salads.

And cheese sticks.

Every so often, I go through a phase where I bake huge lasagnas, big pots of spaghetti and meatballs, and baked chicken with roasted potatoes. Then I'll portion it out, divide it into freezer containers, and eat those for a while.

Usually I do all that after watching the Food Network.

Those phases never last long.

Probably because I usually stick with HGTV.

I load my cart with two pizzas, three bagged salad mixes, and a few of those soups that are already in the microwavable bowl for lunch at work.

Then I buy a package of Oreos, just because I'm an adult now and I can.

The total is higher than I expect, which is always true at the grocery store, and I drive home to put the food away. I don't even bother putting the Oreos in the pantry.

I just leave them on the end table. They'll be gone in three days anyway.

I should really look into some of those workout DVDs.

Chapter 13

I spend the rest of the afternoon doing stuff around the apartment. I straighten up and while I'm straightening, I find a book I haven't read in a couple of years and get distracted.

By the time I look up from the book, it's five o'clock and Tyler will be knocking on my door to pick me up for the double date in fifteen minutes. I gasp and run for the bedroom.

Layla always dresses up, so I have to look semipresentable. I've already decided on a cute deep-red sundress and flats and I'm going to bring a denim jacket with me in case it gets cold in the restaurant. Give me enough sweet tea and I'm immediately freezing.

Tyler knocks at 5:20. I got ready in record time so I could finish the chapter I was on.

"Sorry I'm late," he says in his typical hello, looking nice in dark-rinsed jeans and a button-down blue-and-white pinstripe shirt over a white undershirt and boots.

I shrug. I got to finish the chapter and I figured he'd

be late, which was why I told him to come a few minutes early.

I'm learning.

"Thanks for picking me up, Tyler."

"Sure thing! Hey, so on my way over here, I was thinking. We still need to go to that baseball game."

I nod. I thought of it earlier this week. I was actually starting to get excited about it, even though I won't be able to watch the game in my pajamas. I looked the team up on the Internet and they do fireworks at some of the night games.

Fireworks are a pretty good reason to get out of your pajamas.

I'm not sure that a hot dog is, but I can handle getting dressed for fireworks.

We get to the steak house and Peter and Layla are already there. Layla looks adorable in jeans and a black lacy top. "Oh, this is *so* exciting!" she squeals, grabbing my forearms when we walk in. "Our first official double date as an engaged couple!"

I'm assuming the "our" is referring to Peter and her.

Peter and Tyler shake hands and we get called to our table a few minutes later. It's crowded tonight. Country music is blaring over the speakers, the whole restaurant is dimly lit, TVs are glaring silently whatever game ESPN is showing, and peanut shells crunch under our feet as we walk.

We are led to the very back corner of the restaurant and the hostess points to a corner booth. "Does this work?"

I have no idea why they ask that question. Do people really say no when there's a twenty-minute wait for a table?

Layla and I both slide in and the boys take the outside.

The hostess hands us the menus and leaves. Layla is giddy. "Oh this is so fun! This is so exciting!"

I just laugh at her and open my menu. I haven't eaten here in a very long time. I do, however, remember their incredible rolls and delicious fried onions with some type of awesome sauce.

Which leads me to my first Double Date Dilemma of the evening: Are fried onions acceptable on a date?

Layla sighs at the menu. "Oh my gosh, the Deep Onion Dipper. Guys, we've *got* to get this. Maybe two of them." She fans her face. "I'm salivating just thinking of it."

And that answers my question.

Peter, in his usual outgoing, chatty way, nods at Layla. "Sure."

Tyler thumps the menu. "Rib eye. Going with the rib eye for sure. And the loaded sweet potato with the marshmallows. And the cinnamon apples."

"And the heart attack," I say.

"There now. I don't wish ill tidings on you."

"I'm not wishing it, I'm just predicting it," I tell him. "It doesn't help that you like your steaks blinking at you when they get to the table." Tyler's steak was barely warm last time he ordered one.

Not me. I don't always eat steaks, but when I do, I eat them well done.

Not to sound too much like a beer commercial.

My dad instilled that in me at a very young age. Mostly because every time we had steaks, he would burn the snot out of them until they resembled charcoal more than edibles.

You always end up eating like your parents.

I decide on the chicken kebabs, mostly because I just enjoy the word *kebab*.

"So!" Layla lays her closed menu on the table. "Let's talk wedding details!"

She is so happy, her smile has to be hurting her eardrums. Peter just smiles over at her in one of those placating "isn't she precious" smiles that sort of bothers me, only because I've seen people look at their grandchildren the same way.

I move on. "What details, Layla?"

"Wait a second." Tyler holds up his hands surrender-style. "Don't tell me that you brought me here to eat rare steak and listen to lace descriptions."

"Raw steak. I've seen you eat beef before, Tyler. And yes," Layla nods. "Okay. Now obviously Paige here is my maid of honor."

"Obviously," Tyler and Peter say together.

"She's therefore going to need some directives about how I want the ceremony to be."

"Yeah, but Layla, you aren't getting married for what . . . another five months?" Tyler asks, counting the months off on his fingers. "Isn't that a little overkill?"

Layla just gapes at him, and I roll my eyes before turning to her. "Remember he's male. And single."

She just shakes her head at Tyler. "I'll forgive you. Just this once though, so listen up."

Tyler grins.

"Anyway, I'm trying to nail down a location. I think we are wanting to get married outside, since it will be October and that's typically decent wedding weather here. What I think would be really super cute though is to get married at that farm right outside of Frisco — remember that one, Paige, with the great red barn?"

I nod. We were lost trying to find some craft fair when we drove past it. They were having a little pumpkin patch thing that day.

"Anyway, I might call them and find out if they hold weddings there."

The waitress comes by then to get our order and leaves us with two baskets of sweet, hot, delicious buttered rolls. "I'll be right back with the Onion Dipper."

I don't know why I bother ordering food at this place. I should just eat the rolls and the onion thing. I'm always stuffed by the time my actual dinner arrives.

"So, how is premarital stuff going?" I ask. Layla and Peter had their first appointment with Rick this last week.

Layla rolls her eyes. "It was ridiculous. We went to Starbucks and I casually mentioned I like when Peter laughs so hard he snorts. So then Rick spent the rest of the time trying to see if he could get Peter to snort up his hot chocolate." She rolls her eyes again, shaking her head. "I mean, seriously. We're preparing for marriage here. Supposedly anyway. Aren't we supposed to be talking about birth control or how to handle fights about closet space?"

I laugh. But considering I've barely seen Peter smile, I kind of want to see him snort from laughing too.

I glance at Tyler and I can tell he's thinking the same thing. A mischievous look flints across his eyes. "So. Spill the beans, Pete. What makes you snort?"

Peter shrugs. "I don't know. I probably have to be in a specific mood."

"Which he wasn't in on Thursday night. Particularly after listening to Rick tell 164 jokes. The last ones were just awful." Layla rubs her temple. "I'm wondering if I really want Rick to perform my wedding."

"It'll be entertaining." I've been to a wedding that Rick did. He started the ceremony like the priest on *The Princess Bride*. "Mawwiage."

The poor groom just stared at him like he was speaking Italian.

"I don't know that I want my wedding to be entertaining," Layla says.

"Going for boring?" Tyler asks her, finishing his roll.

"Not boring."

"But not interesting," Tyler says.

Layla and Tyler should never converse with each other.

"So you're going for like a plain-popcorn-with-salt wedding," Tyler says to her. "Not boring, but not interesting either."

"No, Tyler. I want it to be interesting."

"But not *exciting*. You don't want people shaking some delicious chili-spice mixture all over that popcorn."

Layla makes a growling noise in the back of her throat. "I want it to be interesting and exciting without being awkward and awful."

"If you want to not have an awkward wedding, don't give anyone spoons," he tells her, buttering another roll.

"What?"

"Spoons. Just leave them out of the silverware on the tables."

Layla rubs her cheeks with both hands. "Why, Tyler? Why would spoons make my wedding awkward?"

"Have you ever seen a more awkward utensil? If you use it to stir sugar into an iced tea or a coffee, you can't set it on your plate because then it drips iced tea or coffee all over the meal. You can't set it on the table because then you're the guy who messed up the tablecloth. And have you ever seen some-one eat anything with a spoon? If you slurp, you're the guy who can't drink his soup quietly. If you eat ice cream and you don't suck all the ice cream off the spoon, you're the nasty guy leaving his germs all over everything."

Peter grins. Layla starts laughing and then grabs two fistfuls of her hair. "You make me crazy! I don't know why I'm encouraging this!" She waves a hand between Tyler and me.

He smirks at her. "Because. I make your life *interesting*. Like popcorn with —"

"Just quiet, Tyler. Quiet now. And I would really appreci-ate it if you'd stop referring to my wedding as popcorn."

"I wasn't talking about your wedding right then, I was talking about your —"

"Shhh," she interrupts again. "Shh, Tyler."

I look at Peter and shrug. "It doesn't seem like we were needed to discuss the wedding after all."

And for the first time ever, Peter laughs at something I say.

* * * * *

We end up talking at the restaurant until nine o'clock, and then Layla decides we all need to get coffee. The Starbucks nearby closes at nine, so we head over to a locally owned coffee-house not too far away.

"That was a very fun dinner," Tyler says as he drives the five minutes to the coffeehouse.

"Yeah it was." I nod, blocking a yawn with the back of my hand.

"I'm not sure how I will fit a coffee in my stomach too." He rubs his rib cage.

I'm not sure how he's going to either. I only have a sister, and my dad doesn't eat a lot. I've never seen someone put away food the way Tyler does. He ate four rolls, a side salad, about half of the onion dish, the entire sweet potato, the entire bowl of cinnamon apples, and the whole steak.

I would be dead somewhere if I were him right now. I have no idea where they take people whose stomachs explode, but it can't be a happy place filled with laughter.

"You could have taken some of that home with you, you know." I tap the Styrofoam container on the seat next to me. Most of my dinner is in there.

"I don't believe in leftovers."

I believe him.

We get to the coffeehouse and Tyler looks over at me, smiling sweetly. "This is really fun, Paige." He reaches over to squeeze my hand.

I smile at him, suddenly very thankful that I hadn't finished that onion-dipper thing.

Layla and Peter are already in line when we walk in. This place is known for their coffee, their desserts, and their fireplace. People are at almost every table, reading books, clicking around on laptops, or chatting with friends.

"What are you going to get?" Layla asks me.

"I don't know. I'm stuffed."

"Me too. I just didn't want the evening to end, and the waitress at the steak house was giving us the evil eye."

I end up getting a cup of decaf, because if I'm already

getting wrinkles beside my eyes, I probably shouldn't be drinking caffeine past nine. Isn't that a rule somewhere? I feel about ninety-seven years old, though, as I carry my little cup to the table Layla found.

"How's this?" She sets her mocha on the table. Peter and Tyler are right behind us with their drinks.

Tyler's holding a piece of chocolate-mousse pie too.

"I thought you said you were completely stuffed," I say to him.

"Yeah, but the pie looked good."

Maybe all guys are like this, except for my dad. Or maybe they all start like this.

Whatever the case, I bet my parents are very thrilled that they only had to feed two girls.

Whoever says girls cost more to raise didn't factor in food, I bet.

"So, Paige, how's it going with Preslee?" Layla asks as we sit.

I sigh. I'd conveniently put tomorrow's dinner date out of my mind tonight. "Thanks for bringing it up, Layla."

"No problem." She grins cheekily.

"I've got dinner with them again tomorrow," I say. "I guess Wes and Preslee found a house they really like in Waco."

"Waco isn't too far," Tyler says.

"No. No it's not."

I guess Layla hears the "I'd rather not talk about this" that is behind my words and changes the subject. "How about that job Rick offered you?"

Tyler looks curiously at me and I realize that other than him hearing that I was thinking it over at youth group, I hadn't mentioned a lot of details to him. "It's nothing big.

Rick just wants me to quit the agency and start working for him with the youth group."

"Wow," Tyler says, raising his eyebrows. "That's definitely big, Paige. What are you thinking about it?"

In all honesty, I was trying not to. I'm not good with change.

A change of jobs is a Big change.

Capital *B*.

I shrug. "It would be the same amount of money." Rick e-mailed me a potential salary yesterday. At least I assume it was a potential salary. The subject of the e-mail said *For Your Consideration* and he just wrote a dollar amount in the message.

No hello, no good-bye, no sincerely or anything.

It's like I'd be working for a covert op dealing drugs or something. All I need is a second e-mail to appear that just has some guy's name and address in it.

Really have got to stop watching *NCIS*.

"Same hours?" Tyler asks.

Tyler was pretty instrumental in helping me clear up my schedule. I'm sure he's not asking just out of curiosity.

"So Rick says," I tell him.

"See, I think you need to really decide if you want to work for Rick," Layla says, sipping her mocha. "Have you heard his knock-knock jokes? They are not good at all."

"Hey, Layla. Knock knock," Tyler says.

"Go away."

"Anyway," I say loudly. "I'm still deciding. I feel like I would be letting the agency down if I quit there, and I feel like I'd actually be able to use my degree if I start working at the church."

"For Rick," Layla clarifies.

"Yes. For Rick."

"All I'm saying is that he's got to be about the weirdest boss on the planet. And I wouldn't consider my boss a piece of normal cake," Layla says.

"Hey, Layla. So these two penguins are sitting in a tub and one says to the other—"

"Look at that nice table over there!" Layla exclaims, interrupting Tyler. "Tyler, wouldn't you love to go sit with them?"

Peter grins.

"So you wouldn't take the job?" I ask Layla.

"I don't know. I mean, I know you've wanted to counsel people since you were in high school. I just don't want you to end up in a shrink's office yourself, you know?"

I smirk. "Don't forget, I do know Rick pretty well. And Natalie has made it this far."

"That's because Natalie is a freak of nature." Layla shrugs. "All I'm saying is think about it. That's all I'm saying," she says again.

"Hi, guys."

We all look up and Rick is standing there with his arm lazily draped across Natalie's shoulders. No baby is in sight.

"And speak of the freak of nature." Layla smiles at them. "No Claire?"

"The perk of working as a youth director, Layla, is I have instant access to literally thousands of kids who would love to babysit," Rick says.

"Thousands, huh?" I say.

"Yep. Sadly, only three of them are qualified to watch my daughter."

I laugh.

Natalie looks at Layla. "Out of curiosity, is Rick the freak or am I?"

"You are."

"Huh." She shrugs. "I've been called worse."

"Do you guys want to join us?" I ask them. "We can pull up more chairs."

Rick shakes his head. "Paige, you'll understand this someday. And I hope you don't take offense to it right now. But if I have three uninterrupted hours with my sexy wife, I'm not going to spend them with other people there too."

I hold up my hands. "No more information needed."

"Please," Tyler tacks on.

Natalie smiles warmly at Rick.

"But. We did want to come say hi before we left," Rick says.

"Hi," Layla says.

"Hi," I say.

"Hello." Rick waves one hand in a big arc across his body. "Well. Let's go, Nat. Peace out, homies." They walk for the exit.

Tyler watches them go, takes a bite of his chocolate-mousse pie, and then looks over at me. "Sorry, Paige. I'm going to have to side with Layla on this one."

I just laugh.

* * * * *

I pull my Bible onto my lap later, shivering under the covers. Somehow my thermostat got bumped and it is now fifty-three degrees in my apartment. I cranked it up as soon as I got home, but I still feel like someone is going to come to my door in the morning and find me all Han Soloesque — frozen in some desperate position, hands up.

I am not looking forward to this month's power bill. I have the weirdest thermostat. It took me two months and a three hundred dollar bill to figure out how to use it when I first moved in here.

I hate being an adult sometimes.

I also dislike having to decipher what the apostle Paul is trying to say when I am cold and tired. Paul should have hired an English major.

Maybe this is blaspheming the Word of God.

I murmur a quick apology to God and ask Him to pass it on to Paul. Then I flip to Galatians and try my best to pay attention.

"Therefore you are no longer a slave, but a son; and if a son, then an heir through God."

Tonight's isn't so difficult. I can follow that logic, even with my brain cells quivering from the arctic frontier that is now my bedroom.

An heir. Through God.

As cool as my room is, that is even cooler.

Chapter
14

Sunday, I'm once again standing beside my car in the church parking lot, debating about "accidentally" driving my keys into my tire and having to skip out on family dinner because of the flat.

A very long time ago when I first moved to Dallas for school, Dad took me out to the driveway one day and tried to teach me how to change a flat tire. All I remember is something about hex nuts.

Or was it hex bolts?

Regardless, if I ever have a flat, my line of action is probably going to include sitting on the side of the road helpless for a while.

Hopefully this will never happen in the rain.

My mother always tells me that she got married purely to have someone take care of problems like that. "And to keep my grass looking nice," she always adds on.

I clear my throat, rubbing my fingers along my lymph nodes, gauging for scratchiness or swollenness. Because nothing can spoil a family dinner faster than someone there with some awful flu or meningitis or cholera.

Sadly, I appear to be in excellent physical condition.

And I'm not sure I even know what the warning symptoms of cholera are. As far as I can remember from high school history, it included being on a boat.

I will never go on a cruise.

"What are you doing?" Luke suddenly materializes next to my right bumper.

Apparently God thinks I need a good dose of Luke whenever I'm about to see my sister. It's like the double whammy right from heaven.

I never used to see God as the type to deal out double whammies.

"I'm thinking about cruises," I tell him, hoping the icicles forming off the words as I say them will convince Luke to be friendly somewhere else. I'm remembering what I read last night in my Bible, and I'm trying to silently remind God of it as well. *Remember, Lord? You said I was now an heir. Remember? Like a son? You don't give snakes to sons. You give muffins. Or something like that. Remember?*

I thought a lot about Luke since he brought the doughnuts over. It was hard not to since I had a doughnut for breakfast every day this week.

My pants are getting tight.

I thought about the past. I thought about the word *then* that Luke tacked on to his last sentence. I thought about how it was a lot to think about before I really woke up in the mornings.

Luke is smiling at me, his eyes shaded behind some very nice sunglasses. He's wearing straight-cut dark jeans, some fancy leather shoes, and a plaid button-down shirt over a

T-shirt. All I can read on the T-shirt behind the button down is *SMO BEA*.

Unless it's a shirt that says something like *I WANT S'MO' BEACH*, I'm going to assume he bought it at Pismo Beach.

I should not do this much thinking right before a two-hour drive.

"Cruises, huh?" Luke says, his smile flirtatious. "Who are you going to go with?"

"No one. I don't like boats."

"It's not really a boat, kid. It's more like a ship."

There's his old nickname for me coming out again, if you can call "kid" a nickname. Either way, it makes something very old and familiar curl around my heart and squeeze.

Cholera. It's starting.

"Boat, ship, whatever. I don't go on boats. People die on boats."

"It's a cruise ship, Paige. People sail on them all the time."

"They probably said the same about the *Titanic*. I'm very happy on the ground." I look under my feet. "Or the asphalt. Or whatever this stuff is."

He squints at the ground as well. "Looks like concrete to me."

"Sure."

He looks up and pulls his sunglasses off his face, flashing another sparkling smile my way. Luke always has had the whitest teeth. It used to make me crazy in high school because he would drink coffee like his arms would fall off if he stopped, and his teeth never showed any signs of it.

It's so annoying.

"You look beautiful, Paige."

I am wearing jeans and a purple drapey shirt thing.

I skipped the whole hair-washing routine this morning because I was running late and I decided that I've already met Wes and seen Preslee again, so I don't have the same desire to showcase how well I'm doing without her.

So my hair is falling around in haphazard waves and I'm about three seconds away from just putting it up in a bun.

I do not look beautiful.

"Luke," I say, ready to tell him that the tree has been chopped down and he can go find some other tree to bark up.

"Well. I'm late for service. See you later, Paige. I'm still holding you to that coffee date."

I watch the back of his head as he heads into the building and roll my eyes. What coffee date?

I am glad to see he's going to the third—and last—service. I usually go to the second one.

Maybe we can be some of those people who go to the same church and never interact.

I slide into the driver's seat, abandoning hope of a flat tire or a sudden case of smallpox. After backing out, I leave our church's parking lot and head for the interstate.

Again.

I flip the radio to country and start making a mental list of topics I can talk about with Preslee and Wes.

First up, the weather. I squint out the windshield, and while it is fairly sunny right now, there are some big clouds building up in the north. I will likely be driving home in the rain.

Hurray.

Maybe that will be my excuse to leave as soon as dinner is over.

Mom called me this morning and told me that Wes's favorite food to eat is barbecue, so we're going to be eating at a little local barbecue place right outside of the campus.

"I figure we should probably get there early," she told me. "Those restaurants around campus always fill up quick."

"How often do you eat in Waco?"

"Remember when we helped you move to Dallas? We tried to stop at Long John Silver's on the way back and it was just packed."

That was a good five years ago.

I reach for my can of nuts in the passenger seat.

Preslee is getting married.

The thought stopped me a few times this week. Getting *married*. My *younger* sister is getting married.

I feel both old and young at the same time, but way too young to be the older sister of the bride. I remember when Preslee and I were tiny and we'd pretend to be the brides or have our dolls be the brides marrying emaciated-looking Ken dolls.

Ken never said much.

It just makes me wonder . . .

I pull out my phone when I start getting close to Waco. Mom gave me the address and I put it in the maps app on my phone instead of trying to write it down. I don't do well with the whole watch-for-street-names thing. It's better if I can just hear some woman's voice telling me when to turn right or left.

I really wanted a British man's voice telling me directions, but I didn't want it enough to pay for it.

Layla likes to remind me that I'm cheap on all the things that count.

I get off the freeway inside the city limits for Waco but before the real city part starts. The bodiless woman leads me through an old neighborhood, past a park filled with huge and likely rotting trees, and under a bridge covered in graffiti.

Seems like a classy area.

Finally I'm told that my destination is on my left. I pull over and park at the curb across the street from an old red brick house with peeling white eaves. There's a knobby old tree in the front, crumbling cement steps leading up to a porch, and a faded yellow wooden door.

Well. The house fits into the area, I guess.

I really doubt I will ever own a house. Mostly because I am a snob for newness. I am the first renter to ever live in my apartment. I got it brand-new way back in college, and even though it's small, any dirt there is *my* dirt.

None of this 90 percent of dust is dead-skin-cell yuckiness to worry about every morning when I get out of the shower and walk around barefoot for a little while.

I don't see Mom and Dad's car, and I'm sure not going to go up and ring the doorbell and visit with Wes and Preslee by myself. So I sit in my car, listening to someone crooning about harvest moons in Kansas over the radio, picking through the can of nuts to get out all of the pecans.

It will be a sad ride home if all that are left are almonds and those weird Brazilian nuts, but at least I'm happy now.

There's a knock on my driver's window and I jump about eight feet in the air, knocking cashews and almonds all over my steering wheel.

It's Preslee and she's laughing. "I didn't mean to scare you," she says after I mash the button to roll down the window. She's grinning though, which likely makes her first statement a lie.

Preslee was always one for the practical joke.

Wes is standing right behind her, looking like a transplant straight from the coast of California with his sandy blond hair spiking up in a faux hawk, ratty plaid shorts, flip-flops, and a polo shirt.

I turn my car off and mentally cheer on myself. I can be alone with Preslee and Wes. I can.

I probably can.

I shoulder my purse, cap the nuts, and climb out of my car, standing next to them on the sidewalk across the street from their potential new house.

Preslee is glowing. "Isn't this such a wonderful neighborhood?" She gasps, holding her hands to her chest, her eyes sparkling. Preslee has always been beautiful, and today she seems even more so. Her hair is long and wavy, she's wearing white shorts and a blue shirt, and it's killing me that she's already got such a great tan.

I nod rather than share my true opinions about this particular part of Waco.

"It's so quaint! I love it. I wonder if there are any original home owners left on this street." She looks around, pulls a pair of sunglasses out of her shorts pocket, and slides them on her face.

Wes shrugs. "I guess we'll find out."

"So did y'all already buy it then?" I ask, finally speaking.

Preslee nods happily. "We're in escrow."

I have no idea what *escrow* means. Aside from sounding like a slightly more disgusting form of those snails, if anything can sound more disgusting than that, I haven't got a clue. But I nod and manage a nice fake smile, pretending like I'm in the know.

That's half the job of being a secretary right there.

Mom and Dad's Tahoe pulls up and Mom gets out, hands clasped together like Preslee, already oohing over the house. "What a *beautiful* neighborhood! I just didn't even know this area existed! What a perfect, quaint little street! And the trees! Oh!"

Mom and Preslee are cut from the same cloth.

Preslee runs over to Mom, loops her arm through Mom's, and then leads her around, happily pointing out every wonderful thing about this street. "And I just love the lawns and the brick and the cuteness!" Preslee squeals.

Dad gets out of the Tahoe and pulls his sunglasses off, frowning at the crumbling concrete front steps. "There might be structural problems. Did your Realtor say anything about those steps? And that oak tree is planted way too close to the house for my comfort. A good stiff wind and you're looking at major insurance headaches."

I think we can all see where I come from.

We all cross over the street and stand there, looking at the brick house. It's old. That's all I can think about it.

"We're obviously going to need to repaint." Preslee points at the faded, peeling eaves, the dinged-up shutters. "But I just love the porch. And the yellow door, actually. I might keep it yellow. It's just so happy and cheerful!"

Another car pulls up and a woman with big hair and a pale blue suit gets out, waving and grinning a toothy grin.

Must be the Realtor.

"Hello! You must be the family. I'm Wenda, this delightful couple's Realtor." She hurries over to the lockbox swinging from the front door.

Dad is on his hands and knees now, looking at the steps, feeling the crumbs and smelling the concrete. I watch him for a second. "You can tell something about the foundation by the way it smells?" I ask him.

"No, but smell this for me." He holds a handful of powdering cement at my face.

I wrinkle my nose and hurry up the steps. "No thanks, Dad. You never know how many dogs have found that step super attractive."

Dad laughs.

I follow Wenda, Mom, Preslee, and Wes into the house. Mom is just beside herself with enthusiasm, Preslee is all smiles and giggles, and Wes is obviously unsure if he should stay back with Dad or continue on with his fiancée.

The carpets are orange shag, the walls are dingy and gray, the kitchen dark and greasy.

"Obviously it needs a little work, but I figure we have the time and ability to do it, so why not?" Preslee says.

"Exactly." Mom nods. "Why not?"

"When was the last time the plumbing was updated?" Dad echoes from under the sink.

Two very long hours later, we are finally talking about heading to the barbecue place for dinner. I spent the majority of the last hour in the only place in the house that wasn't just awful, which was the backyard. Whoever lived here last had something of a green thumb. Flower beds are erupting in color and there is a little swing hanging off a big tree outside.

Preslee comes outside and joins me on the lawn furniture that whoever used to live here left.

"So, what do you think?" She holds up her hands as I get ready to shrug out my platonic answer. "And I want an honest opinion."

No pressure there. I sigh. "Well, I mean, honestly, it looks like a lot of work for you guys. But if you're up for it, then I think it's fine."

She smiles. "We're up for it."

We sit there quietly for a few minutes, my stomach rolling. I am sitting on the back porch of an ancient house with orange shag carpet with my sister.

The whole thing is just weird.

"So, Paige . . ."

I look over at her and Preslee is playing with her sunglasses, a slightly nauseous look on her face. "What?" I ask her.

"Well. I have a question for you, but I'm a little nervous about what your answer is going to be."

I just look at her, waiting for her to ask it. No sense in me promising that my answer will be to her liking. The odds are good it won't be.

She finally sets the glasses in her lap and takes a deep breath, looking over at me. "Will you be my maid of honor?"

I'm pretty certain I've lost all feeling in my legs. I just look at her, no intelligent thoughts anywhere near my brain.

"Oh, Paige, it would mean *so* much to me! I honestly can't tell you how much."

Even if I wanted to answer, I can't. My lips are numb, words are gone.

Preslee wants me to be her maid of honor.

Me.

Ten years ago, I wouldn't have thought this was a weird question at all. Actually, I might have thought it was a weird question just because it was so obvious. *Of course* I am supposed to be Preslee's maid of honor. I'm her only sister.

Now, it's just awkward.

She's quiet, both of us just staring out at the flower beds, and my brain is furiously working.

On the one hand, she is my sister, no matter what she did to me or our parents. And a tiny part of me is really trying to remember that, even though the rest of me wouldn't mind too much if she just moved into this crappy house and didn't bother us again.

On the other hand, there is the whole past to consider.

Maid of honor. I never knew such a seemingly sweet phrase could seem like such a long, tired sentence.

"You don't have to give me your answer right now," Preslee says after we've sat there for ten minutes in silence while an argument ensues between my heart, my brain, and the Holy Spirit.

I feel like I've been arguing a lot with Him lately.

I nod. "Okay."

She stands and gives me a sad smile as she disappears back into the house. Last time I was in there, Dad was shining a flashlight into the attic and declaring that it looked like there had been a large extended family of squirrels living there at some point.

Reason enough to stay out of the house.

I stare at a cute little bunch of pansies and think about Preslee's question again.

I am going to be Layla's maid of honor. If nothing else, I will be a pro MOH by the time this is all over with. Maybe I'd even be able to list my maid-of-honor services on Craigslist.

*Does an excellent job of holding up bride's dress while bride
pees.*

Dad pokes his head out the back door. "How's everything out here?"

"Oh, you know. Just amazing. Wonderful. I can't believe
it hasn't sold before now," I say, mimicking Mom and Preslee
in a monotone voice.

Dad laughs. "Don't worry, I'm just about done poking
around. Just need to check the laundry room and I'm done.
A house is a big investment, Paige. It's good for Preslee and
Wes to know what they are getting into."

"That's why I'm going to buy new."

Dad sighs and wipes a soot-covered hand on a red wash-
rag he brought with him. "I wouldn't mind that." He goes
back inside.

A few minutes later, Mom comes out to tell me that
Dad's done and everyone is starving, so we're going to eat.

I bring up the rear in our little caravan to the restaurant,
and by the time I find a parking space, everyone else is
already following the hostess back to a table.

"This is my favorite kind of restaurant," Wes says as the
hostess sets a huge basket of buttered rolls in front of us and
then leaves a three-inch-high stack of napkins as well. "Any
place they need to leave fifty extra napkins should be considered a five-star joint."

Dad chuckles. "You and me both, son."

I've never heard Dad use the word *son* before, and it
suddenly hits me that Dad and Mom are getting a son-in-
law. And I'm getting a brother-in-law.

So weird.

I don't know what to think of it.

"I'll have the full rack of baby back ribs," Wes tells the waitress. "And a Coke, please."

"And your two sides?"

"Mashed potatoes and cinnamon apples."

I know someone Wes would really like. He and Tyler order basically the same kind of dinners.

I eat my roll and listen to the conversation around the table. Mom and Preslee are talking wedding details; Dad and Wes are discussing football.

There's still a knot in my stomach that tightens anytime I look over at Preslee. It's just strange that she's back.

Mom and Dad are soaking it up, though. And I guess I can't fault them for that. She is their daughter.

We leave the restaurant stuffed at seven o'clock. Mom looks at her watch and smiles. "Well, this is just perfect timing! Honey, you text me as soon as you get home," she says to me.

I nod, pulling my keys out of my purse. "Well. Bye all."

Dad and Mom give me a hug and Wes waves. "Nice to see you again, Paige." He smiles.

He is a nice guy.

Preslee comes over and gives me an awkward hug.

"Just . . . well, just let me know about what I asked earlier." She puts her hands in her shorts pockets.

I nod again. "Sure."

I climb into my car and the others are still chatting in the parking lot. I turn the ignition, and set my gallon-sized to-go cup of Coke in the cup holder for the drive home.

I might be making a few bathroom stops along the way.

I'm about an hour into my drive when my cell phone starts vibrating in the passenger seat.

"Hello?" I answer it, not looking at the number first.

"Hey, Paige." It's Tyler.

I smile, turn down the radio, and switch my left hand to the top of the steering wheel, settling in for a chat. Tyler moved here from Austin. He knows how long and lonely this stretch of highway gets.

"Hey," I say. "How was your Sunday?"

"That's what I was calling to ask you. Mine was boring. I just sat around and watched football with Rick and Natalie. Natalie made tacos and then Claire spit up all over me."

I grin, secretly very pleased that he's fitting in with my friends. "Sorry about that."

"Eh. I was the one who asked to hold her. So, how was the house?"

"It's old. And in a very old neighborhood." I tell him about the likely plumbing problems and the orange carpet.

"Do Preslee and Wes like it?"

"Yeah. I think they see it as a fixer-upper."

"I guess that's all that matters then. My dad was the fixer-upper type. He lived for projects."

"Not your mom?" Tyler's parents got divorced when he was a kid.

"Nope. Sometimes I wonder if that was the last nail in the coffin. No pun intended."

I smirk. "Sure. No pun intended."

"How was dinner?"

"Good. I think you and Wes would get along really well." I clear my throat. "So, Preslee asked me to be her maid of honor."

"Wow. You know, Stef always says that the best part of

being in someone's wedding is not having to figure out what to wear to the wedding."

Stef is Tyler's sister.

"There is that perk." I sigh.

"You didn't say yes?"

"I don't know what to say."

"How come?"

Sometimes, I really don't like talking to Tyler. I sigh all loudly into the phone, but it doesn't make him recant his question.

"Take your time," he says, instead.

"I don't know," I say finally. "I mean, yes, I feel like I should."

"So why don't you?"

"Because, Tyler. I feel like I'm being guilted into this, and being a maid of honor is more than just standing up there in a very expensive dress and holding the groom's ring."

"What else is it?"

"Haven't you ever been to a wedding and the preacher is like, 'Okay, I'm now charging the people standing up here as well to keep these two to the vows they are making'?"

"No, but I have to tell you that I've only been to one wedding where I wasn't busy decorating the getaway car during the ceremony, and that was Stef's, and I wasn't necessarily focusing on what the preacher was saying."

"Well, my point is that I don't even know Preslee anymore. She's a completely different person than she was five years ago."

"So get to know her."

That wasn't necessarily the answer I was looking for.

"Look, Paige, I can appreciate that she hurt you deeply,

but look at it from her side. If you had done something awful against me and I wouldn't forgive you, how would that make you feel?"

I really don't like talking to Tyler sometimes.

I sigh again. "Not good."

"So. Get to know her. What can it hurt? She lives close enough that you could easily meet halfway to get coffee or something."

I think through that. Coffee. Alone with Preslee.

It sounds terrifying.

"I don't know, Tyler," I say, slowly.

"It's your call. I'm just saying to think about it. Well. I'll let you focus on your driving. Want to have dinner with me tomorrow night?"

"Can we not talk about Preslee?"

I hear his gentle laugh. "Sure."

"Then yes."

"Drive safe, Paige."

I hang up and toss my phone back on the passenger seat, thinking.

Preslee.

A potential job with Rick.

Luke.

I rub my head, crank the radio, and then grip the steering wheel with both hands. And then I try with everything in me to focus my aching head on the song blaring over the speakers.

Chapter 15

The week drags by.

And not just because somehow this ended up being the week when every mundane task that my job could possibly have ended up all together.

I sigh at my work computer again.

"Bad day?" Candace asks, walking by. She's carrying a bag of carrot sticks.

"Whose wedding?" I ask her instead, trying to take the focus off me and my sad problems. I have another job offer, my estranged sister wants me to be in her wedding, and hey, hey, my ex-boyfriend's back.

And I have nine hundred bills to write checks for and process in the agency's online budgeting system.

Hip hip hooray.

Candace shakes her head slightly. "Bar mitzvah. Friend of Bob's son."

"Isn't Bob's son your son?"

She frowns and looks at the ceiling tracing invisible lines with her finger. "A friend of Bob's from work, it's his son."

"Oh."

"Yeah. Too many trails there. Anyhow, I've got to fit back into The Dress."

I grin. Candace has one dress she wears to every wedding, funeral, and apparently bar mitzvah she goes to. And she goes to a lot of events.

"When is it?" I ask.

"Saturday."

Today is Thursday. But considering that Candace has been on some sort of diet since January, I'm not real concerned. She and Peggy are constantly going on some new fad diet. No meat and all vegetables. No dairy and all meat. No carbs and all proteins.

It gets hard to keep track of, so I've just stopped offering cookies when I bring them into work and set them on the desk. If people want one, they'll come get one.

Mark, however, is always up for cookies. Cookies and Sonic tater tots.

I look at the clock on my computer, waiting for the inevitable Thursday "Oh, Paige, could you run to Sonic?" question that is likely coming.

It would be a welcome relief from writing all these checks.

Unless my name is in the "To" line, I'm not that fond of check writing.

Sure enough, ten minutes later, after Candace has gone back down the hall, Mark comes out of his office, walks over to my desk, and looks around at the stuff on it. "What are you up to, Paige?"

Mark, in general, is a very good boss. He does his work; I do mine. He doesn't look over my shoulder, and he doesn't call me on the weekends. I feel like we have a good working relationship, and if all I wanted out of life was to be a secretary, I think we could probably work together for the next twenty years without any problems.

"Bills," I say, trying to keep the moaning out of my voice. I am semisuccessful.

He grins at me. "Want to take a break?"

"What do you want this week?" I reach for a Post-it note.

"How about the double cheeseburger and a Diet Coke? With tots, of course. And get something for yourself." He lays a ten and a five on the desk, and I look up at him, shaking my head.

"It's fine, Mark, I brought my own lunch."

He shrugs. "You've been running to Sonic for me for the last . . . how long have you worked here?"

I smile.

"Get yourself lunch. Sheesh. It's the absolute least I can do."

Sometimes I think Mark picks up on my I'm-not-exactly-content-being-a-secretary vibe.

Thus the raise. And the free lunch.

My bagged salad can definitely wait. There is not much better or worse for you in life than a Sonic cheeseburger, tots, and a cherry limeade.

There's no sense in asking Peggy or Candace if they want anything because both of them always say no.

Peggy just waves her hand at me when I stick my head through her door. "Begone, temptress, I'm saving myself for Christmas pecan pie."

"But Peggy, Christmas is like seven months away."

"When you are old and gain weight just by looking at a

picture in a magazine, you can come talk to me about all the buts."

I smirk. "The butts?"

"Go." She points to the hallway.

Candace just sighs at her carrot sticks and then hands me a couple of dollars and asks for a Diet Coke. "Just a small one."

There is doubt ringing in her tone, so I know if I don't bring back at least a large, she'll be moping around here the rest of the afternoon.

I drive to Sonic and there's a line all the way around the building. I'm craning my head out the window, trying to see if they're offering free fries or something and that's why everyone has suddenly decided to risk coronary heart disease today.

I can't see anything so I just sit back in my seat and yawn, preparing myself for a long wait.

I pop open the console beside my seat, looking for the tin of mints I keep in the car, and that's when I see it.

My old planner.

I think I shoved it in here a while back when I finally stopped overscheduling myself and I could actually remember more of what I was supposed to do every week.

I pull it out and flip through it, sort of missing the feeling of it in my hands. It is really cute. I covered it in denim and added all kinds of fun appliqués to it, back when my sewing machine was new and I was experimenting.

I flip over to this week, the end of May, and there isn't anything written there since it's been several weeks since I scheduled anything.

Come to think of it, I have a couple of things I could

write in here. I mean, it wasn't the planner that everyone was so upset about. It was that I barely had time to eat.

I find a pen in my purse and write down Saturday's end-of-the-year barbecue with the youth group. All that means is small groups are over for the summer. It has nothing to do with the activities of the youth group. If anything, Rick stays busier than ever during the summer.

Sunday, I am teaching the two-year-olds again. So I write that down.

Tonight I'm meeting with Nichole. She's been sick the last couple of times we were supposed to meet, something about allergies leading to bronchitis or something that just sounds miserable during the spring when everyone is supposed to finally be well again.

Tomorrow night I'm going to the baseball game with Tyler. He said he might ask Rick and Natalie if they want to come and bring Claire.

Yet more time for Rick to keep trying to convince me to come work at the church on yet another day when he could very easily win the argument after a day consisting of nothing but paperwork.

I am making a difference in people's lives, but it is the people at the power company for paying our bill and not making them come down to our office and shut off our power.

I guess in that sense, I am making a difference in Mark, Peggy, and Candace's lives too.

"Welcome to Sonic." The voice on the other end of the speaker sounds about as content with his job as I am with mine, and I realize things could be worse.

At least I don't leave my job and smell like work the whole

rest of the evening. People working here must hate the smell of tater tots.

What a terrible life.

Could you file a workman's comp claim for altered smell enjoyment?

"Hello?" the voice says.

"Oh, sorry." I tell him my order and then wait to get to the window, then hand over Mark's and Candace's cash to a kid who doesn't look like he should be old enough to have a job.

"Here's your change. Let me get your drinks," he says in a monotone.

This guy is too young to be so depressed.

"Long day?" I ask him when he hands me my cardboard drink carrier, full of three huge cups.

He just sighs. "The three cars before you all yelled at me that I wasn't going fast enough and that's why there is this huge wait. When really, it's that our grill randomly shuts off for no reason and wasn't working for about ten minutes."

He must see the scared look cross my face as thoughts of death by salmonella found in a cheeseburger start cycling through my head because he starts talking faster. "But don't worry, we got it fixed and everything is cooking all the way through again."

"That's good. Sorry about the yelling."

He shrugs.

"So do you still like the smell of tots?" I ask him out of curiosity when he hands me the grease-stained paper sack with our food it.

"Not at all."

"Sorry about that."

"It comes with the job. Have a good day."

"You too."

I drive back to work, loving the smell of grease in my car right now, but when I walk back out to my car to leave tonight, the smell will make me want to puke and then wash out the pores on my face.

There's something about consuming a lot of oil that never sounds like such a good idea after you've already done it.

I park in front of the agency, carry the bag and drinks inside, disperse them around the office, and then go sit at my desk and stare at the online banking system yet again while I eat my tater tots.

The afternoon passes very slowly. I sit there in my chair, writing checks and answering the phone, thinking about how I am twenty-three years old and most likely developing the secretary spread as it relates to my lower half.

This is not good.

I always have these thoughts after an unhealthy lunch.

At four thirty, my phone buzzes with a text message. I glance over at it while pulling out a calculator.

HEY PAIGE. I STARTED RUNNING ANOTHER FEVER TODAY. WENT TO THE DOCTOR AND THE BRONCHITIS IS STILL THERE, SO THEY ARE GIVING ME A STEROID SHOT NOW. ☹ NOT GOING TO MAKE IT TO COFFEE TONIGHT AGAIN.

Poor Nichole.

I write her back quickly. Mark doesn't care about cell phone use at the office as long as it's not constant or in front of clients. At this moment, there's no one in the front room except me.

SO BUMMED TO HEAR THAT! PRAYING YOU FEEL BETTER SOON!! ☺

For some reason, I always become very fond of the exclamation point and smileys when I text.

I leave the office right at five, not wanting to see another
decimal point for as long as I live or at least until tomorrow
morning at nine o'clock.

I call Layla as I climb into my car. A wave of stale tater-
tot smell runs for freedom when I open the door.

"Nichole is still sick and I need something healthy for
dinner," I tell her when she answers. "I'm going to that new
salad-bar place."

"You know, they say that the average salad in one of
those self-serve places contains over two thousand calories,"
she says.

"Who is they?"

"I don't know. *They*. The invisible people who tell us
poor ignorants how to live."

"They can't be right this time, Layla. A salad should be
like twelve calories."

"It should be but I guess it's not. Something about the
calories in the dressing. I think they were advertising for oil
and vinegar instead."

Ick. The thought of more oil is turning my stomach,
particularly since I am now sitting in the grease-soaked air of
my car.

"Well. Surely there are other options."

"Don't call me Shirley. And I assume you are asking me
to dinner," she says.

"Well, you know what they say about assuming," I tell
her, clicking my seat belt.

"No, Paige. What do they say?"

I look out the windshield, bite my lip, and then shake my

head. "That you, uh . . . shouldn't do it."

"Well, that's a great saying." I can hear the grin in her voice. "All right. Peter is watching Thursday night football anyway. Did you know it's on like nine nights a week now?"

Layla is fairly decent at math so I figure she's just making a point. Either that or I need to tell her that *someday* and *one day* are not part of the calendar week.

In my opinion, Sleeping Beauty should have been singing, "In April, when spring is here."

Or was that Snow White?

Either way, it's beside the point.

"I'm heading there now," I tell her.

"I'll get my shoes back on. See you soon."

Ten minutes later, I'm loading a water-spotted plate onto a plastic tray and standing behind two people who are picking through every bowl of lettuce on the counter, while I listen as Layla tells me about her day.

"So, then, I called the caterer I really liked and of course she's booked until July six years from now or something insane like that and I was like, well, why did you have me taste your food in the first place if you knew I wasn't going to be able to use you for my wedding? And the lady's all, people have changed their wedding dates for me, missy, and I was like, yeah, that's not going to be me, ma'am." She sighs and dumps a tongs full of romaine lettuce on her plate. "Is it just me or is that just ridiculous?"

I honestly got lost somewhere around the fourth comma, so I just nod. "Yep. Ridiculous." Plus, I'm distracted by these people in front of me, who are now picking through all the cherry tomatoes looking for ones with absolutely no yellow on them.

If only I'd made that one yellow light, I could have beaten these people in line.

Should've gone with the V-6 instead of the V-4 like my dad recommended when I was shopping for my Camry.

"I know, right?" Layla picks her commentary right back up. "And then I called the church because we decided to just do the ceremony there, and I talked to Geraldine and of course they need our deposit like yesterday because apparently every other couple in our church who is currently engaged wants our weekend too and I'm like, look, Geraldine, I am at work right now and you'll be gone when I get off and you won't be there before I have to be at work tomorrow, so other than tossing my check into the offering plate and marking it *save the date*, I have no idea what to do. What do you think, Paige?"

Here's what I want to say: "Come on, people, it's a tiny bit of yellow and it's *fine* like that and it still tastes like a tomato!"

Here's what I do say: "That is an annoying problem, Layla."

She just sighs and dumps a spoonful of cold peas on her lettuce, which I think is pretty nasty.

Peas should be hot.

My two cents.

"I'll just have to skip my lunch tomorrow and run it over to Geraldine then," she says. "I had no idea October was going to be such a popular time to get married. What happened to the good old days when everyone got married in June?"

I shrug. "I like the idea of a fall wedding."

"Oh, me too!" Layla is suddenly all smiles and wistfulness and she sighs all dewy eyed. "Won't it be the most beautiful wedding in the world?"

"I think Kate Middleton beat you to that one, Layla. Sorry."
She shrugs. "Okay, other than that one."
I grin.
We finally finish piling our plates full of salad toppings and I put the low-fat raspberry vinaigrette on my salad to compensate for the Sonic today.
We pay and find a booth in the back.
"So, wedding plans aren't coming as expected, huh?" I honestly haven't talked to her that much about the wedding, which is weird considering I'm the maid of honor. I think since I helped so much with her parents' anniversary party, Layla is very sensitive about not having me do work now.
Which is thoughtful but still weird. I am the maid of honor. I should be involved in the wedding.
I bite my lip thinking of Preslee and her question again.
"Eh." Layla shrugs, putting a big forkful of salad in her mouth. "It's all right. Engagement sucks," she says, after she finishes chewing. "Pardon my French."
"I don't think that's a bad word, Layla."
"My mother definitely washed my mouth out with soap at least once for saying that word. Anyway. I don't want to talk about it anymore. It just stresses me out. And who really needs embossed napkins, huh?"
Apparently, this is a question that needs an answer because she's looking at me expectantly. "I don't know," I say. "People who don't remember what wedding they are at?"
"I mean, I don't necessarily like the idea of people rubbing their frosting-covered faces or blowing their noses into mine and Peter's names." She stabs a cherry tomato in her frustration and it shoots off the table, skids across the floor, and winds up under a toddler's high chair. The toddler just blinks at us.

"Well. That was lucky," I tell her.

"No more wedding talk. I'm tired of being engaged. You talk."

I shrug. "What do you want me to talk about?"

"I don't know. Tyler. Luke. Preslee. Your potential new job." She points her fork at my head. "You can start with telling me how you curled your hair today."

"Same as I always do. I left the ends out of the curling iron though. I was going for the beachy look." I rub my hair. "It looks okay?"

"I'm doing my hair like that tomorrow."

It's a high compliment if style-savvy Layla wants to copy something I did on my person. Apartment décor is a different story. Layla doesn't believe in putting work into a temporary dwelling.

Meanwhile I have four different front door wreaths for the four different seasons, pictures up all over the walls, and I even talked my apartment manager into letting me paint one of the walls in my living room a chocolate brown, as long as I repaint it white before I move.

I've been there five years though. I think they're just happy I'm still buying into the illusion that an apartment is the lifestyle I want for myself, when really, I'm just not brave enough to buy an actual house by myself.

Being a single woman is hard.

Layla is looking at me, crunching her lettuce. "Well?"

"Hypothetically, if you weren't getting married, do you think we could live together?"

She chews her salad, motioning with her fork at me. "I can honestly say I never thought I would get propositioned at Fresh Choice from you, Paige Alder."

"Come on." I roll my eyes. "You know what I meant."

"Like roommates? I don't know. For how long?"

"I don't know. What if we moved in together back when we first moved here for college?"

Layla purses her lips. "Mm. No. No, I don't think that would have been a good idea."

"How come?"

"You would kill me." She stabs another piece of lettuce. She chews it while she talks. "I would wake up in the morning and find you'd poisoned my cereal with a bottle of iocaine powder or something."

"I don't think living with you would make me stoop to murder."

"You can say that because you've never lived with me."

"Do I need to warn Peter?"

She waves her fork. "Oh, I have. I have so many times that I think he's a little scared he's going to be living in that *So I Married An Axe Murderer* movie."

"I never saw that."

"Dude. It's terrible."

I sigh. "Please don't start saying that."

"Saying what? Dude?"

"Yes. Every single person in the youth group uses it like every other word. It makes me crazy." I roll my eyes. "Even Tyler says it."

"There was a nice little segue." Layla grins. "How are things going with him?"

I shrug. "Fine."

"Fine." Layla just looks at me and frowns. "Fine?"

"Sure."

"Fine is how you describe the weather or a dog or even a

TV show that's just so-so. Fine is not how you should describe your boyfriend."

I shrug again. "We've never officially said anything about making it official."

"What?"

"I wouldn't say he's my boyfriend."

"What would you say then?"

"I don't know." I think about it, staring at the ceiling tiles. "I'm seeing him."

"Like dead people?"

I give her a look worthy of that comment.

"No, like we see each other. Sometimes he comes over and we get dinner and watch a movie or, I don't know . . . he just hasn't ever clarified what we are doing."

"And you haven't asked?"

"No."

She shakes her head. "Paige, Peter asked me out like three times before I was like, 'Look, seriously, what are we doing here because if you aren't interested in the long haul, I'm going to be looking at other trailers,' you know what I mean?"

I laugh. "You are ridiculous."

"And yet, you can't get enough of me. You were even asking me to move in a little while ago." She grins.

I just shake my head.

We leave the restaurant about eight and I run by the Starbucks in the same parking lot and get a decaf vanilla chai tea. I drive over to Nichole's house and rap quietly on the door.

Her mom answers it, looking confused. "Hi, Paige. Nichole said she texted you . . ."

"Oh, she did," I say quickly. "I just thought I'd bring her a drink anyway. Would you mind telling her that I hope she feels better soon?"

Her mom smiles softly at me and then takes the drink and nods. "You are a godsend for Nichole, Paige. I just need you to know that."

Words can't even describe how that one sentence makes me feel.

I get home a few minutes later, change into my pajamas, and plop on the couch for a little HGTV before bedtime. I'm working on a burlap wreath for over my mantel, so I plug in my glue gun and sit on the floor in front of my coffee table, gluing folded strips of burlap and watching an interior designer make a big mistake in staging a house.

I would never buy a house with fabric stapled to the wall. I don't care what they say about not thinking about the cosmetics when buying a house — can you imagine filling all those holes to repaint?

I finally unplug the glue gun at ten thirty and go brush my teeth before bed. Climbing in, I grab my Bible and flip over to where I was reading before.

"But now that you have come to know God, or rather to be known by God, how is it that you turn back again to the weak and worthless elemental things, to which you desire to be enslaved all over again?"

The thought of my planner fills my head and I wince.

Sorry about that, Lord.

I don't think God has something against planners. I just think He has a problem with me relying on my own power to control my life.

There are times when my prayer life could be summed up in a text to the heavenly realm.

MESSAGE RECEIVED.

Chapter
16

I am home a good thirty minutes before Tyler is coming to pick me up for the game on Friday after work. It didn't take much convincing for me to leave right at five.

Okay, it took no convincing at all.

I change into shorts and a T-shirt, pull my hair into a ponytail, and make sure my sunglasses are in my purse. It's the end of May and that means it's so hot you feel like you are slowly turning into a steaming sponge here in Dallas.

I've got time to kill before Tyler gets here, so I sit on the floor in my living room, find a bunch of Post-it notes and a black Bic pen, and start writing.

Pros of Being Preslee's Maid of Honor

Cons of Being Preslee's Maid of Honor

I put the pros note on my right on the floor and the cons on my left.

Then I sit there.

Well, obviously, the big con would be that I don't feel like I know Preslee or Wes enough to stand up at their wedding. Not in support and not against. I won't be screaming, "No!"

and I likely won't be giggling sweetly as he kisses her.

What's the word for that?

Complacent.

I write it down and put it on the cons side of the floor.

It would make my mother happy.

Obviously, this one would be a pro.

I wouldn't have to find a dress for her wedding.

Pro.

I would have to be at the wedding.

Con.

I write out a few more and at 5:37, there's a knock on my door. I grab my purse and open the door.

"Ready? Wow, what are you doing to your floor?" Tyler asks.

"Nothing really," I say, lightly pushing him out onto the porch so I can close the door and lock it. Tyler pries too much for me to show him my sticky-note system. "Doesn't the game start in less than an hour?"

"Yeah, but we aren't too far. And I figure you probably aren't one of those girls who likes to get to a baseball game hours in advance."

"You figured right. Are Natalie and Rick coming?"

He nods. "They picked me up. They're waiting in the parking lot."

Before Natalie was pregnant with Claire, Natalie drove a really cute little blue Mustang. It was likely the best youth pastor's wife's car ever. But when they got pregnant and Natalie started having trouble getting in and out of the car with her big belly and they started thinking about how fun it would be trying to get a baby car seat in the back, they sold the Mustang and bought one of those crossover SUVs.

I think it still brings tears to Natalie's eyes when she thinks of it.

Regardless, it's not a minivan and that seemed to be the biggest issue. I remember being at their house for dinner when Rick casually suggested they look into a minivan. "I am *not* going to drive one of those," Natalie said, hyperventilating. "You would have to kill me and stuff me to get me in there, and I guarantee that my corpse would still fight you the whole way into that van."

Rick is in the driver's seat and Natalie waves at me through the windshield from the passenger seat. "Hi, Paige!" she says as Tyler opens the driver's side back door for me.

"Hey, guys." Looks like we'll be on either side of Claire. I squeeze the baby's foot. "Hi, Clairey girl! How's life this week?"

The baby just blinks at me, cheeks moving lightly as she sucks on her pacifier.

"She's decided to just not waste any time with those little dribbly spit-ups and go straight to full-force projectiles," Natalie says from the front seat.

"My daughter," Rick says proudly, driving out of the parking lot. "We aren't raising a little sissy girl over here, folks."

I look at the baby, who is developing some really cute, little round cheeks and she's now got some blonde wispy hair around her head. "She looks pretty girly to me, Rick."

"She can be girly. I just want boys to be scared of her."

Tyler grins. "Ah, what every girl hopes her father says about her."

We drive to the baseball stadium and Rick tells us about the summer program he's got coming up for the kids. "Well, the first Saturday after Memorial Day weekend, I'm going to start a new thing on Saturday mornings I'm calling Doughnuts and Da Word and we're going to start going through the Psalms of Ascent. Two a week for seven weeks."

I laugh. "Why not like, Doughnuts and David or something, so you could still be grammatically correct?"

Natalie looks back at me. "See? Rick needs you, Paige."

"I need you, Paige," Rick echoes.

I just shake my head and shrug it off, but Nichole's mom's words float through my head again and so does the warm feeling I got in my chest when I talked with her.

Rick parks about eight blocks away from the baseball stadium in the closest parking spot we can find and we all unload. Tyler and I watch as Rick and Natalie pull about eighteen bags out of the car and start strapping them on.

"What in the world are you bringing?" Tyler asks.

"The essentials, man."

"Your daughter requires a lot of things."

Natalie unrolls a huge piece of fabric and starts twisting it around herself until I recognize the Jedi Knight thing she had on for dinner a few weeks ago. She slides Claire into it and then looks at Rick.

"Diapers?"

Rick nods. "Check."

"Wipes?"

"Check."

"Extra paci?"

"Check."

"Toys?"

"Um . . ." Rick looks through one of the bags he's carrying. "Got a set of plastic car keys and an elephant teether."

"That's fine."

"Food?" Rick looks pointedly at Natalie's chest.

I grin. Tyler flushes.

"Time to start walking," he says.

We hike up to the baseball stadium and by the time we get there, I'm beet red and exhausted. The game has already started, so at least we aren't fighting a crowd to get in the gates.

"I'm getting a hot dog," Rick declares as soon as we reach our seats and he deposits his bags. "Want anything, babe?"

Natalie shakes her head, sweat glistening on her temples. "No thanks." She fans her face and sighs. "It is like 112 degrees inside this wrap."

Claire looks content, though. She's completely passed out. Either sleeping or unconscious from heat exhaustion, but I guess Natalie's convinced she's fine.

Tyler goes with Rick to get food and I settle into my seat by Natalie.

"I like him," Natalie says.

"Your husband? I've heard that makes the home life better," I say.

"No. Well, I mean, yes, I like him too, but I was talking about Tyler."

"Oh." I nod. "Me too."

"How are things?"

Apparently we have reached the point in the number of times we've been seen together that people now feel the need to ask us how the relationship is going. I look at her and shrug. "We still haven't defined anything, if that's what you're asking."

"Sheesh. Boys these days are just slow as Christmas."

Natalie digs a piece of paper out of her purse to fan herself with.

Something happens on the field and everyone except me and Natalie goes crazy in the stands.

"Did you see anything?" she asks me.

"Nope. That lady over there with the blue hair distracted me." She looks similar to Thing One and part of me wonders if maybe baseball games are supposed to be attended in costume. Sort of like a backward version of horse racing.

"Oh. I was looking at that guy a few rows down." She lowers her voice and tries to point all discreetly. "That's totally what Elvis would look like if he were alive today."

If I were my grandmother, I would say, *"If?!"*

But I'm not, so I just grin, because she's right.

"Holy cow, it's like the world is running out of hot dogs." Rick scoots through the seats and sea of legs to get back to us. "Or maybe these aren't 100 percent beef and in that case, holy half-ground-up pig parts."

"Ew," I say, trying not to gag as Tyler settles down in the chair next to me, holding a hot dog.

Natalie is apparently too used to Rick and his awful descriptions. "That smells good."

"Which is why I went ahead and got you one, beautiful." Rick hands her a hot dog slathered in mustard and relish. He looks over her at me. "And that, oh ignorant one, is what marriage is all about."

"Hey, just because I'm not married I'm ignorant?"

"Yep. Rule of life, kid, rule of life."

Tyler leans over and hands me a huge plate of nachos. "I figured you were probably more of a nacho girl." He smiles sweetly at me.

He figured right.

I am touched.

"Thank you, Tyler," I say. He didn't even put jalapeños on it. I have no idea why some people like to eat food that hurts, so I'm thankful he abstained.

The game is entertaining for about fifteen minutes and then after the ninety-seventh pitch to the same batter, I start to lose interest and get distracted by the crowd. A lady three rows down is doing a crossword puzzle, so I'm apparently not the only one here who isn't a big baseball fan.

Natalie elbows me sometime during the fourth inning. "How long do these things last?" she asks me in a low voice.

"Nine innings," Tyler and Rick say together, eyes on the field.

"Thank you, *Paige*." She sighs. "Man, we aren't even halfway there." She elbows me again. "Want to play I Spy?"

"You must be torture on a road trip." Tyler grins over at her.

"Hey! Wait until my husband comes to my defense." Natalie pokes Rick in the arm.

"I don't know why you're poking me. He's the one who said it." Rick rubs his bicep. "And it's not like he was telling a lie or something. You are torture to take on a road trip."

Natalie narrows her eyes at Rick.

He returns her look steadily and just shrugs, then looks back at the game. "Sorry to burst your bubble. Asking 'where are we' every twelve seconds doesn't qualify you as a good road tripper."

"Yeah, well, you telling me 'we're in the car' isn't helpful either," Natalie says, using air quotes as she deepens her voice an octave.

I laugh. Tyler grins. Rick and Natalie have a way of making marriage look much less scary to me, somehow.

Rick pats his wife's knee. "How about some kettle popcorn?"

"That would be lovely."

"Anyone need anything?" Rick asks us, standing.

"I would like chocolate ice cream." I dig down in my purse for some cash, but Tyler puts a hand on my arm.

"I'll get it for you, Paige. I asked you to come here." He stands as well. "Anything else?"

Someone in the row behind us hands Tyler a couple of dollars. "I'll take a water."

I laugh. Tyler takes the money, half grinning. "Uh. Sure."

They leave.

Natalie sighs, arches her back as best she can in the stadium chair with Claire strapped onto her chest, and looks at her watch. "Wow. She's sleeping really well. Apparently she likes baseball games."

"Or she's just bored out of her mind."

"Or that."

The guys get back in about ten minutes. "One chocolate ice cream." Tyler hands me a mini plastic baseball cap turned upside down with three huge scoops of ice cream inside.

"Holy smokes." I gape at it. "I meant like one scoop."

Tyler settles in the chair with another three scoops of mint chocolate-chip ice cream for himself and shrugs. "There was like a twenty-five cent price difference from one to three. I'll eat what you don't," he says, passing me a spoon.

I watch Tyler take a bite of ice cream, waiting to see if he passes my eating-ice-cream-with-a-spoon test. He puts the whole spoon in his mouth and pulls it out clean.

Passed.

I absolutely, positively, cannot stand when someone puts a spoonful of ice cream or yogurt or whatever into their mouth and pulls it back out with some of the ice cream still on there.

Makes my stomach hurt even thinking about it.

"So, Paigey," Rick says, crunching some of Natalie's kettle corn. "How long are you planning on thinking about this job offer?"

I sigh into my chocolate ice cream. "Rick."

"No, I'm just curious. Because it is a real job, Paige. I really do need to hire some help and the church board just approved it. So, if you are thinking you'll be thinking about it for another year, I need to hire some help before then."

I look over at him. "I need some hard numbers."

"One million, seven hundred and twelve thousand, six hundred and eleven divided by four hundred and sixty-two," Rick says.

"What?"

"I'm giving you hard numbers."

I rub my head. "I meant, I need to know specifics. How much does it pay, how many hours will I be working, and what all the job entails."

"Well, honestly, a lot of what you already do now is part of the job. Teaching, leading a small group, meeting with girls . . . it'll basically be what you do right now but more of it."

"And more of you," Tyler says.

"Dude. That's the best part of the job." Rick grins. He shrugs at me. "And we can talk money, but I remember you mentioned once what you made at the agency and let me just say, you'd be making the same, if not more."

"And hours?" I ask.

"Forty a week. You can schedule them whenever you want to. If you want to work every night between six and two in the morning, I don't care."

I eat my ice cream in silence for a few minutes, watching the pitcher throw pitch after pitch to the batter, and think.

"*And*," Rick says, overannunciating the word, "you would get to be making a difference in girls' lives. You would be counseling, praying with the girls, and studying the Bible with the girls."

That part sounds nice.

Natalie elbows Rick. "Honey. I think we got her."

"Hush. You are breaking the spell," Rick whispers loudly. "Dude, I am a genius for asking her over ice cream."

Tyler laughs. I smile. "I can hear you, you idiot. The only part about this that concerns me is forty hours a week with you."

Natalie grins. "It is a scary thought."

"It wouldn't be all with me. You'd maybe spend ten hours a week with me. Maybe. Probably closer to five. We'll have a staff meeting once a week, and I'll see you on Wednesday nights, and then just if you need to do things in the church office."

I keep eating my ice cream, thinking.

"Okay—" I start.

"What?" Natalie gasps.

"Really?" Rick grins.

"You didn't let me finish." I hold up my spoon. "I was saying, okay, can I give you my final decision this time in two weeks?"

Rick looks at me and nods. "Two Fridays from now. Why don't you come by the church office around five thirty or whenever you get off work?"

"I'll be there."

I have a lot of praying to do between now and then.

* * * * *

I climb into bed at eleven o'clock. The game went into extra innings, something Natalie and I were just thrilled about. Poor little Claire just sat there, teary eyed with her bottom lip poking out, for the last twenty minutes of the game.

I look at my Bible on the bedside table and pull it over, smoothing my hand across the leather cover.

"Lord," I start, praying out loud tonight. "I need some direction here."

A few months ago when I was so overwhelmed with everything, I took a day off work and spent the entire day reading the Bible, praying, crafting, and watching mindless TV while I thought about my life.

Maybe I need another one of those days.

It isn't that I am overwhelmed necessarily though.

I'm just not content.

Every day I wake up, take a shower, go to work, pay bills, answer the phone, go home, eat dinner, go to bed, and do the same thing all over again the next day. I have a boyfriend, but I don't. I have a best friend, but she's distracted with getting married. I have a sister, but I don't know her anymore.

I have a list a mile long to be thankful for and a list a Post-it note's length of what I've done with my life that has made a difference in anyone else's life.

I'm stuck.

I sigh and look at my Bible again. Maybe this is one of those moments when the first verse I read when I flip open my Bible to some random spot is going to be like the words written in the sky just for me.

I carefully balance my Bible on its spine and let it fall open. It opens to Daniel chapter 4.

"All this happened to Nebuchadnezzar the king."

Well. That did not help me very much.

Chapter
17

Saturday morning, there's a knock on my door right as I finish putting my makeup on. I'm planning a day of cleaning, grocery shopping, and working on this little hat I found online to make for Claire—a busy day before the youth group end-of-the-year party tonight. I walk through the living room and peer through the peephole.

It's Luke.

Again.

I open the door, trying to push the annoyed look away and aim for something a little more curious, just to be polite.

"Luke."

"Hi, Paige! I'm glad you're home." He's all smiles and dimples and sweetness, holding a paper sack from Starbucks with one hand and a drink carrier with two coffees in the other hand.

Apparently we have started some kind of Saturday morning tradition. At least I'm dressed decently and have some makeup on this time.

"You look beautiful!" he says exuberantly. "Can I come in?"

I've already had coffee this morning and I was considering the half and half I poured in there to be my breakfast. But I can smell the sweet bread smell coming from the sack, so I let him in, already disliking him because he knows my weakness for bread and doughnuts.

He makes himself at home at my kitchen table, setting out coffees and napkins. He opens three of my kitchen cabinets and finally pulls out a plate, goes back to the table, and sets three old-fashioned chocolate doughnuts on the plate and two of those artisan breakfast sandwiches.

"What are you doing?" I ask him finally, still standing in the living room.

He looks up at me and waves to the table. "Breakfast," he says, like we do this every day. "I didn't know if you'd want the doughnut or the sandwich, so I just got both."

I can't decide if that is kind or presumptuous.

After all, we aren't dating. We are hardly even friends.

"Luke," I start, taking a deep breath and crossing my arms over my chest.

He holds up his hands. "Breakfast is getting cold. Let's pray." He doesn't wait for me to come over there but ducks his head and tucks his hands into the pockets of his straight-cut jeans. "Lord, thank You for this food and for this time with Paige and may You bless our conversation. Amen."

I just look at him after he finishes praying. I haven't heard him pray in a very long time.

He's holding one of the chairs out from the table and I sigh and go sit in it. "Thank you for breakfast. But Luke, you really can't—"

"Starbucks has just really done a great job on these

sandwiches," Luke interrupts before I can tell him that this is not going to become a weekly occurrence.

"They have, but Luke—"

"And this cheese . . . gouda, right? It's amazing! I don't even know what kind of animal makes gouda cheese, but I like it just the same."

I sigh. He's not going to accept what I say even if I say it a million times. "I think that would be a cow, Luke."

He nods. "I figured. Just didn't know if the name was a veiled reference to goats or something."

"What are you doing here?" I ask him as he takes a sip of coffee. I try mine. It's a caramel-laced mocha and it's delicious.

He looks at the table, at the food in front of us, and then up at me. "Eating breakfast?" It's a question.

"Why are you eating here? Again?"

He shrugs. "I like eating with you. I miss when we would hang out all the time and talk."

He seems to forget that we were doing those things because we were *dating*.

It's a new era, buddy.

"Luke," I start again.

"Paige." Luke's voice is suddenly very serious and he looks at me, dark eyes sober. "I know what you are going to say."

"What?" Maybe if he hears it from himself, he'll get the message more.

"Look, I messed up. I know I did. I let you down, I hurt you, and I'm so sorry." He pauses and reaches for my hand, sorrow filling his expression. "So very, very sorry."

I just look at him.

"I can't change the past, but I can change the future. And I've grown up. I have. I know what I want now."

I'm scared to find out what that is.

"I want *you*, Paige. I want you back in my life. I've changed, I swear I have. I'm back in church, back reading my Bible, back to trying to walk with God." He lets go of my hand and looks away for a second, which is good because controlling my expression for so long has made the muscles around my mouth start twitching.

I pull my hands into my lap and take a deep breath. My stomach is trembling, my heart racing.

He rakes his hands through his hair. "Look, I know that you've been seeing . . . what's his name . . ."

"Tyler," I supply, feeling a little miffed that he can't even remember his name. Luke spent an entire lunch with us after all and usually manages to sit around us at church. You'd think he would have learned Tyler's name.

"Right." Luke shakes his head slightly. "I know you've been seeing him. But I haven't heard if y'all are exclusive or anything yet. And this is coming from just a casual observer of you guys, but you don't seem too . . . excited to be with him. I mean, I remember when we were first dating. I could hardly hold a fork because I was so busy holding your hand the entire time we were together." He shrugs. "You guys don't even hold hands in church."

He's right about the early days of me and Luke. I remember when it started becoming obvious that we were both attracted to each other. He sat beside me one night at his house when I came over to watch a movie with Layla, reached over, and wove his fingers through mine.

If shivers running up and down your legs and into your

lungs could kill someone, I probably would have died that night.

I shake that thought away.

"I'm just saying, you just don't seem . . . happy. You seem . . ." His voice trails off again and he sighs. "You seem a little discontent."

Luke has always been able to see right through me.

"I don't like seeing you like that." He reaches for my hand again, but I quietly weave my fingers together in my lap and he nods, laying his hand on top of my clasped hands.

"I just want you to think about this. Okay?" He looks at me until I meet his gaze and then he stares so strongly into my eyes that I feel my right retina start detaching.

"Fine," I manage to whisper, since he's obviously not going to leave without an agreement from me.

"Thank you. I'll leave the rest of this." He stands, picks up his coffee, and walks for my door. "Just . . . think about it, Paige."

Then he walks out, leaving me sitting at my kitchen table looking at a latte, three doughnuts, and a bacon breakfast sandwich.

I have lost a little weight since we were dating. Probably due to all the cheese stick dinners. Maybe Luke is trying to plump me back up.

I sigh into the empty apartment and rub my temples, squeezing my eyes tight.

Lord, I really didn't need that today. Don't I have enough to think about?

* * * * *

The youth group party is at a huge park sort of close to my church. I drive down the street, trying to find a place along the curb that doesn't involve too many parallel-parking maneuvers.

That wasn't necessarily my most shining moment in driver's ed.

I finally find a spot big enough for me to creep up between the two cars and just stop rather than having to do the whole forward, backward, forward, and then backward again thing.

The park is already a mess of people and I'm fairly early. Rick asked all of the leaders at the last leaders' meeting to try to make it here about ten minutes before the start so we could help get things situated.

Rick is busy setting up a couple of tables to put food on. There's a huge grill we're borrowing from the church set up and already turned on to cook some burgers. I stopped by the store on my way here and picked up a few bags of chips and a couple packages of Oreos.

I leave one bag of each in the car. I can go get them if we need them and if we don't, then I'll eat them.

I am selfish when it comes to Oreos.

Natalie is here. She has Claire in the wrap thing again and she's busy pointing out directions of where to set up a volleyball net they brought to two of our high school boys. Another couple of kids are setting up a horseshoe throw and still a couple more are carting bags of ice from Rick's truck over to a massive cooler.

I get out of my car, trying to push all thoughts of Luke and his little talk this morning out of my head. I barely got anything else done all day, I was worrying over it so much.

"Hey!" Tyler is suddenly beside me, grinning sweetly at me and reaching for the chips I'm carrying. "How was your Saturday?"

"Oh, you know," I say, trying to shrug the question off. "How was yours?"

"It was fine. I ended up working a half day." He sighs. "I'm very ready for these presentations to be done."

Rick waves us over. "I've just been informed by my beautiful wife that I am not allowed to cook the burgers tonight."

Natalie is crunching on a carrot stick, nodding. "He burns them. I like my burgers juicy."

"I was raised here in this great state of Texas to burn my burgers and a charred burger is what I'll eat," Rick says, hand over his heart.

"I'll cook them." Tyler shrugs. "I'm all about the moist burgers."

"Ew. Do not use that word," Natalie says, gagging.

"Burger?"

"*Moist,*" she whispers, making a terrible face. "Oh, I can't hear that word without feeling like someone is poking the back of my ankles repeatedly with a corn-cob skewer."

I grin. "Not to be dramatic or anything."

"I'm never dramatic."

"Never." I roll my eyes at Natalie. Right then my phone buzzes in my back pocket and it's a text. From Preslee.

Hi Paige, quick question. I'm in Dallas tonight doing some wedding shopping. I've got two more places to go and it's just getting late to drive back to Waco. Can I stay on your couch? You won't even know I'm there.

I sigh and look at Natalie. "I'll be right back." I walk over to a tree so I can be frustrated in private.

How am I supposed to respond to that text?

If I say, "Sure, Preslee, come on over," then I have to spend the evening awkwardly tiptoeing around my apartment and all the baggage that will be piled everywhere, thanks to our past.

But if I say, "Actually, I don't think that's a good idea," then I have to spend the evening sliding around on my guilt complex that will be spilled all over my house.

And it's not like it's six hours to Waco.

I sigh but it comes out more like a growl.

"Full moon tonight?" Justin, one of my favorite kids in the youth group, is suddenly standing behind me.

"What?"

"You just sounded like a . . . never mind." Justin shakes his head. "Everything okay?"

"Fine," I say shortly, flashing him a quick "please leave me alone" smile.

"Sure," he says and walks over to join the quickly multiplying mass over by the food tables. About ten guys are playing a pick-up basketball game on the court, and a few girls are tossing a Frisbee around.

I look down at my phone and chew on the inside of my cheek.

A pox on my stupid guilt complex.

Sure, that's fine. I'm at a youth group party. Should be home around nine thirty.

Maybe earlier. This park doesn't have any lighting. Once the sun goes down at eight thirty, everyone scatters pretty quick.

At least I won't have to spend the entire evening with her. Bright sides and all that.

She texts back right away. THANK YOU SO MUCH, PAIGE!!! SEE YOU TONIGHT!!!

Based on the number of exclamation points, you would have thought I was throwing a fun slumber party or something rather than my plan of walking in my apartment, handing her a blanket, and then going to bed.

Seriously, Lord? Preslee and Luke in the same day? Isn't that a little overkill?

Chapter
18

I pull into my apartment complex at 9:05. The kids, as per usual, all started dissipating at eight thirty, stuffed with Tyler's amazing hamburgers.

I know that the actual making of the burger is a big part of the taste, so probably Costco should get some recognition here, but they never tasted like that when Rick grilled them.

No offense to Rick.

I even ate two burgers and I usually barely choke down one.

I think I heard Natalie asking Tyler if he would come join their household as a live-in chef.

She even offered to do his laundry in return.

Tyler looked like he might consider it just for that, but then he shrugged. "Sorry, Nat. I think I'm more suited toward computers."

"I know suited, and you missed your calling, Emeril." She closed her eyes as she took another bite of her cheeseburger.

I left with plans to have lunch with Tyler after church tomorrow.

I park in my designated spot at my apartment complex and hold my breath, looking around to see if Preslee is around or if she is sitting on my porch. I couldn't see all of my steps when I drove into the lot, but I didn't see her standing in the parking lot.

Which is good. People milling around in apartment parking lots after nine o'clock at night are usually about to get into trouble.

My mother always told us growing up that nothing good happens after eight o'clock at night and we should just go on to bed and get ready for the next day. I remember sneaking out of my room when I was seven, walking into the living room, and seeing Mom and Dad eating a huge bowl of popcorn and watching some movie they were both laughing at.

It took me a long time to trust anything my mother said after that.

I climb out of my car, tuck my keys into my purse, and walk over to my steps.

"Paige?"

Preslee is poking her head out of a little silver sedan in the parking lot, waving to me. "Hold up, let me get my purse." She ducks back into the tiny car.

A sedan. The old Preslee would never have been seen in something so generic. The old Preslee was all about standing out and being different and ticking everyone off.

I wait for her and she emerges from her car a few minutes later holding about eight bags that are full to the brim.

I might as well be polite. She's already spending the night. I walk over and meet her at the curb, holding my hands out. "I can help." I take half of the bags. Preslee's eyes are sparkling.

"Oh, I found the most wonderful things, Paige! Thank you so much for letting me stay with you. I am probably the worst nighttime driver on the planet. Wes panics every time I tell him I'm going somewhere after dark." She smiles at me. "He's going to sleep so much better tonight knowing I'm safe with you."

"Sure," I say because it's that awkward moment when someone is genuinely thanking you for doing something that you didn't want to do in the first place.

We cart the bags upstairs to my apartment and I let her in. She's been here once for about three seconds, so I don't bother showing her around. Not that it would take too long to do so. I've got the big room with the living area, dining area, and kitchen, and my bedroom.

And we have now reached the end of our tour.

Preslee sets all of her bags down by the TV and then sits on the couch. "This is such a cute apartment, Paige. It looks just like you."

"Don't look too close. I can't guarantee when the last time I vacuumed was."

She just waves a hand. "It's fine. How much mess can one person make? How long have you lived here?" She stands and goes over to my bookshelf beside the TV and looks through my collection.

"A while." I go in the kitchen and pull down a couple of glasses for us. "Since about my sophomore year of college."

She points to one of the books on the shelf. "I didn't know this was a series!"

"I didn't know you read."

She looks over at me and shrugs. "I've started picking it up. This book was great. I didn't realize there was a sequel to it."

"Borrow it then."

"Really?"

She sounds like I just gave her the keys to Splash Mountain. She pulls the book out of the shelf and sets it on her purse.

"Thank you, Paige."

I walk over and hand her a glass of water. I'd offer something else but other than coffee that I'm rationing to last for the next three days, it's all I've got.

"Thank you, Paige."

She's starting to sound like she got stuck on repeat.

"Well," I say, preparing to tell her good night before I go into my room to pretend she's not here.

"So," she says at the same time and then stops. "Go ahead."

"No, you first."

"Want to see what I got for the wedding?"

She looks so hopeful, brown eyes all big and pleading, her face all rosy. I can tell she's a little bit nervous and somehow this almost makes me feel a little better.

Sometimes it's nice not to be the only one a little off-kilter.

"Sure." I give Preslee maybe the first genuine small smile since she came back a few weeks ago.

She grins so wide I worry she might pull a cheek muscle, and then she runs for her bags, carrying them to the kitchen table. "Okay, so that home-goods store close to Frisco? *Amazing,*" she gushes, pulling all kinds of white knickknacky things out of the bag.

There are distressed-style tall, white wooden candlesticks, white metal lanterns, four huge bags of white tea-light candles, and a bunch of other stuff.

I look at the tiny wooden place-card holders that clearly say $2.50 on each of them and think about how we could totally have made those ourselves for about ten cents apiece. If that.

Preslee is ecstatic, though. She sits at the table so we can look more closely and I join her. "I'm going for the whole shabby-chic thing," she says. "We're going to get married in the cutest little church in Austin, but I haven't found a reception area yet. I want something eclectic but cute, you know? Like an old barn or something we could totally dress up."

It seems like an old barn would be an easy find on the outskirts of Austin, but I guess I've never looked for one.

It wasn't exactly a high priority back in high school, when I was more concerned about what the humidity was currently doing to my hair and whether or not Luke liked me.

Best to move off that thought train.

"You know," I say, taking a deep breath because I know I'm basically handing her the proverbial olive branch. "We could make these for a lot cheaper than two dollars."

She just looks at me, eyes wide and bright, and all of a sudden there are tiny lakes hovering around her lash lines. "Really Paige?" she whispers.

I would take that to mean she's recognizing the branch between us as well. We might as well change into pajama pants, start brushing each other's hair, and tune up my old guitar so we can sing "Kumbaya."

"I mean, it's just a dowel rod and a couple pieces of wood they've cut down, sanded, and painted white," I say, looking at it. "I'd say three hours, maybe four tops, of good work and you'll have a hundred of these for ten bucks."

I can see the wheels turning. "Meaning I could have one for every guest," she says.

"What were you thinking?"

"I was thinking about putting little note cards with verses special to Wes and me on them and just kind of scattering them on the table."

I shrug. "Or you could do that. You don't have to make them. I just like . . . making stuff," I say, feeling weird that I'm telling my sister something so well-known about me.

"I knew you liked drawing."

Drawing. I haven't drawn anything since high school. I'll doodle when I'm on the phone, but I've turned more to crafty things. Wreaths. Sewing projects. Sometime, hopefully in the near future, I want to learn to knit.

Not like anyone needs knitted caps here in our winters.

Such a sad, depressing thought.

"I've kind of moved on to other things," I tell her. "I like doing a bunch of different stuff now." I fiddle with the place-card holder in my hands. "Do you . . . like doing anything . . . uh, creative?"

This could not be more awkward.

She shrugs and pushes her long, dark hair off her shoulder so it swings around to her back. "Well, Wes says I'm very creative at dancing."

And apparently my earlier statement was wrong.

She freezes and then blushes about 112 shades of red as she realizes what she just said. I'm pretty sure I'm at least a nice coraly pink that would make my general practitioner request a blood-pressure reading on me.

"Oh my gosh," she stumbles, gasping, her hands over her mouth. "Oh that's not what I meant *at all*. I just meant that we like to go to this place that does country line dancing and . . . oh my gosh . . . I am so . . . I didn't mean . . ." She crosses her arms on the table and drops her face down onto them.

I'm giggling now, and even though there is still a big part of me that is resisting this, I have to admit, it is really nice to be laughing with Preslee again.

She starts grinning at me too, eyes sparkling, and shakes her head. "So, *no*, I don't do anything crafty. I've tried to be more crafty, but even walking into Hobby Lobby makes my head hurt."

She's so sad about it that this makes me laugh too.

"How did you even start wanting to do this kind of stuff?" Preslee asks. "It's not like Mom is all crafty."

No, Mom is not at all. I could pretty much bet money that she's never held a hot glue gun in her entire life.

I shrug. "I don't know. I moved here and decided I wanted a front door wreath, but no one had one that was exactly like what I wanted for the price I wanted to pay. So I went to Hobby Lobby, bought all the stuff, came home, and made it myself."

"You've always been a self-starter," she says, all Dr. Phil on me.

"You're the one who started a band," I say before thinking, then I mash my lips together, wondering if it's safe to bring up the past.

After all, the band was one of the bigger reasons Preslee left.

Or rather Spike or whatever his name was who was in the band with her. He played the electric guitar if I'm remembering right. The only thing I remember 100 percent about him is that he had an inch-long silver spike sticking out of his chin.

It was gross.

Preslee looks at me for a long moment and then nods slowly. "Yes. Maybe you tend to be more creative in the arts and I tend more toward creativity in music."

"Probably." She hadn't seemed to mind the last question, so I ask another. "Do you still play?"

Preslee played mostly drums in high school, but she was also pretty good at guitar.

She shrugs. "I don't really play the drums anymore. I sold my set when the band broke up." Sadness crosses her expression briefly, but she blinks it away. "Every so often my church needs a fill-in for music, so I'll play the guitar or piano for them. Honestly, it's been kind of hard not to be around music anymore."

Preslee always lived with her iPod plugged into her ears.

I'm not like that. I enjoy silence. I think I always have. When it's just me at the apartment, I rarely turn on music.

There are a lot of holes in my story about Preslee. I look at her as she settles against the chair back. "Are you up for answering a few things?" I ask her quietly.

Her face becomes very serious and she nods. "I was praying we would get a chance to talk about everything, actually."

"Oh."

She takes a deep breath and sits up. "Could we move to the couch?"

"Sure." I nod to her half-empty glass. "Want more water?"

"I'm fine, thanks." She stands and goes into my living room, sits on one side of my couch, kicks her shoes off, and curls her feet up underneath her.

I refill my water glass and then join her, sitting on the other side of the couch, feeling very weird that I am in my apartment with Preslee and about to hear her side of the story that broke so many hearts.

Doesn't seem real.

"So . . ." She rubs her face. "I guess I'll just start at the beginning."

Suddenly Maria from *Sound of Music* is singing in my head.

"I know I was awful growing up," she says. "I don't know exactly where all the rage was coming from, but I do know that I made your life a living hell, and for that, I want to apologize." She gives me a very sad look. "You have no idea what I would do to change the past."

I nod. "I know. Keep going."

"So, when Spike came into the picture, I thought I was in love. He was cool, he was edgy, he was very unpredictable. It was . . ." She takes a deep breath. "Well, at the time I thought it was exciting. It was like a constant game of figuring out what his mood was going to be like that day."

It sounds exhausting to me.

"So anyway, there was this potential gig in Indiana and a potential agent who was potentially willing to listen to us." She rolls her eyes. "We were so stupid. Risking everything for a potential. I remember thinking that this was it. We were going to break out, and I'd never have to come back to Austin again, unless it was to perform."

She's quiet for a few minutes, staring at my blank TV, lost in memories, I assume. I don't try to rush her. I just sip my water and wait.

"There wasn't anyone waiting for us in Indiana," she says.

"But we tried to do some things there anyway. We played a few times. We were completely broke. There were four of us and all the equipment all crammed into this van, sleeping there, living there. I took showers at road stops for a while. I don't know how we managed to keep gas in the van. Then one of the guys' aunts said she would pay us to play at her daughter's wedding if we could make it to Chicago and learn some tame songs."

She shakes her head. "Spike was livid. Said we would be selling out if we went there and played some crappy wedding songs." She looks down at her hands. "I remember thinking then that maybe he wasn't the guy I wanted to live with forever, but he finally came around. We drove to Chicago and ended up getting a few more gigs from people at the wedding. Bar mitzvahs, anniversary parties, stuff like that. With each one we took, Spike just got more and more angry."

She stops abruptly and clasps her hands in her lap, fingers white from the pressure. I'm pretty certain I don't want to know details of everything my baby sister was going through during that time. "Those were dark days," she says finally. "I didn't know what to do. I couldn't go home. Not after the way I left. I couldn't stay with the band, not with the way Spike was hurting me. So I left. We played a gig, I told the guys I was going to pack up the drums, but instead I just carried them right across the street to a pawn shop, got a hundred bucks for them, and left."

She rubs her face. "I found a disgusting little motel in the heart of downtown Chicago that only charged twenty dollars for a night and stayed there. That night someone was killed in the room next to mine. I woke up to cops surrounding the building and ordering everyone out. One of the cops was sent there by Jesus because he saw me leaving with nothing but my clothes and for whatever reason, he offered to take me to his church's rescue mission."

My brain is spinning. I sit very still, very quiet, but I'm gripping my glass like the Hulk. I'm trying my best not to blink because I might start crying.

What if Preslee had been killed instead of whoever was in the motel room next to hers? What if Spike had seriously hurt my sister? What if I had never seen her again and she had died with such a huge chasm between us?

Preslee tucks her hair behind her ears and continues. "Things changed after that. I lived at the rescue mission for four months and I got very close with one of the ladies who volunteered there. She reminded me a lot of Gram."

I smile. Gram was spunky.

"She kept telling me that I was smart, that Jesus was still going to use me for some wonderful thing. About two months into getting to know her, I became a Christian. I started going to her church, I started reading my Bible, and I started studying so I could take the high school diploma equivalency exam."

"How come you never called?" The million-dollar question.

Preslee sighs. "I just couldn't. I had to come back changed. I couldn't come back and have everything start all over again between Mom and Dad and me. I needed to know I was different." She bites her bottom lip. "I should have called though."

"Yes."

"I'm sorry," she says again. "I started working as a waitress and spent the next two years working, taking correspondence classes through one of the colleges in Chicago, and going to church. I was asked to share my testimony with the youth group, and that day is when I met Wes."

She takes a sip of water and shrugs. "After that, time just flew past. I fell in love. He's really a wonderful man, Paige. I'm so excited for you to get to know him better. He proposed and I told him that there are a few things I need to take care of before I get married." She looks at me and nods slightly.

I assume I am one of those "things."

She takes a deep breath and leans back against the sofa. "And that's the condensed version. Still kind of long. Sorry about that."

She looks exhausted, and I feel completely emotionally drained. I'm not sure I can have a coherent conversation about her long story right now.

I am one of those people who needs to process things.

"Thank you for telling me that," I say in a quiet voice.

"Thank you for listening."

We both just sit there in silence for what feels like an hour but is probably closer to two minutes.

"I think it's bedtime," she says finally.

I nod and go pull out an old comforter and an extra pillow from my linen closet. "Do you want sheets?"

She shakes her head and slips off her shoes. "I'm just going to curl up on the couch. I can sleep anywhere. Don't worry about me." She tucks her hands in her pockets sheepishly. "Obviously I didn't plan this too well, but you don't happen to have an extra pair of pajamas and an extra toothbrush, do you?"

I smile. "Follow me." I lead her into my room and dig out an old pair of gray pajama shorts that have coffee cups all over them and a black T-shirt. I point to the cabinet under my sink. "There are a few toothbrushes in there." I hate the toothbrushes my dentist gives out, but I just have issues throwing away a perfectly good toothbrush, so I just stockpile them under my sink. I always have this vague idea of donating them to a homeless shelter, but I never remember to do it.

I should do it.

She comes out of the bathroom a few minutes later all ready for bed. "Good night, Paige." She clasps me in an awkward hug. "I love you. Thank you for letting me stay here tonight."

"Yeah. Sure."

I shut my bedroom door, change into my pajamas, brush my teeth, and climb into bed, pulling the covers up around my waist. I plug my phone in and there's a text from Tyler that I missed.

HOPE YOUR TIME WITH YOUR SISTER WENT WELL. I'VE BEEN PRAYING FOR YOU. SWEET DREAMS, PAIGE.

He really is very nice. He was all concerned after I told him who was spending the night and even prayed with me before I left.

I look over at my Bible on my bedside table next to my phone and just sigh.

I'll read tomorrow.

Chapter 19

My alarm goes off at seven for church.

I would be very okay with a midafternoon church service. Maybe one that also served Starbucks and freshly made chocolate-chip cookies.

The chewy kind.

I am suddenly remembering the stories the last missionary who visited our church told us about starving children who walked three hours across deserts and through dangerous ravines just to go to church, and I am suddenly hit with good old-fashioned American guilt.

I take a lot for granted.

I take a quick shower and then quietly creak open my door. Preslee is still sacked out on the couch, long dark hair splayed all over my sofa cushion, face relaxed, mouth open.

She looks like she's about twelve, and my chest hurts again for all the years we lost.

Here's an issue. If I sneak into the kitchen to make coffee, she will likely wake up. If I don't, I might get stuck drinking the coffee at church, which has a 50 percent chance of being good coffee.

Fifty percent is not that high when it comes to a ratio of good or bad coffee.

She looks so peaceful that I decide not to wake her up and slip back into my room to finish working on my appearance. The older I get, the longer this takes.

Except for a brief stint in junior high. It took me like two hours to get ready back then.

Sad that Danny Waggerston never knew how much I tried to impress him.

Rick asked yesterday at the party if I would come sit in on the youth group Sunday school again this morning. I've gone a few times in the last few months.

"You just want me to decide I do want the job," I told him.

"Well, duh," Rick said, grinning.

I arranged a sub for the two-year-old class, which is never too hard to find. I just go for the women who have an empty nest and no grandkids yet. It gives them their kid fix and their own kids get a few more months of being spared the "when are you giving me grandchildren?" talk.

I brush on my eye shadow, add some liner and mascara, and then spend the next few minutes putting some curl into my hair. My hair is way too long.

It doesn't help when I see all these girls around with these super-cute short cuts in preparation for summer.

But then I remember every girls' dream of wanting to get married with long hair. Not that that is going to happen anytime in the near future, but it is a concern since it took a few years for my hair to get this long. If I chop it all off now, I'll have to factor that into my dating life.

The thought of Tyler brings a smile to my face, but then Luke's plea yesterday morning wipes the smile right off.

No more thinking about the dating life while looking in a mirror. I've apparently gotten some wrinkles I didn't know I had.

I pull on a pair of jeans and a green Henley-style short-sleeve shirt over a white camisole with brown flip-flops and peek out my door again.

Preslee is still sleeping.

She was apparently on the tired side.

I sneak out into the kitchen, silently pull a notepad and one of my spare keys from the junk drawer, and write a quick note.

I went to church. Main service starts at ten, if you want to join me. Hope you slept—

I pause, pen in the air. Good? Well? English 101 is failing me this early in the morning.

—well. P.S. I will be your maid of honor.

Better to tell her this in writing so that: (a) I can't change my mind and (b) neither of us will cry around each other.

I have this feeling that if we start crying, we just won't stop.

That's not good for maintaining the proper pH balance in your system. Or so says WebMD.

But then again, my PMS headaches always turn into brain tumors on WebMD's symptom checker.

I leave the note and the key in the bathroom where she definitely will not miss it. Then I grab my purse, slip out the door, and lock it as quietly as I can behind me.

I am even leaving a little early, which warrants a stop by Starbucks, I think. I pull out of the drive-thru a few minutes later with a macchiato and then head toward the church.

This will play into my decision about the job, I think. There's a Starbucks directly on my way to church.

I could live with that.

I wonder if I could factor in some coffee money into my salary from the church.

Rick is standing in front of the sound-booth thing in the youth room when I walk in. Our youth room looks like a huge garage, basically. There's concrete floors, open duct-work, and the whole place echoed when they first built it, so Rick finally had them add some of those sound-absorbing boards on the walls, which made conversations and Sunday mornings way more bearable.

A few kids are milling around in the room, talking small talk or staring blankly at the band setup, obviously up a little too early.

"Good morning, Paige," Rick says when I walk over, but he doesn't look away from the computer where he is typing out the lyrics to what looks like "Our Great God."

Great song.

"Morning. So. This job thing," I say.

He perks up immediately and looks right at me. "Yes?"

"I might need a coffee allowance."

"Done."

"Because I—" I stop. "Wait, what?"

He shrugs. "It was already part of the job description."

I just gape at him. "You are kidding."

"Nope. You're supposed to be meeting with students. So we are prepared to give you a hundred-dollar prepaid Visa card every month to take you and the girls out with." He waves a hand and goes back to typing. "As long as you make it last through the month and meet with a bunch of students,

I don't care where you use it or what you use it on. Go to Starbucks. Go to Putt-Putt. Go waterskiing. I don't care."

I swear I have not heard this bit about the job before. I knew the meeting with students part, but he did not mention the Visa card.

Suddenly, the job is looking a little better. Using my major *and* doing it at Starbucks?

"Okay." Rick pushes the Save button on the computer. "Words are all set. Remember how to do them?"

The last time I did words, I spent the whole time panicking that I was going to mess up and cause everyone's worship experience to come to a screeching halt. I back away with my hands up. "Oh no. I'm not doing that again."

"It wasn't really a question." Rick smirks at me. "You'll do fine. Cut yourself some slack. Speaking of slack, did you get the e-mail I sent you yesterday?"

I hadn't been around my computer all day yesterday, but I did check it on my phone this morning. One of the only ways I can honestly say that I actually utilize the smartness of my smartphone.

"I didn't see anything from you."

"Shoot. Must have gotten lost in hyperspace."

"I think you mean *cyberspace*."

He shrugs. "Whatever."

"I thought hyperspace was when you were going someplace really fast."

"Oh my gosh," one of the sophomore guys comes over, making the universal signs for choking. "You guys are *killing* me. How does neither one of you know the proper terminology for hyperspace, much less cyberspace?"

Rick and I just look at him and then he proceeds to spend

the next twenty minutes talking about interstellar trade, safe routes, and something about droids being required to navigate. He loses me about ten seconds into his speech, and I just stand there, thinking about how nice it would be to have a conversation with a fifteen-year-old boy that didn't involve a reference to *Star Wars*, girls, or sports.

But really. What else do fifteen-year-old boys care about?

Rick glances at the big clock on the wall and butts into the monologue. "That's all well and good, Logan, but we need to get things rolling here." The band has already picked up their instruments and the room is filling up.

Logan shakes his head and leaves, mumbling under his breath about intergalactic transportation and how he shouldn't have wasted his breath on morons who don't care about anything important.

I think the biggest issue was our definitions of *important*.

Rick starts the hour with prayer and then the band takes over. I manage to make it through being in charge of projecting the words without completely ruining people's worship experience, or so I hope anyway.

Computers are just really not my thing.

Maybe I need a droid. Or whatever Logan was talking about.

Then Rick gets up and talks for about thirty minutes about grace. "We as American Christians have become desensitized to this word. We sing it, half of the girls I know are named it, and we even use it to describe dancers. And the only reason I know that is because Natalie likes to watch that ballet reality show, whatever it's called."

A few of the kids snicker.

"My point, friends, is that we need to get in the habit of reminding ourselves, day after day, night after night, about how great a price God paid to make us His own. We do not deserve it, and yet so great is His love for us that He still did it." Rick weaves his fingers together and cups the back of his head, elbows sticking out. Rick is nothing if not animated as a preacher. "But what do we do? We just go on living like nothing happened. Sure, we come here. Sure, we sing our little songs. Sure, we might even pick up our Bible a couple times a week. But are we really living in grace? Or are we doing what it says in Romans 6 and just going on with our sinful lives, counting on God's grace to save us?"

I quietly flip over to Romans and verse 20 of chapter 5 catches my eye.

"Where sin increased, grace abounded all the more . . ."

For whatever reason, Preslee and Luke come to my mind.

I shove them back into the corner of my brain where they belong, and I try to focus on the rest of Rick's sermon instead.

* * * * *

"Paige! Wait up!"

I turn in the crowded church hallway and see Tyler pushing his way through the masses. For whatever reason, whoever designed our church decided to make the coffee bar area right in the most crowded hallway of the entire church. I'm sure when our founding fathers of this church built it, they saw it as a great place to serve drinks, catch people coming in and out of classrooms and the sanctuary, and create a homey environment, but it just makes everything clogged and chaotic.

He finally catches up to me, trying not to let the crowd smash us into bits. "Hi," he says, eyes twinkling, tiny little smile lines around his eyes and mouth. He's got on straight-cut dark jeans, a gray T-shirt under a button-down shirt that makes his blue eyes look even bluer, and his blond hair would have made Shirley Temple proud.

He looks adorable.

And sweet.

Here's my immediate thought: Luke is completely wrong.

I suddenly don't care that we are standing dead in the middle of a huge throng of people smashing around us, crowding us together, everyone jostling Bibles and coffee and children. I look up into Tyler's blue eyes and my whole chest feels warm, like that time I told my mother I thought I had the bubonic plague and therefore did not need to go to school, and she told me we should smoke it out by feeding me the hottest chili I've ever eaten in my life.

I went to school that day, just in case you were wondering.

I reach up on my tiptoes and lightly kiss Tyler on the cheek. He's got a five o'clock shadow thing that sandpapers my lips, and he blinks at me in surprise as I flatten my feet back down to the floor.

In his defense, it is a weird place to kiss someone's cheek for the first time.

Unless you are one of those dear, old women at church who just kiss everyone's cheeks all the time, particularly if you are under thirty and male and somewhat cute.

Tyler gets smacked a lot by them.

Somehow he finds my hand with everyone shoving around us and squeezes my fingers. "Are we still on for lunch?"

I nod. "Definitely."

"What?"

I motion to him to follow me and then squeeze and press and jostle through the people until the crowd spits me into the hallway leading to about half of the adult Sunday school classes. Tyler is close behind.

He takes a deep breath and then smiles at me. "I feel like we are outgrowing this building."

"Not again. We just added that new wing three years ago." He's right, though. I guess it's a good thing to constantly be busting out of your church.

"So, yes to lunch?" He reaches for my hand again. He weaves his fingers through mine and my stomach reacts like he gave it a carbonation injection.

"Yes, but we have a potential catch. So, you know how Preslee spent the night with me last night?"

He nods. "I was praying for you. How did it go? And I never actually heard why she wanted to spend the night in the first place."

"She was in town shopping for the wedding and it went late, and she didn't want to drive all the way back to Waco. We talked last night. A real talk. For the first time since . . ." I shrug, but only because I start feeling my throat close up.

Apparently I can hold the tears in when it's Preslee, but when it's sweet Tyler, who I would prefer not to see me cry, I can't plug them up. My eyes are burning as huge tears fight to see which one is going to fall down my face first.

Here's the thing. I am not a pretty crier. When I cry, I look like I am contracting some terrible plague that could potentially wipe out humankind, or at least the remaining survivors on whatever ship I'm on. There are no gentle tears, there is only snot, redness, swelling, and huge bulbous, bloodshot eyes.

One of the many reasons I try not to cry in front of people. And everything stays that way for about three hours afterward.

I have spent my life training myself for this moment.

I shove Tyler and his comforting you-can-go-ahead-and-cry-here-because-I-obviously-have-no-idea-what-you-look-like-sobbing arms as far away from me as I can get him and suck in my breath through my nose, carefully, slowly letting it out through my mouth like the lady told all of us to do during that one Pilates class I took in college.

I quickly discovered that I am not into Pilates.

I would much rather just run on a treadmill.

I mash my thumb and my middle finger of my left hand into my temples and keep breathing, eyes closed to prevent the swelling.

"Paige? Paige? Paige?" Tyler is turning into an echo of himself.

In through the nose. Out through the mouth.

Rinse and repeat.

I manage to shove the emotions down deep into my ankles, and while I may walk a little funny for the next few minutes, at least I won't scare Tyler that my happily ever after is like Fiona's on *Shrek*.

I open my eyes and Tyler is just staring at me from about five feet away where I had pushed him to. "Are you okay?" he finally asks me.

"Yes. Now. Thank you." Short and concise. That's the new way to go in sentences.

"I've never seen you do that before."

"Cry?"

"No, shove someone like that. You've got some biceps, girl." He rubs his chest. "I want you on my Ultimate Frisbee team when youth group starts up again in the fall."

Motivation is the key difference here. I care to protect my vanity. I do not care to sacrifice my face for a plastic disc.

Probably because of the vanity thing.

"Anyway," I say. "I left Preslee a note and asked her if she wanted to come to church today, so I don't know if she's coming or not. For all I know, she could still be sleeping. She was pretty out this morning."

He nods. "Well, if she comes, then she'll have to come to lunch with us. I would really like to meet her. I've never met any of your family before."

One of the weirdest parts of being an adult that lives away from your parents is that people don't know you in association with your parents.

I just find that odd.

We join the crowd going into the sanctuary, and I save a seat on the other side of me for Preslee. I check my phone, but there aren't any missed calls or texts.

"Paige!"

Layla is waving obnoxiously two rows ahead and about eight feet to the right of where I am sitting. "Paige! Paige, over here!"

I wave at her. "Hi, Layla."

"I saved seats!"

"So did I." I point to the seat for Preslee and the two on the other side of it.

Layla bites her lips and crosses her arms over her chest. She's wearing a rose-colored skirt and a cream-colored lightweight sweater over a gauzy, loose-fitting top. She has her shoulder-length hair down and curly with a rose-colored headband with one of those fabric rosette things right above her left ear.

And she's wearing glasses.

I've never seen Layla in glasses before, and we've been friends forever.

They are big, black plastic frames like I see on everyone in Starbucks now. She looks cute.

I point to my eyes. "New?"

"Mascara?" she shouts. "I can't tell if it's making a difference, but you do have pretty short lashes," she yells over at me.

I sigh. Another secret blown for Tyler. He is just raking in the information about me today.

"The glasses." I point at her face instead.

"Oh! Yeah." She grins and pushes them up a little on her tiny nose. "They are totally fake. What do you think?"

The people sitting around us are starting to get annoyed.

Layla waves. "Wait, I'll just move. Peter isn't here yet anyway." She grabs her Bible and purse and slides down our row, picks my Bible up off the seat next to me, and sits down. "So," she says.

"Wait, before you start, that's Preslee's seat."

She just gapes at me, mouth open. "You speak to her now?"

"Kind of."

"What is this? It's like I haven't seen you in, like, years!" She shakes her head. "This just isn't good, Paige. We are growing apart!"

I haven't gotten to see her very much lately, but I don't think we are growing apart. "Movie night at my house. Tomorrow."

"I'll get the Panda Express." She nods, fiddling with her glasses and then sliding down a seat.

Peter shows up and stands on the end and talks to Tyler for a few minutes. Considering how little I've ever heard Peter talk, I'm about to bestow Tyler with the title of Miracle Worker.

The band is gathering on the stage, I'm checking my phone for news from Preslee for the ninth time in thirty seconds, and that's when I feel a little tap on my left shoulder. I look up and it's Preslee, wearing what looks like my blue dress and my yellow heels.

"Hi, Paige," she says, looking awkward but at the same time very cute.

"You came!" I jump out of my seat and this huge surge of joy at getting to introduce my baby sister to my friends comes out of nowhere. "You're wearing my clothes!"

She tucks her long, dark hair behind her ear and blushes. "I didn't know how dressy your church was and I felt weird wearing my dirty clothes here. I hope you don't mind."

I didn't at all. She was raised by my mother who taught us that an item of clothing is dirty the second you remove it from the hanger.

"Layla. Tyler," I say, interrupting his conversation with Peter but wanting to introduce Preslee before the music starts. "This is Preslee. Preslee, you know Layla, and this is her fiancé, Peter. And this is, uh—" Oh gosh. We haven't settled on anything official, so I can't call him my boyfriend. I wince and just nod. "Tyler," I say weakly.

Tyler doesn't seem to notice. He smiles his customary big grin and shakes Preslee's hand. "Nice to meet you."

"Thanks."

"Oh, I am *so* glad to see you again!" Layla gushes, pulling Preslee into a hug. "Come! Sit! Music is about to start!" She pretty much manhandles Preslee into the seat between us, chatting a hundred miles a minute. "Welcome to our church! Oh, I'm *so* glad you are here! I hope you like it! The music is so wonderful and you'll just *love* our pastor. He's —"

Right then our music pastor starts to play the guitar and invites everyone to stand up. "Let's come together in worship," he says into the microphone. Then he starts singing.

I try to follow along as best as I can, but it is just so weird to be standing next to Preslee, in church, singing worship songs again. It has been at least ten years since this has happened. Ditching church was one of the first things Preslee started doing way back when.

Now she's marrying a pastor's kid.

It's true what they say about things coming full circle.

Our pastor gets up a few minutes later and tells everyone to turn to Luke chapter 7. He starts reading. *"A moneylender had two debtors: one owed five hundred denarii, and the other fifty. When they were unable to repay, he graciously forgave them both. So which of them will love him more?"*

Pastor Louis looks up at all of us, his eyes scanning the room. Pastor Louis is probably the most pastoral-looking man I've ever met in my life. I sort of doubt this man had a childhood because it's hard to imagine him going through middle school.

"Jesus starts here by asking a question. Who loves the

moneylender more? It's almost one of those rhetorical questions."

If Rick were teaching this message, I'm pretty sure the word *duh* would have been used. Probably more than once.

Probably why he's the youth pastor and Pastor Louis is the lead pastor.

Pastor Louis preaches for another thirty minutes on the verses in Luke. "As Christians, particularly Christians who have been in the church for many years, we have a tendency to look down on those who haven't known the Lord as long or who have sinned in greater ways than us. I pray that we remember what it says here. That those who have had much forgiven often love the Lord more than those who have had little forgiven." He quirks one side of his mouth up. "Room for thought, eh? Let's pray."

Preslee is swiping under her eyes as we bow our heads and a part of my esophagus suddenly feels like there's a lasso around it.

For all intents and purposes, I am the perfect daughter.

I never smoked, never drank, never stayed out past curfew. If Mom and Dad told me to do something, I did it. My bed was always made, my teeth were always brushed, my clothing was always up to my dad's standards for me.

The closest I ever came to cussing was when I stepped on a scorpion barefoot in the seventh grade and said, "Oh my God." Mom sent me to my room for a week, swollen foot and all, and I never took the Lord's name in vain again after that.

I never missed a birthday, never missed my parents' anniversary, and I called my grandmother every single Friday at exactly four in the afternoon until she passed away three years ago.

If I were to die tonight, my headstone would read:

PAIGE ALDER
LOVED BY HER PARENTS. ENVIED BY OTHER
PARENTS. BORING BUT DEPENDABLE.

I never realized how uninteresting I was as a child. While Preslee wreaked havoc, screamed, yelled, and gave my parents early gray hair, I had my name on the honor roll and a steady job since I was fourteen years old.

I'm like the human equivalent of a Chevy truck. Though I hope to heaven I never hear anyone describe me like that. I'll have to immediately go on a diet and get a tattoo.

Preslee pokes me and I blink, suddenly realizing that everyone is up, milling around, stretching, and talking to the people around them. Somehow I missed the whole prayer and closing ceremony, which is just usually a bunch of announcements.

It's not like this is the Olympics or anything.

"You okay?" Preslee asks me, frowning.

"Fine. I'm fine." Aren't I always?

There's a thought needling the back of my brain, and as it surfaces and forms into something tangible, I realize that my problems with Preslee and Luke aren't really with Preslee and Luke.

I have problems with *me*.

What if my issues with them aren't so much because of what they did as much as me feeling . . . maybe, in a small way, potentially . . . jealous of them?

Jealous.

Rick was right.

I'm jealous. I'm jealous of the apparent fun they had. I'm jealous of the way that everyone seems to just forgive them and move on, and I'm jealous that on top of everything else, now they apparently love God more than I do.

"Well, where would you like to eat?" Tyler asks me. He looks over at Preslee. "We would really like for you to join us."

"Oh, that's sweet, but I — "

"Good morning, everyone." It's Luke, looking for all the world like a team of professionals spent hours fixing his hair this morning.

No one should look that good before noon.

He looks at me and there is just straight-up, undiluted longing in his eyes.

Another thing that shouldn't happen before noon.

I bite my lip and look away. Luke's impassioned speech yesterday is hanging in the air like a big old toot that everyone can smell but no one can figure out the source of. Tyler is looking at me and then back at Luke confusedly, and Layla has apparently used her Spidey sense to figure out what happened because she is glaring so hard at Luke, I'm scared his perfect hairstyle is going to melt.

Preslee, meanwhile, is looking at Luke, recognition flitting in and out of her expression. "Are you . . . ?" she starts.

He looks down and sees my sister. "Preslee!" He yanks her up into a big, huge hug like he's been missing her for ages. "I haven't seen you in years!"

Tyler is still looking at me and I take the opportunity to attempt some telekinetic conversation.

Nothing happened. Stop. He is just delusional. Stop. You can stop worrying. Stop.

I don't know the proper format for telekinesis apparently because Tyler is now just making a weird, confused face at me.

Even so, I'm thankful that Preslee intercepted Luke's attention for the moment.

"How about that sandwich place a few blocks away?" I ask Tyler in a quiet voice.

He nods. "Done." He smiles slightly at me.

"Well, Paige, I'll see you tomorrow night. We've got a *family* lunch right now at Birker's. Mom and Dad want to discuss the wedding details." Layla overannunciates, looking pointedly at Luke.

"I heard you and I'm coming," Luke says, shaking his head at Preslee. "I'm not sure why I need to be present for wedding detail talks, though."

"I'm just telling you what Mom said."

Sometimes Layla and Luke don't act too different from how they were as kids in high school.

And yes, to the unasked question about their parents being *Star Wars* fans. Apparently a lot of people were in the 1980s. I think they changed Layla's name just enough to not make people too weirded out.

Or maybe to save her from a life of wearing cinnamon-roll buns over her ears. The jury is still out on that one.

"Well, it was good to see you guys again," Preslee says. "Have a good lunch."

Layla gives me a tight, one-second hug around my shoulders and simultaneously whispers, "You're welcome!" in my ear as she leaves.

Luke gives me one last, long look and then follows his sister and Peter out of the sanctuary.

Tyler stares at me with a quizzical, somewhat sad expression and then wipes his face clear before turning to Preslee. "So, I think we're going to go to a little hole-in-the-wall sandwich place that both of us like. Would you like to join us?"

Preslee looks at me and I nod. "I'd really like that."

"Then sure. Thanks, Tyler."

We end up all riding in Tyler's truck together and get to the sandwich shop a few minutes later. Preslee walks in, inhaling. "They make their own bread?"

"Yep. Aren't you glad you came?" I ask her.

We order our sandwiches and Tyler finds an empty booth in the far corner of the restaurant. It's not busy yet, but the last time we came here after church, the place filled up within minutes of us getting our food.

"So, Preslee, Paige tells me you're engaged," Tyler says.

She nods. "Yes. We are planning the wedding for the end of November."

I don't think I've heard a date yet. Guess that would be good to know as the maid of honor.

"Congratulations." Tyler gives her a genuine smile.

"Thank you." She looks at me and tears build up in her eyes as she grips my wrist. "Paige is going to be my maid of honor."

He only smiles at me, but the way that he does makes everything in my rib cage get warm.

"Order for Tyler!"

He stands and walks over to the counter to get the order. Preslee squeezes my wrist again. It's an awkward place for her to hold.

"Oh, Paige, he is just the sweetest guy," she whispers. "I like him a lot."

"Me too," I say. And I mean it.

Tyler sits back down with our tray of food and looks at Preslee and me. "Can I pray for us? Lord Jesus, I thank You for this meal and for these dear friends. Watch over us today and bless this food. Amen."

"Amen," Preslee and I echo.

"Thank you for lunch," Preslee says to Tyler.

He shrugs. "My pleasure. So tell me about Waco. You've moved there? Are moving there?"

Tyler is a master conversationalist at lunch. He only hits on the good topics, sticking with the future and staying away from the past. He tells stories about his work that make us laugh and then bemoans the fact that he's the only engineer in his office who knows anything about football.

"I promise I did not know this before I majored in engineering."

"Oh please." I roll my eyes.

"I honestly didn't. I didn't know any engineers at all. My computer-lab teacher in high school suggested I look into software engineering and I did."

"Sorry about that. I imagine it was a rude awakening." Preslee grins over her sandwich at me.

"Very rude."

I just shake my head and laugh.

* * * * *

I cross my arms and just stare at my Bible that night, pillows stacked behind me so I'm sitting up in bed, covers up around my waist.

I do not want to open it.

I know what it is going to say.

So I sit there. Staring at the brown leather cover.

On the plus side, things are going great with Preslee. She gave me a hug when she left this afternoon, and for the first time in ten years, it wasn't awkward or rushed or out of some guilt-ridden desire to please our mother.

For the first time in forever, I'm almost excited to get to know my sister better. Where there was once a hard, cold knot of pain in my heart, there is now something soft and squishy.

Hopefully that isn't the sign of some sort of awful heart disease.

I finally sigh and pick up my Bible, turning to Galatians.

"For the whole Law is fulfilled in one word, in the statement, 'You shall love your neighbor as yourself.'"

Luke's chocolate-brown eyes begging me to forgive him fill my brain and I close my Bible hard. I toss a couple of the pillows off the bed, mash the remaining one under my head, yank up the covers, and flick off the light.

"You ask too much, Lord," I whisper into the pitch-black darkness.

Monday night Layla arrives at my apartment at exactly six o'clock, holding a huge bag with a panda bear on it.

"Good night! How much food are we eating tonight?" I gape at her. "Everyone knows Panda makes the worst leftovers."

She shakes her head sadly. She's got her hair up in a sloppy bun and she's changed into baggy sweatpants, an old T-shirt, and fuzzy blue slippers.

I'm willing to bet she walked into Panda in those slippers.

She comes in, sighing. "I can't commit, Paige. I was standing there in the line, planning on getting the orange chicken and Beijing beef and then, all of a sudden, I just started thinking. What if the mushroom chicken is better? What if I really don't want meat, what if I only want fried rice and spring rolls? What if I should have worn real shoes in here? What if I should have had my hairstylist put some blonde in for the summer? What if I shouldn't marry Peter?"

She sets the bag on my kitchen table and covers her eyes.

"What if you stopped overreacting long enough to eat some of this feast?" I start pulling boxes out of the bag. "There's like nine entrees here, Layla."

"What if this is all just a big sign?"

"Layla."

"Like if I can't even decide what I want to eat, how in the world am I supposed to be able to decide who to marry?"

"Layla."

"Woe woe to me." She collapses in one of my kitchen chairs, crosses her arms on the table, and lays her forehead on them.

I sigh. I have too many major life decisions to make myself. I can't be making Layla's too.

"Layla," I say again.

"What?" she moans.

"Do you love Peter?"

"Yes."

"Do you enjoy being around him?" My voice is a monotone.

"Not if he just ate a chili-cheese dog."

Too much information about Peter. I rephrase the question. "Do you have a good time with Peter?"

"Yes."

"Do you have similar beliefs about God, the Bible, raising kids, and how often carpet should be cleaned?"

"Yes."

"Then marry the poor man, Layla." I pop open the lid on a huge container of chow mein noodles.

"Oh." She raises her head. "He's not poor. He's not rich, but—"

"I meant *poor* in the sense that he has to live with you for the rest of his life."

She levels a glare at me. "Mean head."

"Crazy one. We're going to have to be rolled out of here after dinner tonight. Probably on a stretcher."

She shrugs. "You know how Chinese food is. You can only eat so much and then you're stuffed for an hour and then you're starving again."

I find a few paper plates in the back of one of my kitchen drawers, and we load up our plates with food. "Thanks for dinner, Layla," I tell her, carrying my plate over to the couch.

"Thanks for calming me down." She joins me with her own huge plate of food.

"Cute slippers."

She looks down at them. "Thanks. They're really comfy. And they're nice because you don't have a definite right or left slipper. They're unisex."

I choke on a chow mein noodle. "I don't think that's the word you're going for, Layla."

"Uniform? Uniside? I don't know, I just think they're comfy."

I look over at my best friend slurping noodles up with a fork, set my plate on my lap, and hook an arm around her shoulders. "You're crazy, but I love you."

She grins at me. "Right back atcha."

* * * * *

The rest of the week crawls past. I walk into work on Friday and just stand there for a second at the door, taking a deep breath, trying to mentally prepare myself for the day of filing and paychecks.

Yay.

Tonight is also the night that Rick wants an answer from me on the youth worker job. And I still have no answer. I've been scouring my Bible every night for the past week during my evening devotional time, skipping time in my new least-favorite book called Galatians, and I've come up with nothing.

Last night, I didn't even turn on HGTV when I got home from meeting with Nichole at Starbucks. I just sat on the couch, opened my Bible, and looked up every reference regarding careers I could think of. The word *job* just got me a bunch of verses about Job and *work* didn't have too much either, other than letting me know that if I wanted to eat, I'd better work.

I learned that within the first three weeks of living away from Mom and Dad.

I open the agency door and walk inside, set my stuff on my desk, pull the call logbook over, and mash the blinking red light on the answering machine as I pick up the phone.

"Hi, yes, I was just calling to get some information on adoption. My name is Cindy and my number is 972-555-1276. Thanks!"

There are three more messages just like that, which means I'll most likely be spending the morning talking on the phone and working through my lunch break to get paychecks out by three when Candace has to leave.

I write down everyone's messages and then I make a pot of coffee so the clients coming in this morning have something for me to offer them to drink beyond water.

Fridays are typically big counseling days for Peggy and Candace.

Peggy's office door is open so I take her messages down to her. She's checking her e-mail when I walk in.

"Morning, Peggy." I set a small stack of paper slips on her desk.

"Happy Friday, Paige." Peggy grins at me over her bifocals that she has to wear to read anything on the computer. "Busy weekend ahead?"

If I do take Rick up on the job, I will miss working with Peggy the most. She's like my second mother.

"Not really," I tell her. Tyler texted me yesterday about maybe getting lunch tomorrow, and part of me is bracing for Luke to show up with some kind of breakfast and another tearful rendition of "Return to Me."

Sadly, Luke, while he does have a decent voice, does not sound like Dean Martin.

That could have tipped the scales in his direction, though.

I am so shallow.

I look at Peggy and the next thing I know, I'm plopped down in one of the chairs by her desk, pouring my heart out.

"So I have another job offer. And on top of that, Luke Prestwick has been asking me to be his girlfriend again, Tyler hasn't made anything official, Preslee is back in town but we're actually getting along now, Layla's getting married, and did I mention the job offer?"

Peggy just looks at me and then slowly takes her bifocals off. "Okay," she says, drawing the word out. She pulls out a big three-ring binder and starts making some notes. Apparently I am officially on the clock. "Let's start with this job offer."

I sigh and cover my face with my hands, probably messing up my eye shadow, but I really don't care at the moment. "I don't know what to do," I say quietly. "It would be working as a youth intern at my church."

Peggy nods, writing. "Sounds like something you'd enjoy."

"I think it would be." I pull my hands away from my face. It's the first time I've ever really thought about whether or not I'd even *like* the job. "I'd get to meet with girls. I'd get to take them out to coffee, dinners, whatever, and talk to them. I'd get to use my major. And as annoying as Rick can be, I honestly think it would be fun working with him."

Peggy keeps nodding. "I'm not seeing any downsides here, Paige."

My voice is quiet. "I hate quitting."

"Jobs?"

"Everything. I don't quit. If I start something, I finish it." It used to make my mom nuts when we were trying to leave for somewhere and I would beg to stay so I could finish whatever book or puzzle or imaginary plaything I was doing. I never leave the theater until all the credits are done rolling, and milk never expires in my house because if I open a jug, I finish it.

"So, you were planning on just being here until you die?" Peggy asks, hands folded together, eyes on mine.

"I don't know." When I'd taken the job, there were several references to me someday becoming a counselor with the agency and working alongside Peggy and Candace in that capacity. Which is why I originally took the job.

"And then there's the clients," I say.

I do love the people who come in and out of here. I love

seeing the prospective parents coming in for the first time, looking for all the world like lost little puppies and leaving a few months later, joy spilling from every pore in their bodies as they carry out their new baby. I love the birth mothers, each of them with their different stories, different heartaches, different reasons to change their destinies.

If only those things were a bigger part of my job.

Peggy is looking at me, letting me think. She's a good counselor.

"I don't know what to do."

She just studies me for what feels like six weeks but is probably more like a whole minute, silent, eyes thoughtful. "I think you do," she says slowly. "But let's move on. Tell me about Luke."

"Luke." I don't mean for his name to come out in a growl, but it does.

Peggy grins. "That might be enough of an answer right there."

I rake my hands through my hair. "He's just so . . . so . . . so *annoying.*" I shake my head. "He's been coming by the last two Saturday mornings, bringing me coffee and telling me that he wants me back. I've told him it's not going to work, but then he just tells me to pray about it."

"So have you?"

I shrug. "I don't really need to. Luke seems like he's changed a lot and I'm happy for him. But I'm not interested anymore." I mean, I'd be lying if I said there wasn't the occasional spark between us, but Luke is just a very attractive man. He's like a taller, older, more broad-shouldered Zac Efron.

I don't care who you are or what your current romantic settings are in, that's hard not to notice.

Especially when all that is combined with a good deal of charm and it's all focused right on you.

I sigh.

"And on to Tyler," Peggy says, scribbling in her book. "What about him?"

"I like him. A lot. He's very sweet."

"Sweet," Peggy echoes. "Tell me what you mean by that."

"He just . . ." I shrug. "He's just nice to me. We have a good time together."

She nods slowly. "But Luke isn't nice to you?"

"Have you met Luke? He's like the most charming person you've ever talked to."

She shakes her head. "Never met either of them."

"Well, I'll make it really easy for you when you do meet them. Luke is the good-looking, annoying one. Tyler is the sweet, attractive one."

"There's that word again." Peggy points her pen at me. "I've never heard it used so often in a conversation that doesn't involve a golden retriever."

"What are you talking about?"

"The word *sweet*. You've used it like four times now in reference to Tyler." She smiles, though, so I guess it's okay. She walks around her desk and sits in the chair beside mine, then reaches for my hands. "Paige, I've been married for twenty-three years. So I like to think I know a little about this kind of stuff. You seem happy with Tyler, but I don't want to see you become complacent with him. Does that make sense?"

Not really, but I nod like it does. Peggy has clients coming in here in five minutes.

"As far as Preslee goes, I'm glad you got things sorted out

with her. And give Layla time. Things will go back to normal as soon as she's married and settled in."

Married.

It sounds old.

I nod and stand. "Thanks for talking with me, Peggy."

"I'm praying for you, sweet girl. God has big things for you, if you'll let Him lead."

I nod again and walk back to my desk. Peggy's first clients are already in the waiting room and I send them on back.

"If you'll let Him lead."

What does that even mean?

* * * * *

Five thirty and I am standing outside the church, looking up at the white crosses that are positioned on the steeple. They look pretty, which is just weird to me when you consider what they are supposed to be depicting.

But maybe it doesn't draw a lot of people to church to see a real, rough cross hanging from a building.

I walk inside, still totally clueless about what I'm going to tell Rick. I could barely concentrate on any of the phone calls I returned today because I was so consumed by this conversation.

And by thinking about Tyler.

And complacency.

I don't even know what complacent means, really.

Rick is sitting at his desk reading from the biggest book I have ever seen in my whole life. "Hey, Paige." He looks up when I knock briefly on the doorjamb. "Come on in."

"Hey." I walk into his trashed office and push papers, books, Frisbees, and what looks like a to-go container from Olive Garden over so I can sit on the couch. I wrinkle my nose at the container and look at Rick. "Seriously?"

"It's empty. I need to clean."

"You think?"

He raises his hands. "Hey, I'm a very busy guy. With no help. Which brings us to the question of why you are here." He folds his hands on the huge book and looks at me.

I look at him, look at his disaster of an office, look at the book he's studying, and look at my hands.

"Still undecided?" Rick asks after a long minute of me furiously praying.

I shake my head. "No."

"No what? No to the job?"

"No, I've decided." I just have to make sure I know what I'm doing.

He just looks at me, waiting.

I take a deep breath and then nod. "I want the job, Rick."

His face splits into a grin so fast, I think he might have strained his neck. "That is the best news I've heard all day!" He is ecstatic. He comes around the desk and gives me a big hug. "This is going to be great, Paige. Natalie will be thrilled."

I don't have a clue what I'm doing, but for some reason, this seems right. I think it's always seemed right, I just didn't want to admit it.

I smile back at him.

Change is in the air. I can't tell if it's the change I'm smelling or the remnants of whatever was in that Olive Garden container. For hopeful purposes, I'm hoping it's the container because if the change is smelling this bad, I think I need to recant my earlier declaration.

"First things first," I tell him. "If I'm expected to share this office with you, you are going to have to clean."

"For you, Paige, I might even do that."

Chapter
21

I t's nine o'clock on Saturday morning. I'm showered, fully dressed, fully made up, and my hair is even curled into a beachy summer look I'm going to try for this season.

I'm sitting on the couch, arms crossed over my chest, staring at my front door.

Any minute now. I can feel it.

Sure enough, two minutes later I hear someone's footsteps on the metal staircase and a second later, soft knocking on my door.

I march over to the door and yank it open, preparing to give Luke the verbal thrashing of the century that will most likely start with, *"Leave me alone."*

Tyler stands there, hands in the pockets of his jeans, blond hair curling crazily over his head, and a huge grin covering his face. "Oh good! You got my text."

I just gape at him. "Your text?"

"Yeah." He looks at me for a second and then shakes his head at my blank expression, laughing. "And maybe you didn't. Next week is my mom's birthday. I was asking if you wanted to join me for breakfast out and then birthday shopping."

The words are barely out of his mouth before I'm nodding. "I'll get my shoes," I say, leaving him on the porch.

I slide into a pair of flip-flops, grab my purse and my sunglasses, and follow Tyler down the steps to the parking lot.

He stops me right before we get to his truck, reaches for my right hand, slips his left hand under my hair, leans down, and kisses my cheek.

I suddenly am having a lot of trouble getting a full breath.

"I'm glad you're coming," he says, his blue eyes sweet and warm. His fingers are flicking lightly through my hair and a colony of roly-polies have apparently decided to rent out space in my stomach and my knees. "I hate birthday shopping by myself."

He opens the passenger door for me, and it's not until he's walking around to get into the driver's seat that I can finally inhale enough to get some oxygen back into my brain.

Tyler climbs into his seat and by the time he puts the keys in the ignition I'm back to a fully functioning human being.

"So, better late than never, huh?" I ask him, pleased with myself that my voice even sounds pretty normal.

"What?"

"Your mom's birthday is next week?"

"Yep."

"And we're just now shopping this morning?"

He looks at me. "This is early, Paige. Half the time I shop on my way to the post office."

"I'm speechless."

"Priority shipping, babe."

"Really. Speechless."

"Because of how impressive of a son I am, huh?" He grins at me. "Now. What do you think we should get my mom?"

"Tyler, I've never met your mother."

"But you are a woman. Women know gifts for women." He grips the steering wheel. "Or at least tell me what store to drive to."

I just laugh.

We end up at this nice outdoor mall about an hour later after stuffing ourselves with French toast at a cute little breakfast place.

I do not think I ever want to eat again.

The mall is just opening, crowds are low, the temperature hasn't gotten so high that we're swearing off the outside forever, and it's actually nice wandering around.

"Okay," Tyler says. "Mom likes roosters."

"Like live ones?" I'm now worried about the upbringing Tyler has received. I do not mix with barn animals well. One of my friends raised rabbits and that was about as wild as I was willing to be around.

I've told Layla several times that if I'm ever in a Tom Hanks–style accident and somehow get lost on some island and have to fend for myself, she might as well just go ahead and start helping my mother plan my funeral because there is no way I'm making it back alive.

God knew what He was doing when He allowed me to be born into air-conditioning. And flushable toilets.

"No." Tyler grins over at me. "Like ceramic ones. She's got a couple of roostery things in her kitchen."

"I don't think that's a word."

"This from the girl who told me that her eggs were too scrambley today?"

"They were. You have to respect the egg." I sigh, worried about what stores we might have to look in to find something rooster oriented. "What else does she like?"

He looks thoughtfully at one of the window displays we are passing. "She likes Christmas stuff."

"Tyler, it's May."

"I know."

"What about like earrings or home accessories or bath stuff or gift cards?" I throw that last one in there in the hopes that Tyler will say, "Yes, gift card. Let us purchase one immediately." He's going to be shipping this gift to Missouri, where his mom and stepdad live. A gift card would be the optimal thing to ship.

It doesn't work. He just purses his lips and looks at me. "I think she wears earrings," he says very slowly.

I rub my forehead, preparing for a very long Saturday.

"This is fun, huh?" he says, one side of his mouth quirking up.

"So much."

"Bet you wish I had like eleven moms so we could do this more often."

I drop my chin in a fake gape. "Now you can read thoughts too?"

He laughs.

We are wandering through our fifteenth store around two o'clock in the afternoon when I remember I haven't informed him of my news.

I haven't informed anyone of my news.

"So, I'm quitting the adoption agency." Just saying the words out loud makes a nerve under my right eye start shaking.

I am not a quitter.

Tyler's head jerks up. "What?"

"Retiring. I'm retiring from the agency," I rephrase.

He grins, tucking his fingers in his pockets. "You took the job, didn't you? I knew you would."

"How did you know I would? I didn't even know I would until 5:37 last night."

He shrugs. "I know you, Paige." He holds up a digital picture frame that is all shabby chic. Preslee would love it. "This looks like my mom."

I nod my approval. "Done."

I think about his comment as he goes to the back to pay for the frame. *"I know you, Paige."*

It hits me then that he *does* know me. I haven't known Tyler long, but in the few months since I met him, he's become a very good friend.

I watch him walk back with his bag and he holds it up like Rafiki presenting Simba to the animal kingdom.

What a weirdo. I just laugh.

"Okay, now that we have a success on our hands," Tyler lowers the bag and reaches again for my hand, "I want to show you something."

"That sounds ominous."

"You know what I like the most about us, Paige? The trust. There is just this overwhelming sense of trust between us." He stops halfway outside the store suddenly, holding a hand up, looking around. "See? Did you feel that?" He waves his hand around. "Trust," he whispers.

I shake my head. "You are crazy."

"Eh. I've been called worse."

"Where is this something?"

He grins at me all happy and cute, and I think I have a

pretty good idea of what Tyler looked like as a six-year-old when he was making plans to break into the cookie jar.

"You'll see."

We walk back to the truck and Tyler sets his gift for his mom behind his seat. "She's going to flip for that. I'm glad you talked me into coming to the mall."

"You're welcome."

He backs out of the parking space and starts driving toward I-75.

"So about this new job," he says, looking over at me at a red light.

"Yes, the new job." I still am having trouble believing it. When I took the job at the agency, I expected to be there until I left for maternity leave, or something else hugely life changing like that someday light years in the future.

"I'm proud of you."

I look over at him and he squeezes my hand, eyes gentle. "I know it was probably a very hard decision, and I think you're going to be great with the girls. Plus, you'll actually get to do what you have been wanting to do."

I nod. "Yeah, there is that."

"Working with Rick should be interesting."

That was the understatement of the year. Rick sent me a text this morning. CLEANING OUT THE OFFICE PER YOUR REQUEST. FOUND ANT. ASSUME MORE TO COME. SURE YOU DON'T WANT YOUR DESK IN THE HALL? YOU PROBABLY WON'T BE SITTING THERE VERY OFTEN ANYWAY.

I almost wrote him back and told him to forget the whole thing. Then I remembered that the church janitor has been a friend of mine ever since I spent six painstaking hours removing all the crayon that one of our particularly naughty two-year-olds had drawn with all over the nursery wall. I left a voice mail for him at the church this morning.

God willing, two weeks from now I'll walk into a bright and clean youth office at the church.

Tyler turns south onto I-35 and I frown. "Where are you taking me?"

"You'll see."

We keep driving on the interstate, and Tyler tells me about his big project that he's working on. "Basically, I spend the first five months of the year working on this one thing. At the end of June, my team and I have a big presentation for it. The president of our company is coming down from Indianapolis for it." He winces over at me. "I could use some prayers. I'm already sweating at night about it."

"I'll be praying. And have you looked into those cooling pillows? My mom says they work wonders." My mom is also going through menopause, so who knows if they work for average cooling needs.

I like my pillow and bed warm. I know I am in the minority.

Tyler just chuckles. "I'll keep that in mind."

"Are we there yet?"

"I knew you were that kind of a kid."

I fidget in my seat. "No, seriously, how much longer?"

"I don't know. Ten minutes? Why?"

"You really should have informed me we were driving to Mexico. I would have used the restroom at the mall."

He grins. "I'll step on it."

Eleven minutes later, he pulls into a parking lot with millions of trees and bushes and flowers around us.

"Hey, are we at the arboretum?" I look around.

"Yep." Tyler is all smiles.

"I have always wanted to come here and never made it!"

"I know. Layla told me." He reaches behind his seat and pulls out a backpack I hadn't noticed there. "Want to walk around for a bit? With a bathroom stop first, of course."

We walk to the entrance of a huge, grand building. Beautiful flowers are already everywhere. I have wanted to come here since I moved to Dallas. There were a couple of days I almost just drove down here, but it seemed depressing to walk around a huge flower garden by myself, and Layla isn't into the outdoors.

I keep telling her that I'm not either, but flowers are a different story for me. Not for Layla.

Tyler pays the entrance fee, I run to the restroom, then we walk in. Two minutes through the door and I'm already stunned at the beauty. That and the sudden realization that I don't know what any flower is beyond daisies, roses, and tulips.

And sunflowers.

And that's it.

"My sister loves this place." Tyler slings the backpack over one shoulder and reaches for my hand, weaving his fingers between mine. "Every time Stephanie comes to visit me, we always have to come here."

Tyler's parents got divorced when he was little. Neither of them are Christians, which just makes him and his sister all the closer since both of them are. I've never met Stephanie, but he talks so much about her, I feel like I know her. She married one of Tyler's good friends and is going to have a baby in the summer.

"She knows all the names of all the flowers." He points to a particularly pretty patch of some yellow flower I could never identify.

Well, that's one way that I'll never live up to his sister. Might as well inform him of this good and early while things still are in the not-quite-seriously-dating mode.

"I think I know three flowers," I tell him.

"Which one is your favorite?"

"Daisies." I nod. "Definitely daisies."

He shrugs. "That's all you or I need to know. The rest is just nice to look at, don't you think? Honestly, Stef can get a little overwhelming with her 'hydrangea' this and 'flowering whatever' that."

We walk along this huge tree-lined path, and it's hard to believe that just a few minutes ago we were in the middle of a mall. It feels like we might be out in an English countryside now. Wide, grassy fields with flowers and a view of a lake stretch out around us.

"This is incredible," I say, gasping.

"It's pretty, isn't it?" He looks over at me and smiles, rubbing his thumb along the back of my hand.

Families and couples litter the areas around us, lounging on the grass, walking along the pathways, watching the lake, and smelling the flowers. It is a beautiful day to be outside.

We come alongside a huge sea of red, pink, and yellow tulips and Tyler stops, looking at the flowers and then reaching for my other hand. "So, Paige, I've been waiting to ask you this question for a few weeks," he starts, blue eyes focused on me, a slight smile on his mouth.

I just look at him. We have barely started dating. If he proposes, I will have to call a cab home. My shoulders are suddenly aching, and there's this little thought in the back of my brain that shoulder pain can be the first signal of a heart attack.

But really, it wouldn't be a bad way to go, surrounded by flowers, holding the hands of a really attractive man.

He smiles then, looking all shy and sweet, squeezing my hands. "Will you be my girlfriend?"

A mix of relief and something else soft and sticky floods my chest and I grin at him, squeezing his hands back. "Eh, why not?" I shrug, but I'm smiling so wide my cheekbones are threatening to dislodge.

Tyler laughs. "Glad you aren't too distraught by the idea." He lets go of one of my hands, lightly brushing my bangs off my forehead.

My stomach begins twisting.

He leans down and softly kisses my cheek, lightly running his thumbs along the sides of my face.

My chest is so tight, I can't breathe. Potential heart attack threat is reinstated. He pulls back, smiling so sweetly at me I can't help but smile back.

Tyler is about the most opposite from Luke that he can be. Blond hair and all.

And I really, really, really like that.

He takes my hand and we start walking again. I squeeze his fingers. "Hey. Thanks for asking." I'd been wondering.

He nods. "Sorry it took me so long. I've been waiting for the perfect moment. When Mason asked Stef to be his girlfriend, they were sitting in the airport pickup line, waiting for his roommate to arrive." He rolls a shoulder. "I just wanted it to be a little nicer than that."

I grin. "It seemed to work for them."

"You don't know Mason. He was going to propose at Golden Corral until I told him that Stephanie might appreciate something a little more upscale." He rolls his eyes. "There are reasons not to let your college roommate marry your sister." He adjusts the backpack on his shoulders.

"What's in the bag?"

There's the sweet, shy smile again. "I thought we might have a picnic for an early dinner, if that's okay."

If that's okay. Like I am going to say no.

We find a little spot surrounded by trees and flowers overlooking the lake, and Tyler pulls a blanket from the backpack, and tosses me two corners of it to spread over the grass.

We sit on the blanket and Tyler unearths a cooler from the backpack. "Okay, so I wasn't sure exactly what kind of stuff you liked, so I just kind of brought everything I could think of." He pulls out crackers, six different kinds of block cheese, summer sausage, grapes, strawberries, and a box of assorted chocolates. He even has a bottle of sparkling cider in there.

I just sit there. "Wow!"

"Let me pray and then we'll dig in." He reaches for my hands. "God, thank You for this day with Paige. Please bless this food and bless our conversation. In Jesus' name, amen."

We eat half in silence, watching the lake and soaking in the flowers around us and half talking about details around my new job and having to share an office with Rick. "I hope Gary will clean it before I officially start," I tell Tyler, talking about the church janitor.

"I'm sure he will."

The arboretum closes at five, and by the time we are headed back to my apartment, I'm stuffed full of cheese and crackers and feeling very sleepy. I lean my head back on the headrest in his truck and look over at Tyler. "Thanks for today."

"You're welcome." He smiles over at me and reaches again for my hand. "I'm glad we spent the day together. Sorry if you had a lot you needed to get done today. I kind of kidnapped you."

I grin. "This was way better than cleaning my toilet."

He laughs.

He walks me up to my apartment door about thirty minutes later, and I unlock it and wave him in. "If you don't have some place to go, you're welcome to stay. I can make decaf and we can watch a movie or something. If you aren't completely sick of my company by now, that is." This is the longest we've ever been around each other.

"Eh." He shrugs. "I've made it this far. I think I could make it a little while longer." He goes into my kitchen. "Want some water?"

"Sure. Thanks, Tyler." My cell phone buzzes right then and it's a text from Rick.

ARE YOU COMING WEDNESDAY NIGHT?

I just stare at the text for a minute and finally write him back. WHAT?

YOU NEVER GOT THAT E-MAIL, DID YOU?

NOPE.

PARTY AT THE CHURCH WEDNESDAY NIGHT. IT'S MOST OF THE KIDS' LAST DAY OF SCHOOL FOR THE SUMMER. THERE'S GOING TO BE A CHURCHWIDE POTLUCK. COMING?

I look over at Tyler. "Did you know about the party on Wednesday?"

"Oh yeah. I think Rick said something about maybe even using the projector and doing a movie night too since a lot of the families in the church are coming."

"Huh. Are you going?"

"I was planning on it." He brings two glasses of water in from the kitchen.

I write Rick back. SURE. I'LL BE THERE.

GREAT! SEE YA THEN, NEW HIRELING!

Behold, my new boss.

* * * * *

I climb into bed that night around eleven. Tyler and I ended up watching two movies, making two batches of popcorn, and finishing off the chocolates from the picnic.

He kissed my cheek again as he left, pulling me into a gentle hug.

I pick up my Bible from my bedside table and just look at the cover. New job, new boyfriend, basically new sister.

It is a new me from all external evidence.

I turn to Galatians, my heart tensing with the one issue that still remains unsolved.

Luke.

"If we live by the Spirit, let us also walk by the Spirit. Let us not become boastful, challenging one another, envying one another."

My breath catches in my throat and I think I might cry.

Boastful. Challenging. Envious.

Three words that have described me these last many weeks.

I thought I was better than Luke and Preslee. Thought I

was a better Christian, a better person, a better citizen. That I rarely sinned, and when I did, it wasn't nearly as bad as they had. I am proud. So very proud.

I was difficult for them to be around. I didn't give them forgiveness, I didn't listen when they wanted to talk, and I put up walls when they wanted to apologize.

And I envied them. Oh, how I've envied their ability to screw up completely and still find happiness.

I close my eyes, tears filling them.

Oh Lord, how I've failed.

Maybe I didn't run away. Maybe I didn't turn my back on God or my parents or my friends or my morals. Maybe I didn't hurt feelings, smash relationships, decimate hearts. Maybe I was, in a lot of respects, the perfect daughter.

But oh how I have held on to this seedling in my heart. How I planted it, cared for it, and fed it.

For years and years and years. Until at some point, it became such a part of my thoughts and life that I didn't even recognize it for what it was.

A weed. A thorn. A root of bitterness.

I look into the Bible and see only a mirror reflecting back at me. How much bitterness is in my chest, in my head, on my hands?

Toward Preslee for leaving first. For forcing me to have to be the older, wiser one who cleaned up her mess.

Toward Luke for choosing the world and its lusts over me. For breaking my heart and making me doubt God's control in my life.

Toward Layla for marrying Peter, who, for all purposes, is a wonderful man who loves my friend. But she is moving into the next stage of life and I am left behind.

Stuck.

Right where I have been.

Tears are coursing down my face, tracing tiny rivers down my cheeks, dropping single file into my lap, watermarking my Bible in small circles of grief.

God, forgive me. Help me remove this bitterness from my heart.

Chapter

22

Monday morning and we have a very conveniently timed staff meeting. I record our standard, "We're here, but we're not available" message for the voice mail and then join Candace, Peggy, and Mark in his office.

I look terrible. But I guess that is to be expected. I was up way into the small hours of the morning, praying, reading the Bible, praying more, and crying. I finally ended up just getting out of bed and making myself a pot of decaf, sitting at the kitchen table, writing my thoughts in a journal.

God has forgiven me.

I can feel the lightness from my heart all the way down to my shoes today. So despite my miniscule makeup and yanked-into-a-bun hair, I still feel wonderful. Beautiful.

Loved.

"All right, let's start." Mark shuffles his pile of notes around on his desk. "Candace, how are things with the Bakerson family?"

Their birth mother just had their new little daughter after thirty-six hours of labor and an eventual C-section.

Candace was at the hospital with the girl the entire time.

"Good," Candace says, looking even rougher than I do. She rubs her hand through her blonde hair, and tucks it behind her ears. "Tori is still in the hospital but recovering. Baby Gianna is settling in nicely, and obviously, the Bakersons are tired but overjoyed." There are several state-sanctioned visits that have to be done right after a child is placed in a home. Those are always Peggy and Candace's favorites.

Mark nods. "Great. They were a cute couple."

"Still are," Candace says.

We talk details about a few more families. I make notes about new couples coming in and new birth mother matches and new due dates. Finally Mark looks at me.

"All right. I think we can wrap this up. Am I forgetting anything, Paige?"

Now is the moment I've been dreading since I woke up from my frightfully few hours of sleep last night.

"Well, actually," I say, slowly, clasping my hands in my lap. "I have some news."

All of them just look at me. Peggy has a knowing look on her face, but Candace's eyes are wide with worry, and Mark is just looking at his notes with concern, like what I'm about to say is something he overlooked.

I take a deep breath, incredibly nervous. My hands are clammy.

"Y'all know I love working here. I love the clients; I love being a part of something so life changing. And I really do love working with you all." I look particularly at Peggy and Candace as I say that.

I inhale another deep breath. "Recently, I've been offered the opportunity to work with younger girls, and it is going to be working in a setting that will allow me to do actual counseling, which you all know is something I've wanted to do here since the beginning." I gnaw on the inside of my cheek for a couple of seconds, looking down at my lap. "So, I'm going to be turning in my two weeks' notice today."

The room is quiet. Mark is just looking at me, shocked. Candace has tears spilling out of her eyes and down her face. Peggy has both hands clasped under her chin, a sad smile on her face.

Mark is the first one to speak. "W-Wow," he stutters. "I honestly did not see that coming."

I nod. "I know, sir, and I am so sorry for the surprise. It's something I've been praying about for a while now. And I don't want you to think I am in any way ungrateful for all the experience and wisdom you have taught me."

He nods absently, and I can tell that a million thoughts are running through his head.

Candace comes over and pulls me up into a crushing hug, crying and swiping her tears and telling me she is so excited for me but so sad for herself.

Peggy just gives me a gentle squeeze on my shoulders and nods. "I knew you would," she says quietly and chucks my chin lightly. "You'll be an amazing intern."

"Well, uh, I guess with that . . ." Mark says a minute later. "Um. Meeting adjourned."

I walk back to the front room, suddenly seeing everything with new eyes. My desk that I never bothered to decorate with pictures or plants or fun pen holders. My chair I hated that I inherited from the last secretary.

That awful, horrible, leviathan of a copy machine.

I pat it as I walk by. "I will not miss you, friend." Nor the hours I spend every week wrestling it to get it to work.

I sit down, look around, and decide that maybe, somewhere deep in my soul, I always knew this was a temporary job.

The phone rings and I pick it up, cradling it between my shoulder and my ear, reaching for the call logbook. "Thank you for calling Lawman Adoption Agency, this is Paige, how may I help you?"

And the countdown begins.

* * * * *

Wednesday passes in a blur of e-mails, phone calls, and clients hugging me once they hear the news of me leaving. "Oh no, this is terrible!" one hopeful adoptive mom says.

I smile. "I'll be back to visit," I say all placating. I'm sure I'll have thoughts of coming back to visit at least.

I run home after work and change into jeans, a white eyelet top that feels summery, and a pair of ballet flats before heading back out the door to the church. I pull in right as Tyler does across the parking lot.

"Hey," he says, walking up to my car, pocketing his keys.

"Long time no see." I climb out, holding the single person's contribution to church potlucks. Chips and Oreos.

"How was work, T-minus eight days?" He grins. "Oh, don't let me forget. I've got something for you in my car. I'll give it to you afterward."

I nod and then shrug an answer to his question. "Long. I know why people dread the two weeks of notice now."

He wraps an arm around my shoulders. "You'll make it."

We walk inside and there are already a ton of kids and

parents in the fellowship hall, laughing, talking, goofing around on guitars, playing board games. Cheyenne is manning an espresso machine that I've never seen before and is serving up all kinds of frothy drinks while Justin stands beside her, refilling cookie trays.

Rick waves me over. "Meet Garinda." He points to the machine.

Cheyenne groans. "*Glinda*, Rick. Glinda. As in the popular one from *Wicked*."

"I have no knowledge of this," Rick says.

"It's a musical retelling of *The Wizard of Oz*." She sprays a healthy helping of whipped cream on top of what looks like a caramel macchiato. She nods to me. "I named her that because Glinda is popular, and I feel like this baby will be too."

"Good idea. I think you're right," I say right as Rick goes, "Oh, no, we are *not* naming my new youth expense after a musical!"

I grin at Rick, have Cheyenne make me a cinnamon latte, and then start socializing. Rick plays a Pixar movie and after it's over, everyone starts talking again, pulling out card decks and strapping back on the guitars.

It's an end-of-school fiesta.

I grin at one of the girls I was talking to and happen to glance up at the doorway. And that's when I see him.

Luke. Standing there, looking forlornly at me. He waves sadly and I nod to the girl. "Hey, I'll catch up with you in just a minute." I walk over to Luke. "Are you not going to come inside?"

He shakes his head. "I'm not staying long. I just got off work and I haven't eaten yet."

"There's plenty of food here," I say, pointing. I look at

him, at his dark-chocolate eyes, his ever-perfect hair, his designer clothes, and suddenly feel very compassionate toward him.

Proof, I guess, that God is really doing a work in my stubborn, stubborn heart.

I keep both hands on my cinnamon latte refill that is nearly gone but smile a friendly smile at him. "Stay, Luke. You might make some friends."

He looks in the room, glances around at the food, the drinks, the games, and then back at me. "Maybe . . ." he hedges. He clears his throat, eyes tortured. "Paige . . . I . . ." He sighs and shakes his head. "Look, could you please just step outside with me? Just for a minute. I just need to . . . talk and I don't want to do it here." He talks quietly, people are coming in and out, kids are bumping into us, jostling my empty cup.

I can see why he wouldn't want to have a heart-to-heart right now.

I bite my lip and then nod slowly. *God, keep me civil, if not forgiving.* I toss my paper cup in one of the trash cans. Tyler catches my eye from inside the room and I try to wave sign language at him. *I'm going outside!* I mouth in his direction. He nods and holds up two fingers at me.

Peace?

I nod confusedly and then follow Luke's wide back out into the fresh air. The humidity is high but the night is nice. It's cooled a little bit and a very small breeze is blowing, causing little pieces of my hair to fly up and tickle my face.

Luke stops by my car, standing on the sidewalk, looking at the hood of the car, hands tucked in his pockets, face pensive. I stop a foot or so away, not sure what to do with my hands, so I weave them together so I'll stop fidgeting.

"So, look, I'm sorry," he says finally in one breath. "I shouldn't have said what I said that morning in your apartment. I meant it, but I shouldn't have said it." His face twists and he looks like someone who has been told that he just ran over his best friend's dog.

Pity is creeping up my spine and wrapping around my chest. I nod and take a deep breath. "It's okay, Luke." I make sure he looks me in the eyes before I say the rest. "It's okay. I forgive you." I swallow. "For all of it." He knows that I don't just mean these last few weeks.

I mean it, too. The next breath I take is healing, cleansing.

Fresh and clean.

He looks at me, brown eyes wide, and the next thing I know, he's got me wrapped up in his arms, tucking me close to his chest, whispering in my ear, "Thank you, Paige. Thank you, thank you," he says, voice full. He slides his arms just a smidge, moving me back far enough to see his face.

Then he kisses my cheek, one hand tucking my hair behind my ear, the other arm snugly around my waist. I just gape up at him, shaking my head, pulling out of his reach. "What are you——?"

Right then I see him. A dark figure, turning back to his truck, a bouquet of flowers dangling from one hand as he climbs inside.

It's Tyler.

About the Author

Erynn Mangum is married to her best friend, Jon. They have one adorable toddler here on earth and one precious baby in heaven. Erynn loves to spend time with her family and friends, particularly if there is coffee and chocolate involved. She's the author of the LAUREN HOLBROOK, MAYA DAVIS, and PAIGE ALDER series. Learn more at www.erynnmangum.com.